WHERE WE BELONG

A NOVEL
BY
MIRANDA SHISLER

ISBN-13: 978-0996561907
ISBN-10: 0996561900
First edition published 2015

Cover art © 2015 Kathleen Kirtland Photography
kathleenkirtlandphotography.wordpress.com

Miranda Shisler
mirandashisler.blogspot.com

For my writer dad.

We didn't know you would go to bed one night and wake up in the arms of Jesus, but I know you aren't sorry. You are where you always wanted to be.

I'll take up your mantle until I get to be there, too. I miss you.

LITTLE SICILY, OHIO
1890

ONE

Amelia Farnsworth, being the daughter of a clergyman, had never set as much as a toe in a saloon before. She'd been properly scandalized by all those who did.

As twenty-one-year-old Amelia approached the long bar, almost as high as she was tall, she could hardly believe just that morning she had been standing in the parlor of the parsonage, saying goodbye to her sister and father. If this day was the measure of her ability to live on her own as a schoolteacher two states away, she'd already failed before she even started.

The barkeeper leered at her. He glanced at patrons sitting close by and all eyes turned on her. Her face went hot when she realized they were perusing the entirety of her person.

"I think you have the wrong place, miss," the bartender said in condescending amusement. "You're not from around here, so we'll forgive the intrusion."

Indignation prevented her from swooning as the men around her snickered. She tried to raise her chin with some semblance of confidence. "I'm looking for Mr. Harold Hagaman. I'm afraid my train was quite late and the clerk suggested I might find him here. Not being *from around here*, I had no choice but to follow his direction. I would appreciate your prompt assistance so that I might be on my way."

His indolent smile didn't budge. She sensed he would not tell her the whereabouts of Mr. Hagaman until he had his fun with her.

She debated her options. She could return to the train station and take the next train back to Portland, Illinois. There she could continue to be safe Amelia, working at the library and playing the piano for services. She could pretend this ill-conceived journey never occurred.

But Father might be disappointed in her. And anyway, could she go back and continue on as though nothing had happened? She would not forget the failure. She would carry it with her.

She took a deep breath and cleared her throat, planning to give the entire vicinity a lecture on their lack of manners and moral character. But before she could utter a sound, a loud voice from the other end of the bar shifted attention away from her.

"If you don't like the way Daisy and I are getting on, you go ahead and stop me," a man said. He tipped a bottle and drank deeply.

Amelia gawked as the man wrapped his arm around the neck of a girl – a girl wearing a revealing red dress with black lace edging. Embarrassment heated Amelia's face. She knew drunks and saloon girls existed. But she had never actually *seen* either.

The saloon girl winced. Amelia's outrage that any young woman be treated in such a manner overwhelmed her initial shock at the girl's clothing.

"I said to stop," a second man said.

Amelia's attention shifted to the protester. He sat at the bar, his face hidden under his Stetson, holding a small glass of amber liquid. Amelia assumed it to be whiskey, only because whiskey was the drink of choice for men in saloons in many novels she had read and re-read.

The man – Amelia decided to mentally refer to as *The Rogue Outlaw,* although the title was redundant and she would eventually need a more satisfying method of address – set down the glass so hard the liquid sloshed over his hand and onto the bar. "Leave her alone, Turner."

Turner laughed. "William here thinks he's the sheriff, boys."

Amelia reassigned The Rogue Outlaw the name of William. She organized her thoughts into sentences for later when she had a pen and paper. She was writing a novel.

Writing secretly, of course.

Some men like The Rogue Outlaw – er, William – went quiet when they were in their cups. Fools such as Turner gave drinking a bad name for everyone.

Amelia couldn't help a grin.

"The way I hear it, you've been on the wrong side of the law more than the right," the barkeeper said to William as he wiped up the spill.

Amelia gave herself silent congratulations for being correct in her verdict. By his tone, Amelia guessed the barkeeper was taunting William. Maybe it was a dare.

William appeared to belong to the setting. His hat was slung low, leaving his face in a shadow, yet his revolver was obviously displayed in its holster on his belt. Amelia assumed it was a warning. But why would an outlaw need anyone to dare him to act like one?

An outlaw attempting to turn over a new leaf? Now, that was interesting.

Amelia gulped as she studied the weapon. What was it like to hold one? Or fire it? What did one think when staring down the receiving end of the barrel? The whole scene jumped right from the page of a book and compelled her to stay long past the point of her better judgment.

For nothing was as dear to Amelia as a good story.

She did move a little closer to the door in case she might need to escape, and she positioned herself behind a rather large gentleman who would be able to take any stray bullets that might come her way. But she stayed, committed, unable to miss the ending to this scene. Her heart pounded in her ears and her throat went tight as she peeked around the large man, holding her breath.

William looked toward the saloon girl whom Turner had called Daisy. His hat pointed downward, as if he studied the lace around the hem of her dress, nearly touching his leg. He spoke without looking up. "You know I can make good on my threat, Turner."

"You can't. Not anymore."

William took a long swallow of the harsh liquid in his glass, gritting his teeth like he was in pain, yet sighing with satisfaction.

3

Amelia wished she knew how it felt to drink a mouthful of alcohol. Was it cold and refreshing like lemonade, or did it burn all the way down?

The latter, she decided.

The burn traveled down his throat, offering a sort of cleansing for the pain of his soul.

Amelia watched him intently as words swirled through her mind and tried to find appropriate places on the paper that framed her every thought.

William stood and turned. A tell-tale flash of fear sparked in Turner's eyes as William's hand hovered near the capable walnut and steel of his Colt.

"You're going to shoot me?" Turner gave a short laugh of disbelief. "Over a soiled dove?"

"Last chance." William's fingers made contact with the gun. "Let her go."

Amelia waited for Turner to move away. Instead, he turned and pressed the girl against the counter so her back curved across the polished wood at a painful angle. Turner assaulted the girl with a vicious kiss that made Amelia lightheaded.

The blast of a gunshot mingled with the girl's strangled cry. Amelia felt the vibration through the floor and wondered if she had gone deaf from the sound. The whole room stilled, as if everyone was tensing for a fight.

But before Amelia t for the exit, she realized it was over. William's gun rested in its holster and Turner writhed, holding his knee and bellowing curses as blood seeped through his fingers and dripped to the floor.

William flipped the barkeeper a coin as he sauntered to the door. He headed out into the night with the air of a seasoned gunfighter. His face was still hidden by the hat and he didn't look at Amelia as he passed.

She had almost hoped he might.

Two

Mr. Harold Hagaman, as it turned out, was not in the saloon that evening. He came in and rescued Amelia only seconds after the "outlaw" left the scene. With burning cheeks, Amelia followed the school board representative to his wagon.

As they drove down Main Street, the sights of the town tempted her away from her shame.

It beckoned to her almost as a memory, but a distant dream. She felt at home, but a stranger, all at once.

Amelia dug in her reticule for a pencil and paper to write down her thought. She had learned early to keep them close. There was nothing she loved so dearly as words. At the age of four, Amelia had taken it upon herself to decipher the alphabet code while sitting on her father's lap as he studied the Bible. As soon as she could string sentences together, she began to write stories.

Amelia watched the shopkeepers standing under green and white striped awnings. Most were closing up for the night.

"There's a nice lake just beyond the Second Methodist Church. You can see it from the schoolhouse." Mr. Hagaman gestured in the general direction. "And the town is surrounded by woodlands. We have some rather large caves if you are an explorer."

"How lovely," Amelia answered. She doubted the nature around Little Sicily could compare to the stunning canyons and waterfalls of her beloved home town, but she didn't voice her incredulity.

Boys played in the street, catching her attention. Her eyes

5

wandered to a couple on the bench by the dry goods store, pushing accepted boundaries of propriety as they stared into each other's eyes.

Would Amelia ever feel that way about someone? The picture of her future husband had always been well-defined in her mind. She was determined not to settle for anyone less. Her younger sister Ella said she expected too much. Amelia wanted marriage and family, but not without love.

Her father had loved her mother that way. He loved her still, though she lived in a sanatorium as consumption slowly stole the life from her body.

Was love worth the incredible pain it was capable of producing? Amelia had pondered the question for a long time with no answer.

She shook her head as if she might shake loose the image of her languishing mother from her mind. As she did, someone else caught her attention. A man walked toward them on the boarded sidewalk.

He was tall, though not too tall. His face was shaded by stubble. His eyes were narrowed and his forehead lined, as if he might be staring down an enemy.

Another outlaw? Goodness, but Little Sicily seemed full of shady characters! Yet something about him seemed familiar. She placed a hand on her chest, feeling breathless, and not just from the summer humidity. No, she decided. Not an outlaw. He wasn't wearing a gun, but rather a leather apron.

She looked away. Something about him intimidated her down to the toes in her sensible black boots. But she couldn't help looking back, and this time, his eyes met hers. He was scowling at her with accusation. But what had she done to offend him when she had never met him? How dare he judge her without knowing a thing about her?

She glowered back and stuck her nose in the air. Shame on *him* for staring at *her*.

I am not a sideshow, sir.

"Evening, William," Mr. Hagaman said, causing Amelia to startle. *William?*

She gasped. The Rogue Outlaw! Despite her intimidation, she could not resist peeking once more at him. The desperado had stopped walking just to glare at her. Why had Mr. Hagaman been so friendly? Didn't he realize only minutes before this man had shot someone in the saloon? Shouldn't they find the sheriff?

"Hagaman." William nodded without taking his eyes off Amelia.

When he disappeared from her view, she still sensed him watching. Not only that, but it seemed William's disapproval of her had spread down the street faster than an influenza outbreak. All eyes were focused on her. What were they thinking?

It's obvious why she's teaching. Look how homely she is!

"Never mind them, Miss Farnsworth," Mr. Hagaman said, smiling. "They're just curious. We go through teachers awful quickly, and they want to see how sturdy you look."

His explanation was not comforting.

William watched Hagaman's wagon lumber as it turned onto Ash Street and disappeared. He figured Hagaman was taking the new teacher to the Ables where she would live for the school year. But where in the world had he seen that girl before?

The only place he'd been that evening was the saloon, and he didn't think the new schoolmarm would be the sort to frequent the watering hole.

Maybe he was just feeling guilty.

He frowned and went into his shop, closing the door behind him. Unlike Turner, William hadn't gone in to the saloon to get drunk and mistreat women. He'd just needed something to take the edge off the pain.

Come to Me.

He knew he shouldn't have been in the saloon in the first place, but he wasn't sorry for shooting Turner in the knee. The drunk had no right. William saw past the look of disinterest on the saloon girl's face. He knew better. He could look straight into her eyes and see the fear, because he'd seen it in a different saloon girl a long time ago.

He recalled the black lace fringe of Daisy's dress, and it brought a rush of memories.

Stiff and feathery all at once as it clung to satin.

He pushed the memory away. It beckoned from another time and place. One he kept trying to forget.

It was nearly impossible for a house to be uninviting with two little girls playing in the front yard, Amelia decided as she surveyed the house at the end of the lane.

In the fading daylight, Amelia observed the white Carpenter Gothic with a triple-arched window on the third floor and a cozy wraparound porch. Bushes and trees dotted the spacious yard, and a long vegetable garden flourished on the side of the house.

The sight caused a lump to form in Amelia's throat. The scene reminded her of her childhood, when she had spent happy summer days with her sister while their mother worked in the garden. Now her mother could barely lift her spoon to her mouth. Amelia felt a prick of conscience that she was not there to help her.

She shouldn't have gone so far away. What had she been thinking? Tears stung her eyes.

Mr. Hagaman stood at her right with his hand extended. "Shall we?"

She scrambled to clear the wheel and find the foot rest with her boot.

"There's a school board meeting tomorrow night," he said as they took the steps up from the road. "You aren't required to be there, but if you would like my advice, I think the town would take it as a gesture of good will."

She wondered about the meaning behind his words, and why the town required an extra measure of good will in the first place.

"We appreciated the fact that you went to the normal school, so we voted to give you six dollars a month," he said.

Six dollars didn't sound like the epitome of generosity, but she hadn't come for the money. The only purchase she had considered, aside from more books, was a velocipede. She had been eyeing them in the Montgomery Ward catalogue and imagining herself flying about town on such a wonderful contraption. She wondered if she would ever have the courage.

No, it was the implied message behind the frugal salary that made her nervous. Did this town doubt she could successfully teach their children?

After apologizing for her husband, Connor, who was away on business, Mrs. Amy Able took her on a tour of the quaint house. The second floor had two doors she assumed to be bedrooms and an indoor water closet. The final staircase was smaller and uncarpeted. She stepped into the attic space to find a cozy room with the arched window Amelia had admired from the street.

A mild breeze rustled the yellow gingham curtains. A wrought iron bedstead graced the far wall, the mattress covered with a wedding quilt. A writing desk and oil lamp sat against the opposite wall, along with a dresser topped with a porcelain washbasin.

A worn leather trunk with a broken latch had been pushed against the wall under the alcove over the staircase. She wondered if it was moved there to be out of her way, or as a signal to her that she should leave it alone. Either way, the item intrigued her.

Amy introduced the children. The two girls seemed as different in manner as their appearances suggested.

"Jennifer is eight and in the second grade. Kathleen is four. We decided she is not quite ready for school yet. Did anyone tell you the school is divided into girls and boys?"

"Yes, thank you."

Amelia turned her attention back to the children, who watched her with curiosity. Jennifer was short for her age, with muted brown hair that matched her eyes, the same shade as her mother's. Her lazy swinging back and forth and swishing her knee-length sailor dress spoke of her easygoing nature.

Kathleen had hair as blonde as could be with deep green eyes. She watched Amelia with an intense expression, as if she didn't quite trust her. Amelia saw subtle glimpses of traits she shared with her mother and sister, but assumed she must favor her father more.

"My nephew, Jon, teaches the boys. You'll meet him at breakfast on Sunday."

9

"I look forward to it." Amelia summoned a mental picture of Jon. Possessing Amy's soft features, serious and scholarly. A bit dull.

The girls were excused, but Kathleen hesitated. She turned back toward Amelia and allowed a controlled smile for a moment.

Amy watched her go with a surprised expression. "I've never seen Kathleen look a stranger in the eye. You must be something special, Miss Farnsworth."

Amelia had her reservations. Perhaps she just was just funny to look at.

The following evening, after a quiet day of settling in and getting to know her host family, Amelia requested directions to City Hall. She would take Mr. Hagaman's advice and introduce herself to the town in person.

The air felt cool after losing the humidity of the afternoon. She breathed a sigh of contentment as she walked, observing her surroundings. For all its staring citizens, Little Sicily was a charming little town. She could imagine how it might be homey to someone who didn't belong somewhere else.

"I think I can do this, Lord. It's only for the school year," she said in a whisper. "Only be with me."

The answer seemed to travel across time and space to surround her.

Always.

But when Amelia noticed a sizable crowd gathering at the door of City Hall, foreboding overshadowed her shaky confidence.

THREE

Amelia entered the chamber as her heart began to beat so loud, she was afraid everyone could hear it. Chairs lined both sides of the room, with a center aisle that led to a small stage and podium in the front.

Fifty pairs of eyes turned. Murmuring commenced.

She took a seat near the back and tried not to mind the whispering. Instead, she thought about the situation from the viewpoint of the character in her secret novel.

"Why must they stare?" Gwendolyn leaned closer to Richard. Close enough to smell his clove-scented breath.

"Because you are that beautiful, my dear." His fingers brushed against hers under the fold of his jacket. It was a conundrum – the combination of peace and upheaval she experienced at his touch.

Amelia's mind's pencil stopped as she caught sight of her own hand. Decidedly *untouched*.

She heard her name.

"Miss Farnsworth's position is not under discussion," said a balding man with spectacles and a long mustache.

"The school board has received a letter from the other applicant, and I move we read it." Another man held up the letter with challenge in his voice.

"It's not the first letter from *that* applicant, but very well," the first man conceded with a sigh. The other cleared his throat as he opened the folded page.

"*Dear Sirs. In regard to the position of schoolteacher for the upcoming year: I realize my application was received after the deadline, due to circumstances out of my control, since I had to wait for my certificate to be mailed to me. I implore the board not to hold so minor a failure against me, or preempt my desire of teaching the young women of Little Sicily. Sincerely, Miss Rebecca Sapp.*"

Murmuring grew insistent on all sides. Amelia felt sorry for the woman, though she wondered if she detected something false in her words.

The bespectacled man held up his hand, trying to reestablish order. When that didn't bring results, he began to stomp his foot on the wooden floor of the stage.

She feared the man might harm himself, so red in the face he was growing.

Amelia made a face. Awkward wording.

Instead: *She feared harm for the man as his face was growing so red.*

Still awkward. Humph.

"It is our honor to have our new schoolteacher with us tonight. She comes from Portland, Illinois, a small mining community, and holds a teacher's certificate. May I introduce Miss Amelia Farnsworth?"

The school board and the citizens applauded. She saw warm smiles of welcome, though some stared at her with obvious skepticism. Amelia stood and gave an awkward curtsy.

"Miss Farnsworth's father is a respected minister, and he has sent her to us with his blessing and a request that she be made welcome. We trust she will be treated with the honor due her position."

While Amelia wondered what would prompt such a charge, the whispering grew louder. She heard the snicker of a gray-haired lady two rows up. She held a Bible, of all things, to her mouth and whispered in a loud voice to her neighbor.

"Respected minister to whom, may I ask? Coal miners?"

Amelia wondered if she was meant to overhear. Her chest felt tight.

I don't know a single hard-working coal miner back home that would be so pompous! I'd like to see you live such a life with half the perseverance—

"Miss Farnsworth, do you have something you wish to say?"

To her mortification, Amelia realized the room had gone quiet and all eyes were focused on her. If only she had the courage to speak her thoughts. Perhaps it was best she did not. She shook her head and gave the woman a reproachful glare from behind before she sat down rather stiffly.

When the meeting finished, she hadn't heard a word. However, she had imagined Gwendolyn's courageous standoff with her naysayers in several possible scenarios.

As she attempted to leave the building, a group of women circled her.

"Look at you, dear. All buttoned up and proper with such a sensible hairstyle. It's obvious you are the teacher our girls need."

Amelia touched her hair. She had no response, but she wouldn't be allowed one, anyway.

"Don't mind that Sapp girl. She thinks mighty highly of herself, all because her ancestors built the town."

Another woman pushed her way to the front of the circle. "Well, I disagree. You should consider stepping down, Miss Farnsworth." She put a firm hand on Amelia's arm. "Rebecca has lived here her entire life. Who are you to be chosen above her?"

Several women murmured their agreement.

"Not to mention what happened to the poor dear's family. It's our duty to take care of her. Her parents would want it."

Before Amelia could ask what happened to her family, an older woman raised her hand to speak. She had a pinched face of wrinkles and a hair knot so tight her eyebrows seemed to point upward. Her withered finger came within inches of Amelia's nose. "You will do well to remember what our Lord saith in the Holy Word: 'Live at peace with thy neighbor's wife.'"

13

Amelia's head started to spin as several women broke into poorly concealed giggles.

"Beatrice, don't use the Bible to beat your neighbor's wife over the head!"

Amelia frowned, certain her words had not come from the Bible.

Some of the women smiled uneasily at Amelia, perhaps embarrassed on behalf of the mischief-makers.

"Please, ladies. Let's not give Miss Farnsworth the impression we are sorry she came," a woman said in a soft voice. "We have no reason to be uncivil, and every reason to believe she will be a good teacher for our girls."

"Just like the others? Mrs. Hubble, you are a dear and always kind, but as soon as these girls are put to the light, the flaws are seen. We have a right to be concerned for the welfare of our students," another woman said with a sharp tone.

"Give her a chance to prove herself before you judge."

"I wasn't judging. I was only saying I was concerned," the older woman huffed. As the crack in civility gave way to bickering, Amelia stepped backward until she had managed to detach from the group.

She walked. Fast. She considered walking all the way to the depot and taking the next train home.

Her plan was thwarted by a collision with something tall and solid. She reeled back and looked up, finding herself inches from the face of the man who had stared her down in the street earlier. William, wasn't it? Had he been inside the meeting? How had she missed him? Unbidden thoughts rushed to her mind, so unexpected she blushed just for thinking them.

He smells like sunshine. And leather. And... pine?

Whatever the combination, it was successful. It made Amelia aware of her already noted "sensible hairstyle" and plain dress. She looked down, smoothing her skirt self-consciously.

"You're just going to run away?"

She glanced up at the sound of his unfriendly tone. "I beg your pardon?"

He nodded toward the group of ladies still arguing behind them.

"If you couldn't stand up to them, how are you going to stand up to a roomful of their children? A pretty face doesn't get the job done."

Amelia gaped, speechless. He shrugged as if he didn't have all day, and if she planned to make some sort of excuse for herself, she better be quick about it.

"I do not see the value in engaging in futile arguments," she managed. She thought she saw a flash of humor in his eyes. Was he serious, or was he teasing her?

She hated to be teased.

He spoke again. "If that's the case, you won't last longer than the last three women who came here to teach."

As Amelia searched for the perfect words to leave him speechless, he gave her person a closer perusal that caused her further humiliation.

"Pardon me. Girl. Not woman."

Her indignity rose to such a level that she made herself a good inch taller and balled her fists at her side. "I'm appalled at your behavior. I expected Christian kindness, being a stranger in a new place, here for the benefit of the children, but I fear the rough miners back home have you quite trodden upon when it comes to manners!"

She realized she was speaking to his back as he walked away. She thought she heard him chuckling.

"I'm twenty-one years old!" She felt girlish just for saying so.

Her shoulders fell. She turned to walk back to her new residence. Her father had told her to go out into the world and find where she belonged, but she faced the inevitable truth. She did not belong in this town.

And yet – William *had* called her pretty.

Four

Amelia's first thought the next morning was to gather her things and sneak away to the train station.

She sat up, forcing herself to be reasonable. It was Sunday, and she would be able to attend church. Surely there would be friendly souls at church.

She talked herself into getting dressed. She eyed her green paisley, set over the chair last night in preparation. Her sister Ella had declared the dress predictable, but Amelia thought it pretty without drawing unnecessary attention.

She pinned her hair back in the usual knot, but something made her let it back down and try several variations of something looser and prettier. She stood back and looked at her reflection with a critical eye. It was lovely. Feminine. Ella would be proud. She smiled and moved toward the stairs to join the others at breakfast.

But she stopped at the top of the stairs and her hand went to her hair. She returned to the mirror and undid the hairstyle, restyling it in her usual bun.

Before going to breakfast, she visited the window. She leaned out and breathed deeply of the late summer morning. Sunshine spilled across the garden, coaxing flowers to open their souls to its warmth. Amelia felt yearning for a different kind of light.

"Lord, you've brought me here. I know you don't make mistakes. I beg you to send me comrades in this place, but I trust you. I know I'm not alone."

She closed her eyes and sighed. "Help me find where I belong."

Her mind drifted back to the conversation at the beginning of this journey.

Her father had returned from the hospital where her mother lived, an hour's ride away. Apparently, her parents had shared a conversation about her lack of direction.

He meant the best for her. She had no doubt he prayed over the matter and gave it the careful thought any father would. He even sat her down and asked if she might be willing to uproot her entire life and move two states away to become a schoolteacher.

She declined; adding a laugh for good measure.

"You see, Amelia," he said, exhaling a thoughtful sigh and drumming his fingers on the arm of the sofa in the parlor of their parsonage. "I believe I'm doing you a disservice to allow you to remain here under my roof."

Amelia was ashamed. She had noticed she was becoming conspicuous, unmarried at the age of twenty-one. No doubt her father felt some embarrassment that she'd failed to turn the head of any young men in the church or community. It wasn't as if she didn't want to be married. But she hadn't met anyone she'd care to share a first kiss with, let alone a lifetime. Her sister said she was far too particular for her own good.

Regardless, she had not expected her father to turn her out. And it had never crossed her mind to leave.

Her father pastored the Baptist church, her sister Ella was in the last year of her education, and Amelia worked at the library. Why couldn't they remain as they were? At worst, she would end up the spinster librarian. A life alone, but filled to overflowing with books, seemed an adequate consolation prize.

"I'm sorry, Father, I didn't realize—" Not sure how to finish the sentence, she clamped her mouth shut and willed her eyes to stop their ridiculous watering. What would he think of her if she burst into a childish fit of crying?

"My dear, you are an exceptional young lady, and whatever you

17

set yourself to do, you do well. But I sense that God has more for you than you will find in Portland. You should go find where you belong."

"Might we give it some time?" Her voice squeaked. "I'd hate to leave Mrs. Tracy without help at the library. And who would play the piano for services?"

He smiled and reached over to place his palm against her cheek. She leaned against the sturdy hand of her father. Sensed his confidence and good intention.

"Trust me, my little dreamer. This will be a good thing. One day you will smile and kiss my wrinkled old cheek. You'll say I was right and you're so glad I insisted."

"Will you pardon me if I don't quite believe it yet?"

"I will pardon you your inexperience."

She took a deep breath, gripping the arm of the chair as if holding on for her life.

"Relax, child. I'm not asking you to become a pirate and go marauding on the seven seas," he said with a laugh. "I'm only suggesting you fill the position of teacher for the town of Little Sicily, Ohio, for the school year. I met a man at the mercantile who was traveling on business from Little Sicily, and he told me of their dire need for a teacher. I've already written the board to tell them you would be a perfect candidate. All you need to do is apply."

"I've never taught school before."

"You were trained as a teacher. The library was only temporary, until you could find a position."

"But that was two years ago."

"And that is my point, dear. I don't want you to be so safe that you forget all your dreams."

"I haven't forgotten them," she said. "I only expected them to take place here in Portland. Near Mother."

"I know." His voice held tenderness. "But if your dreams aren't found here, but in Little Sicily, don't we owe it to your future to find out? Your mother wants the best for you, and it would hurt her to know you are keeping your life on hold because of her."

The room was as quiet as the true source of her doubt. She

searched for words in which to frame her fear.

"What if I become ill? Like Mother?"

His face softened considerably, and he nodded.

"Sometimes I forget you were so ill as a child. You are doing so well now." He paused and she searched for the relenting she hoped to see in his expression. It was not to be.

"We can't let our past define us," he continued. "Your mother's path is not yours. Sometimes God means for us to grow out of the place where we are comfortable."

Amelia could see his mind was set, so she sent in the application. When she received the letter of acceptance and realized the nightmare was becoming reality, she promised herself it would be temporary. She would prove she belonged at home. She would survive the school year, and be welcomed back with open arms.

Amelia shook herself from her reverie and descended the stairs. An unfamiliar male voice spoke from the dining room. She stopped on the last stair, stricken with a sudden case of shyness. She didn't mean to eavesdrop, but his story caught her attention.

"It happened this past Friday evening. The story came from Hilda Hagaman, so who knows how much is based in truth, but she said that Doc spent the evening stitching up Mr. Turner."

"What was the altercation about?" Connor Able asked.

"Apparently over the way Mr. Turner was treating one of the... women," the stranger said.

"William was in the saloon?" Amy's voice sounded dismayed.

"Not only there, but dead drunk, to hear Mrs. Hagaman tell it. He told Turner to stop and Turner persisted. William shot him in the knee."

Silence invaded the kitchen. Amelia shivered, remembering the night with complete clarity.

The girls bounded down the stairs behind Amelia, breaking the tension. She turned around the corner at the bottom of the stairs as everyone in the dining room looked up. Timidity made her stomach flutter as she traded first glances with a handsome young man. He stood as she entered the room.

Amy turned from the stove where she was transferring sausages from the skillet to a serving platter. "Good morning, Miss Farnsworth. You look rested."

"Yes, thank you." She sat down next to Kathleen and gave her a smile.

"May I present Mr. Jon Hastings?" Amy gestured to the young man as she returned to the table.

He gave Amelia a pleasant grin. "So pleased to meet you, Miss Farnsworth."

"Likewise." She felt her cheeks warm. As they sat down and prayed over the food, Amelia found herself wondering what Ella might think of Mr. Hastings.

"Jon's mother, my older sister Elizabeth, lives in Indiana. He came to us last year to teach." Amy smiled at her nephew as she passed the coffee. He offered to pour a cup for Amelia, but she declined.

She also turned down the sausages, as good as they smelled. She reached for a plain biscuit.

"I hear we are to share a schoolhouse." Mr. Hastings smiled amiably.

Amelia dared to look at him, noticing his brown hair, slicked back with Massacar oil. It was the style, but it was not her favorite trend. It did nothing to detract from his pleasant features.

She sensed the lull in the conversation and searched for words. Ella would know what to say. Amelia was too aware of her faults, and couldn't help but wonder if everyone else was thinking about them as well. It made conversation difficult.

"May I offer you some advice?" Mr. Hastings asked.

"Of course." Amelia's voice faltered.

"When you walk into that schoolroom, come ready to give it your full chisel. There are a few old hens in this town that are expecting to see you fail. I would rather they were disappointed."

"I will do my best, Mr. Hastings. Thank you."

"Jon, shall we refrain from name-calling on the Lord's Day?" Amy rebuked him in a mild tone.

"Of course, Aunt Amy. I apologize."

Amelia cast a few more glances his way, but by the time they rose to leave for church, she was sure that someone as intelligent and attractive as Mr. Hastings would not look at her other than in social politeness. He would have his sights set higher. As he should.

But as she confronted the truth, she felt a twinge of regret. There seemed to be no man in the world who felt like home.

Amelia felt strange walking in the opposite direction of the Ables and Mr. Hastings. They attended the First Presbyterian Church on Main Street. She supposed she could have gone with them, but the little white church on the edge of town called to her. It reminded her of home and family.

As she stepped into the small sanctuary, the smell of oak filled her with calm. She touched the embellished end of a pew, noticing how the soft grain of the wood gleamed with the particular shine that came from many years of being touched.

An older woman sat at an upright piano that looked and sounded as if it had seen better days. Amelia felt the urge to play again. She missed the feeling of the ivory keys, cool and smooth beneath her fingers.

The melody being played was sweet enough to make amends for the instrument's lack of beauty. She hummed the tune as she found a seat by the window halfway up. A man she assumed to be the pastor raised his hand and signaled that they rise and sing the hymn.

Stand up, stand up for Jesus,
Ye soldiers of the cross
Lift high his royal banner,
It must not suffer loss.

Amelia felt the words within, bursting up through her spirit and renewing her frazzled mind. She wished it was appropriate to dance for joy. By a quick survey of the room, she thought it best to keep

21

her elation to herself.

Following the song service, the sermon focused on the wise man building a life in Christ rather than seeking selfish gain. She heard the Spirit's whisper as her eyes rested on her Bible, open to Luke.

If any man will come after me, let him deny himself, and take up his cross daily, and follow me.

If any of her actions or attitudes here in this new place were not for the glory of Christ, it was for nothing. Worthless.

After the service, to her chagrin, the pastor called her to the front. She dutifully went forward, stomach churning.

"Dear people, we are blessed to have our new schoolteacher with us this morning. Please make Miss Farnsworth feel at home and pray for her as she ministers to our children." The kind eyes of the pastor turned to Amelia as he spoke. He went to the door to greet the people and left her standing alone in front of the church.

She fidgeted and stared at the floor until someone came to her and embraced her.

"I'm glad you're here, dear. You seem to be just what our girls need. A beautiful young lady who will lead by example."

Amelia looked into the cheerful brown eyes of an elderly lady. She reminded Amelia of her grandmother.

"How can you tell all of that?" Amelia squeezed her hand.

"I just know. You'll do fine."

Amelia wished she possessed her confidence.

As she shuffled away, a tall, sober woman stood in her place, her hands folded in front of her. Amelia felt the disapproval before she spoke a word.

"Good day, Miss Farnsworth. Might I have your qualifications and philosophy of teaching?"

Amelia opened her mouth to answer but found she wasn't sure where to begin. She swallowed hard.

"I attended a normal school in Illinois –" Amelia began.

"Illinois?" The woman curled her lip, as if Amelia had told her she went to school in a swamp.

"I'm from Portland, Illinois."

"Is that near Chicago?" She looked over her spectacles, as if to suggest Amelia had made it up.

Amelia was not allowed time to respond before the woman continued.

"So, you attended a normal school. How will your teaching and behavior differ from the pattern of ineffectual young women who have stood at your post?"

"Well, I..." Amelia scrambled for an answer at the same time she wondered about the other teachers. "I subscribe to a rather new pedagogy that involves activating the whole child in the process of learning rather than just their mind."

The woman appeared horrified, as if Amelia had suggested she might teach them voodoo and hexes in place of numbers and letters. At this uncomfortable moment, Amelia realized someone was watching her. Intently. It took her a moment to locate the pair of eyes she could feel burning into her person.

When her gaze locked onto his, she felt a prickle of fear. The horrible man called William lounged in the back row, smirking through his frown, if such a thing was possible. She had the impression he could hear every word of her conversation. It was plausible, given the size of the room. She felt dizzy when she recalled the scene in the saloon. Why would he be in church?

She tried to focus on the remainder of her speech. "I will, of course, complete the expectations of the parents and school board. The lessons will be learned, only in a different way than we are used to associating with the school environment."

The woman sniffed and turned away. Amelia repressed a sigh and managed to greet the others who had come forward before she made her way to the door.

She kept as far to the right of the aisle as possible to avoid the man still staring at her. She felt like a schoolgirl having her braids dipped in the inkwell by the bully.

The handsome bully.

She attempted to shake her head of the unwelcome observance and, with a fleeting glance, checked his belt for the infamous gun that caused so much trouble. She saw no evidence that he wore one.

He didn't move. He sat with his leg crossed over his knee and

23

his arms stretched across the back of the pew, as if Amelia had entered his domain and was at his mercy.

The man was, without a doubt, the worst excuse for a human being Gwendolyn had ever met.

No. *The man was simply the most horrendous person Gwendolyn had ever had the unfortunate occasion to meet.*

By the time she reached the house, she thought she might lose her breakfast. The burning sensation in her stomach became so strong she had to stop and sit down on the step. She leaned forward, trying to relieve the pressure.

"Miss Farnsworth, are you ill?"

Gwendolyn prayed the voice did not belong to the certain man she did not wish to see again…

She looked up and saw Mr. Hastings. At least it wasn't William what's-his-name.

"I'm fine, thank you. I do need to go inside and get my medicine. Might I impose on you for some assistance?"

She hoped she didn't sound too forward. Would he think her motives impure? He reached for her hand.

"Of course."

Amelia leaned on his arm as they climbed the stairs. The pain of the corset pressing into her stomach took her breath away.

"May I ask what ailment you suffer from?"

"A stomach ailment. It's aggravated by stressful situations. The doctor called it an ulcer."

She worried she had been crude, but he made no comment until they went into the parlor. She sat down on the settee.

"Might I offer to retrieve your medicine?"

At first the notion surprised her. Something about him entering her room seemed improper. But she had left it tidy, and it would be a great help not to have to climb two flights of stairs.

"That would be most kind. It's the bismuth powder on the desk."

He nodded and left. She considered him as he took the stairs two at a time. He seemed to be the kind of man she had always hoped to meet. Ella said she hadn't found a husband because she couldn't find someone as perfect as the prince inside her head. But what if Mr. Hastings turned out to be that prince? She smiled in spite of herself.

He came down the stairs and headed into the kitchen, returning moments later with a glass of white liquid.

"I took the liberty of mixing it. My mother is a surgeon, and I have assisted her."

Amelia accepted the glass and drank it down fast, steeling herself against the chalky taste. "I have heard of lady doctors, but I've never met one."

"Quite a few of them these days." His voice seemed casual, but she wondered if misgiving was hidden behind his words. "There is a college for women in Pennsylvania. My mother was trained by her grandmother in healing, but when my father passed, she decided to go the whole hog and become a doctor. She attempts to employ her grandmother's teachings alongside the modern treatments."

"How interesting," Amelia said. "Though I am sorry to hear of your father."

He sat down across from her. "Don't be. I hardly remember a day when my father didn't come home with a brick in his hat, if you know what I mean."

Amelia noticed tension in his voice. "I don't think I do."

"He was a drunk. He lived for the bottle, and it's what killed him."

"I'm sorry." She wished she could say more. Clearly, speaking of his father caused him pain.

He grinned abruptly. "Enough about me. Tell me what caused your stress. Was the Baptist church not to your liking?"

"It was nice," she said. "Just like home. But afterward a woman approached me. She could not see my vision for teaching."

"And?" He eyed her as if she might be holding something back. She shifted her gaze and looked down at her cup.

"Well, I… I saw someone I didn't expect to be there."

He smiled a devilish sort of grin. "Here under a week and already you have enemies?"

She caught his playful tone and chuckled uneasily. He stood.

"I'm joking, of course. I meant what I said this morning. Stand up to them. They have it coming."

"What about you?" she said with challenge. He scratched his chin.

"Let's just say I pick my battles."

After a pause in the conversation, Amelia asked the question she had been wondering. "What happened to the teachers that came before me?"

"Oddest things." He scratched his head. "The first one became so ill she had to return home to be cared for by her mother. The next one was accused of stealing from the mercantile and let go, though she insisted she was innocent. The most recent one left because she was frightened by something that happened at the home where she was boarding. She described it as a ghost."

Amelia could hardly believe the tales. He shrugged as if he knew how it sounded.

"And this is all in the past year – since I started teaching. One after the other," he added.

"Doesn't that seem strange?" she asked.

"Incredible, I know."

"Thank you for telling me, Mr. Hastings," she said with a wobbly smile. He went to grab his hat from the stand by the door.

"I think we've moved past Mr. Hastings, don't you? Call me Jon."

"And you may call me Amelia."

"I don't think I will." He opened the front door. "I've already decided I'm going to call you Em."

FIVE

On the night before the first day of school, as she paced in her room well after midnight, Amelia found the letter.

She was trying to read *Sherlock Holmes: The Sign of Four*, the book Ella had hidden in her suitcase, as was their tradition. It was something Amelia might stay up all night to finish, but she found herself too agitated to sit still. She tried to work on her novel with the same results.

As she paced, the old trunk with the tattered edges caught her eye. She wanted to take a peek inside. But what if they discovered her rifling through their belongings?

The trunk had been left in her room. If it held something they didn't wish her to see, wouldn't they put it somewhere else?

Before she could reconsider, she slid to her knees next to the trunk. She breathed deeply of the old scent. Mildew and dust – the smell of an aged mystery. Her heart beat faster at the possibility of a story hiding within.

She flipped the broken latch and pushed open the lid, disappointed when she saw the folded quilts inside. She ran her finger down the length of the satin and lace trim of a baby quilt. This must be where Amy stored her daughters' baby things.

She lifted the quilt on the top, seeing tiny dresses and pinafores, bonnets and hair ribbons. There was no mystery here. She noticed there were only a few dresses, but it wasn't so strange. Amy would have reused them for Kathleen. Ella had always fumed about being made to wear Amelia's castoffs.

It wasn't until Amelia slid a hand to the bottom, touching her fingers to the leathery base, that her excitement was renewed. Her fingers brushed against paper and she pulled out an old letter.

She knew she should put it back. Propriety demanded it. It was not her concern and she had jumped straight over the line to full meddling as she sat back and read each astonishing detail.

The manner and manuscript was decidedly male, she observed. As she whispered the scrawled words on the crinkled page, she drank up the essence the author had left. Not just the words he chose, but the deliberate writing style that suggested every word had come at a cost. He had paid a high price, and he carried a secret with him.

He addressed the letter to no one, and did not leave a signature. She gathered it was written to someone who had died. Was it intended to follow her into the afterlife instead of stay hidden beneath a quilt in an old trunk? Amelia read it again, her hands shaking with excitement.

I'd been there before, my love. You know I had. Lying there in all that blood, staring up at nothing but sky. Blue sky with pretty white clouds. I remember them because the beauty of the day mocked me, helpless, without hope. I smelled the gunpowder, so strong I could taste the bitterness. I felt the lace of your red dress in my fingers, stiff and feathery all at once as it clung to satin. I heard the child whimpering.

I'd been shot before, and nearer to death. But it was that moment when everything fell into place. For the first time I felt guilt. I'd always been proud, ready to take my punishment like a man, ready to stare down the Almighty while he tried to make me ashamed of the life I lived.

I could feel him in that moment, Beloved. Feel him! He was there, and my eyes could almost see him. The strangest panic came over me, like I'd been wrong about everything.

He wasn't an enemy to face with arrogance; instead, he was more like family. The sum plus infinity of all the love I'd ever had in my miserable life. I didn't want to die. I didn't want to face him before I had a chance to sort it out.

I asked him for another chance. I knew I was out of them, but I asked him anyway. I said if he'd let me live, I'd promise to find out why he gave me life. And what I could do about the rotten mess I'd made of it so far. That was the last thing I remember. I closed my eyes and succumbed to whatever fate I'd be dealt. If I opened my eyes again, I wouldn't waste that second chance.

Not one minute.

Amelia covered her mouth as tears stung her eyes. She'd never felt so close to someone as to this unknown author whose heart she had just held in her hands. Oh, to find this man who had loved with such beautiful passion!

Were it the sole reason to leave her home and travel east to a new life, it would be well worth the distress the whole affair had caused her.

Six

Before the sun rose on the first day of school, Amelia was at her window again, breathing in the smell of fall. It was invigorating, with that mysterious and unsettling hint of winter's inevitable arrival as the remnants of summer began to give up their life to the cycle of the seasons.

It was beauty in death.

She wondered if God had planned the seasons just so they might remind people of his love. Even when death seemed to conquer the world, when winter covered all in a frozen blanket of silence, still they could be sure spring would come, and nature would rise again. Just as the Savior did.

"You've written your love everywhere." Amelia whispered to the stillness.

She dressed in her simplest white blouse and navy twill skirt and set off to the school with an apple in hand.

Minutes later she crested the small hill behind the Lutheran church and saw the schoolhouse, picturesque against the woods, surrounded by a whitewashed picket fence. She walked down the stone path to the stairs and looked up. A bell tower split the building in two sections.

Her footsteps echoed in the long hallway, freshly painted a muted blue color. Hooks waited under long shelves for jackets and lunch pails. Amelia went into the room on the left, where she would spend the next year teaching Little Sicily's girls.

A small stove stood in the corner, its pipe rising up and out of the wall. Her desk, no more than a small table, had been pushed against the wall under the blackboard.

She placed a slate, a piece of chalk and a McGuffey reader on every desk. With no more preparations to be done, she wandered across the hall to the boys' room, curious. It was larger, with plenty of room in the aisles, though the number of desks was about the same as for the girls. From the window, she saw a wide view of the field behind the school, complete with two outhouses.

Steps on the floorboards alerted her to someone's presence.

"You're here early." Jon smiled in greeting. "You'd think it was the first day of school."

"Good morning, Mr. Hastings." Amelia offered a smile of her own.

"No, you are definitely not my student," he said, wagging his finger at her after he set down a load of books and maps on his desk. His rather large desk.

Amelia complied. "Good morning, Jon."

"Good morning, Em. Are you rested and ready for the day?"

Amelia inhaled and nodded, though a pang made her press a hand to her stomach. His gaze softened.

"They're only children."

"I know. It's their parents I fear."

He nodded. "Fortunately, you don't have to teach the parents. You'll do fine. After all, what is teaching? They only need to learn their letters and numbers and everyone will be satisfied."

"I could never be satisfied with that," Amelia said, earning a strange look from Jon and wishing she'd kept the thought to herself.

Hearing the sounds of children just outside the door, she went to her post as Jon moved to ring the bell.

As she stepped back into the girls' classroom, Amelia discovered that the back wall had become lined with solemn parents, arms crossed, murmuring to each other.

It seemed she would have an audience for her first day.

31

As she walked home that afternoon, after a long day of explanations and reassurances, she noticed William standing by the Dry Goods store, flipping through a catalogue. She searched for an alternate route, but she was already too far down Main Street to turn back. She decided to ignore him, but he seemed just as determined to stare at her.

Had he seen the parents filing out of the schoolhouse with their daughters? Was he scoffing at her? Did he think she deserved their mistrust?

She almost made it down Main Street, but was finally overcome with irritation for all the unspoken thoughts he directed toward her in his scathing glances. She marched across the road.

"Pardon me, sir, do you have something you wish to say?"

She noticed humor in his eyes though he did not smile. It made her angrier to know he wasn't taking her seriously.

"I didn't even know you were there." He shrugged and looked back at his catalogue.

Humiliation turned her cheeks pink. She turned to walk away in shame.

"If you like, I'll think of something to say," he offered. She huffed and kept walking. As she turned the corner to Ash Street, she realized he was following her.

"I saw your audience finally left."

She didn't answer. He kept in step. She prayed he would not pull out his gun and shoot her as he had shot the man in the saloon.

"I've seen your kind before, you know. Stubborn as they come," he said.

She chanced a glance at him and thought she saw deeper emotion peeking through the veiled expression. He hid it as soon as she noticed it, but it intrigued her. As he replaced it with a condescending grin, she replied with a soft "humph."

"Sometimes stubborn people have to learn the hard way."

Amelia worried that he was threatening her, so she gulped and increased her speed. He stopped walking and let her continue on alone.

"Look at it this way," he said. "Even if you're stubborn and foolish, at least you're a good view from behind."

She would not be able to get his words out of her head for some time. She reasoned it was only because she was so dismayed at the obvious degradation of his soul.

Seven

Amelia hid behind a tree for a few minutes the next morning until she was sure no parents followed their girls inside.

Without visitors, she was able to get to know her students. She saw anticipation on a few of the faces, but most wore the apathetic expression of a child doing their duty by attending school.

"I know we had a rough start yesterday. I hope your parents were convinced of the truth: I am here to help you learn. I do hope that you will come to see the process as an adventure."

By the end of the day Amelia knew who her secret favorite would be. Thirteen-year-old Laura Spencer was gangly and quiet, but her peaceful spirit and insatiable hunger for books would have been a joy to any teacher's heart.

She was also sure of her challenge. Eleven-year-old Polly Dennis had the curliest blonde hair she'd ever seen, with big blue eyes and a generous smattering of freckles. She eyed Amelia with condescension, as if she had already decided she would gain the upper hand. Amelia had no doubt there would be several showdowns before Polly learned she was not in charge.

Amelia possessed a familiar sense of dread as she surveyed her group of girls. If she gave them her all and loved them as deeply as she was capable, it would hurt when the school year ended and she went home. But how could she keep her distance? It was in the girls' best interest to be loved with their teacher's whole affection.

She could give them nothing less.

As fall turned brisk, the school settled into a routine. Amelia saturated her teaching with long nature walks and plenty of time outdoors to study creation and apply what they were learning. She asked more questions than she passed out facts, hoping to engage their interest.

Not long after school started, Jon asked her to join him at his desk for lunch. She worried at first that she would be in his way, but he insisted, saying that they could see the children play from his window and it only made sense.

She found him easy to talk to. He liked to chat and didn't mind leading the conversation. She listened as he spoke about his mother's medical practice and some of her more entertaining patients. They also discussed books, though Amelia quickly learned Jon did not appreciate fiction to the degree she did. It didn't surprise her. It was a rare find to stumble upon another soul who shared her fascination with imaginary worlds and people.

She almost told him about her novel buried in the top drawer of her dresser. Only Ella had read it. She had been enthusiastic, but what if she was only being a loyal sister? What if it did not measure up to quality literature? For now, it was enough that Amelia loved her characters.

Jon would probably only laugh at her. He might even compare her attempts to a dime novel, and that would be worse than hearing it was tedious. Amelia didn't want anyone to see what she wrote if it lacked the depth she expected in any book she read herself. She would be mortified to be accused of using the same hackneyed theme as all the other ten cent novels stacked on the shelf in the general store.

The day proved bright and warm for early October. Seeing the leaves were beginning to display their brilliance, she wandered into the woods after school and found a secluded pond. She curled up next to a large rock by the water with *Sherlock Holmes*. She breathed in the scent of ink and paper inside the newly bound book, and quickly lost herself in the shadowy world of the quirky detective.

An hour later, as she rushed along foggy London streets beside the genius hero, a deep voice from behind her almost made her fall straight into the pond.

"Watson. The game's afoot."

She dropped her book and grabbed her chest. Her heart pounded, as if enigmatic Holmes had truly taken form in her world, which was, of course, one of her often-considered fantasies. She whirled around to beg mercy from her attacker.

William held up his hands. "I come in peace."

Several things occurred to her. She was alone in the woods. This man had recently shot another soul in a drunken rage, and the last thing he had said to her had been appallingly improper. With an uncomfortable turn of her stomach, she also realized again how handsome he was, especially when inspected up close, with his shirtsleeves rolled up over his elbows. Not to mention all that stubble covering his face. Her cheeks warmed.

He sat down and grabbed the book she had dropped. He leafed through it.

"I read Doyle's first story in a magazine a couple years ago. He's got talent."

She wanted to flee, but she couldn't bring herself to leave her book in his hands. It was too good. She gulped and decided to pretend civility until she could retrieve it. "Most definitely."

"It takes a good author to write in a manner that is not distracting from the story. Don't you agree, Schoolmarm?"

She narrowed her eyes and refused to answer to the title. Or to admit that she completely agreed.

"How far are you?" He opened to the first page and began to read. She remembered it was unladylike to sit on the ground, so she eased herself up into a standing position with her arms across her chest.

"Far enough."

He seemed to forget her presence as he read. She cleared her throat.

"You are quite welcome to borrow it," she said, plucking it out of his hand and quickly stepping back. "*After* I have finished."

He seemed perturbed. "You better be a fast reader."

"I am," she said, with challenge of her own.

"You know what I think?" A savage grin spread across his face, although his eyebrows still lent to the illusion of a frown. He didn't wait for an answer. She had no idea what the impossible man would be thinking, anyway. "You like to make yourself look smart by reading books like this. But when you are by yourself the only books you look at are dime novels."

She exhaled in disgust.

"Seems like I've hit a nerve."

More like jumped up and down on several.

"I suppose you are the well-read scholar of Little Sicily?" She found her voice and surprised herself by making the words ring with an air of indifference.

"I've been known to read on occasion." He shrugged and sat up. "Ask me something."

"I beg your pardon?"

"Ask me about some of these books you read. Give me a quote. Maybe I'll tell you where it comes from."

She tried to think of something random, but had trouble thinking at all with his eyes on her face.

"'*There comes a time in every rightly constructed boy's life when he has a raging desire to go somewhere and dig for hidden treasure.*'"

He scoffed as if she had just asked him the sum of two plus two. "Who hasn't read *Tom Sawyer*? And Clemens was right, by the way. That desire never really goes away."

She couldn't help a small smile.

He stood up. "If that is all you have, I guess I'll be going."

Had she lost this strange but compelling duel? "I suppose you have something better?"

"I could quote Dickens if you'd like." He pushed his hands into his pockets. Again, his partially bare arms caught Amelia's attention. She looked away, but not before he caught her observance.

"Please spare me your nonsense; you are nothing but hot air," she said.

"*An unfinished coffin in black tressels, which stood in the middle of the shop, looked so gloomy and death-like that a cold tremble came over him, every time his eyes wandered in the direction of the dismal object from which he almost expected to see some frightful form slowly rear its head, to drive him mad with terror.*'"

"Is that *Oliver Twist*?" Amelia was side-tracked from her humiliation, impressed that he could recall such a large portion of text from memory. More than that, there was something in the way he said it. Was it ownership? Why would this William speak with such ease of terrifying forms beyond the grave?

The cold tremble to which Dickens had referred prickled her skin.

"Go on, then. Give me another one." He nodded her out of her frightened stupor, and she acquiesced for no other reason than to give him something else to do other than murder her there beside the pond. Her mind scrambled for something, and she was instantly ashamed at the quote that tumbled from her mouth.

"*He recalled every detail of his quarrel with his wife; he realized the hopelessness of his situation, and, most tormenting thought of all, that it was his own fault.*'"

She noticed his eyebrows rise, and felt satisfaction at surprising him. Perhaps it was not her day to die after all.

He took his time answering, an indolent smile passing across his face as he took one step closer to her. She inched back as he replied with maddening haughtiness the next line of *Anna Karenina*.

"*It's all my fault, it's all my fault – though I'm not to blame.*'"

Silence followed. He watched her, smug. Amelia opened her mouth to speak but then shut it when she realized she had nothing to say. He sprang upon her hesitation like a bird of prey.

"I'm surprised, Schoolmarm. Should you be reading such a scandalous tale?"

Her face burned.

"Do you know why it was his fault, but he was not to blame?"

His piercing green eyes leaned in and fixed on hers. She could not imagine what he was thinking, so she decided to open her mouth and let whatever nonsense came forth distract them both from wherever this present battle of wills might take them.

"Frankly, no, I don't. It *was* his fault, and he *was* to blame. Adultery is not excused on the basis of a spouse not looking as well as you'd hope nine years later. Nor for the sake of a man who turns your head or your heart instead of your husband. Anna's demise shows the result of following a path dedicated to self. Marriage is about unconditional love, which is what Levin learned in the end, which makes it a beautiful story of contrasts, and not a lurid tale of immorality."

Amelia realized she had just shared her most vulnerable thoughts on a strange man who already alarmed and intimidated her.

He shrugged. "That depends on what you mean by *unconditional.*"

"What would you know of it?"

She saw a flash of anger. He subdued it with effort. "What would *you* know?"

She swallowed hard, but against her better judgment, she kept talking. "Did you intend to prove my innocence so you could mock me when you found it?"

He smiled. "I did come for another reason, whether you believe me or not. I saw you leave the school and go into the woods and I thought I'd warn you."

"Oh, is that what you thought you'd do?" Her voice held incredulity.

But there had been a hint of sheepishness in his voice. She resumed normal breathing.

"I don't know what good it will do to warn a stubborn girl like you, but you should know some of the parents are unhappy about the changes you've made, and the young lady who thinks you stole her job is taking advantage. She's called a meeting tonight at her home to discuss your teaching methods. '*In the interest of the children.*'"

Amelia noticed the edge of sarcasm in his voice and wondered if he knew something about Miss Sapp that she did not. Then she

39

remembered to whom she was speaking and did not find it odd that he would carry a sarcastic tone concerning anyone.

"Why are you helping me?"

He shrugged. "Nothing personal. I don't like sneaking around or gossiping just because a person's ideas are different. I also don't like the way the last three teachers lost their jobs. Something seems off, and I don't want any more trouble." He gave her a look of challenge. "So, what are you going to do, Schoolmarm?"

She stared into the still water of the pond. "I suppose I'll start by finishing my book."

He chuckled, and she couldn't help but like the sound of it. Rich and throaty, vibrating in a deep tone that seemed to reach inside her and remind her that she was in so many ways his opposite.

"I know you shot a man when you were in the saloon. When you were drunk," she said before she could stop herself.

He paused before he answered, as if she had caught him off guard. He looked across the pond, narrowing his eyes. "Had to. The fool was mistreating a woman."

"A… lady of ill repute," Amelia said to clarify.

"They're people, too." His voice held an edge of defensiveness.

He turned and headed back down the path. She watched him until he was almost out of view, wondering if she should call out a goodbye. He spoke without turning around.

"Put away your dime novels if you want to talk literature again, Schoolmarm. They rot the brain."

EIGHT

When Amelia arrived at the Ables' home, she found Amy on the porch swing, cradling her Bible in her arms. Amelia sheepishly hid her novel behind her back.

"Supper's simmering on the stove." Amy pushed her foot against the painted floorboards, causing a gentle sway of the swing. She patted the seat next to her. "We'll eat in a half-hour. Mr. Able had business in Columbus and will be out of town for a few days."

Amelia joined her, and they watched the girls play on the front lawn. Jennifer took Kathleen by the hand and led her among the fading summer flowers, trying not to scare away the last of the butterflies.

"You have lovely daughters." Amelia felt the need to fill the silence, though she meant the words.

"God is good." Amy's voice was reflective.

"He is."

"What's wrong?" Amy asked. Amelia considered denying it, not sure how to put into words the strange encounter in the woods.

"Did someone tell you of the meeting?" Amy prompted.

Amelia squirmed, ashamed she had been alone in the woods with William. It wasn't as if she had approved the interaction beforehand.

"I wasn't going to go because I disagree with the covert nature of the meeting," Amy said. "But if it will make you feel better, I'll

41

go so that I can tell you what you are up against. Can you watch the girls and put them to bed?"

Amelia nodded with a smile. "Amy Able, detective. Just like Sherlock Holmes."

"Who on earth is Sherlock Holmes?"

Despite the things weighing on Amelia's mind, she enjoyed her time with the girls. As she walked in the garden with them, she mentally penned a few lines.

If Gwendolyn had a daughter, she would possess a fathomless spirit and discerning eyes that never missed anything. And she would learn the wisdom the child had to offer, a treasure hidden in simplicity, and yet a key that unlocked great mysteries of the ages.

"What do you think about when you stare at the sky?" Jennifer asked.

"I'm thinking about a story. Writing it in my head."

"Do you write it on paper?"

Amelia made a show of looking every way to make sure no one heard their conversation. "Sometimes. But you must never tell anyone my secret."

Jennifer and Kathleen both smiled. "We won't."

"Do you girls ever make up stories?"

"We don't know how," Jennifer said with a shrug.

"I could start it and you could tell me how it will continue," Amelia suggested. "Whom shall our story be about?"

"A baker," Kathleen decided, not looking up from the piece of grass she meticulously dissected.

"And what shall our baker be called?"

"Eduardo," Jennifer said with a giggle.

"Where does Eduardo the baker live? What does he do?"

"He gets up early in the morning to bake bread and pastries for the town where he lives way up in the mountain." Kathleen's voice sounded far away, as if she were there in the little mountain village of her mind.

"What problem disrupts Eduardo's happy existence?"

They walked through the backyard, and Amelia reveled in the peace of the rising and falling sounds of the cicadas and the blush of clouds in the western sky.

"The town has run out of yeast. Winter is coming and someone must brave the icy passage to fetch some."

The tale continued until Eduardo had faced his challenge and emerged the victor. The girls were in bed before Amy came home. Amelia sat on the porch swing with a sweater wrapped around her shoulders. Amy sighed as she joined her.

"You have your work cut out for you, Amelia. I hope you don't regret coming here."

"I don't," Amelia said. And as she said the words, she realized she meant it.

"It seems to me Miss Sapp is sore because you were chosen over her. She coaxed them to tell stories on you. John Dennis claims that you upset his daughter by telling her she would go straight to hell if she didn't straighten up and act right."

Amelia gasped. "I would never say something so heartless!"

"I figured."

"Polly demanded I tell her if the devil and hell were real. I said that the Bible is clear on those points, but that Jesus' love is bigger and stronger than either of them, so we must put our faith in his power to save us."

"A wise answer," Amy said. "But it stirred some rather heated debate. About half those present thought it was an acceptable thing to say to Polly Dennis. Or any Dennis."

Amelia caught the humor in her voice, but she couldn't smile. In her experience, the most unlovable were often the most in need of love.

"I hope you know there are good people in this town. We're all weary of losing teachers, and some respond with cynicism." Amy reached across the swing and squeezed Amelia's hand. "You have nothing to be ashamed of. There's no way you could teach in Little Sicily and please everyone at the same time. Stand up for what you believe in, Amelia. You may be just what this town needs."

NINE

Amelia woke the next morning with a sense of resolve. She would visit the Dennis home and speak to Polly's parents. Surely this misunderstanding could be cleared up.

When school was over, she gathered her things as well as her nerve. Jon appeared in the doorway. He leaned on the frame and smiled at her, shoving his hands into his pockets.

"Where are you headed with such determination?"

"I'm going to the Dennis home to speak to Polly's parents," Amelia said, and explained the situation.

He stepped into the room. "I admire you for being so thorough. Most folks just try to pretend the Dennises aren't there. I know from experience those boys are bound and determined to get themselves kicked out of school." He hesitated. "Sometimes I hope they will succeed."

Amelia chuckled. "Well, I don't know anything about the other members of the family, but Polly is smart. She's precocious and prone to cause trouble, but if she learned to apply herself, she would get the best marks in the class."

He nodded. "What are you going to say?"

"I suppose I will just tell them the truth and ask how I may help them minister to their daughter."

"Be careful with Mr. Dennis. He 'don't cotton' to new ideas."

Amelia wasn't sure what he meant. "Fortunately, the Bible is an old idea."

He gave her a surmising expression. "That depends on what part you mean. I hear people going on all the time about things I could swear aren't actually in the Good Book."

Amelia nodded as she moved toward the door. "That is true enough. As the daughter of a clergyman, I've learned that most bickering comes from rules not yet located in Scripture."

He smiled. But he seemed to be distracted from the conversation, and Amelia wondered what had his attention. He held his arm for her to take as they moved from the schoolhouse and down the path.

"I've enjoyed getting to know you, Em. I really have. You are a smart and lovely young woman."

Amelia felt panic cause her chest to tighten. "But…?"

He laughed and reached for her hand, running his thumb along hers. She looked down in surprise.

"There is no 'but,' Amelia. I just wanted you to know. I look forward to pursuing our friendship."

She watched him go, unable to think of a response. She wondered what he was trying to say.

Don't be a goose. He meant exactly what he said.

She agreed with her intuition and ignored the voice that whispered of possibilities. She had heeded that voice before and been disappointed.

How she hated being disappointed. Yet how often she was.

She put it out of her mind and slung her bag of books over her shoulder, heading in the opposite direction of home. She was determined to clear the air with the Dennis family, no matter what anyone said.

By the time Amelia finally found the Dennis farm, she was completely winded and ready to ditch her corset into the creek. Her stomach burned in continuous protest to her journey.

The home was on the outer edge of the woods, settled into the backdrop of trees like a child standing close to his mother, wrapped in the reassuring cocoon of her skirts.

It must have been built many years before, because it was worn. Uneven boards revealed mold between the cracks. The porch sagged with age, and weeds adorned the front walkway. Children seemed to be everywhere, some shirtless or shoeless. Two large dogs eyed her suspiciously and gave a warning bark. A clothesline stretched across the yard from the porch frame to the outhouse, but half the laundry had been pulled off and left in the dirt. Amelia wondered if anyone might be offended if she picked it up and dusted it off.

"Mama! Teacher's here!" One of the children yelled before he took off down the path toward the barn. He dodged rusty bits of wagon wheels and farm tools as he went.

A woman appeared at the door. Her apron was covered in smears of dirt; a kerchief held back her tangled hair. She didn't seem thrilled to see Amelia.

"Come on in and tell me what my kids done now." She held open the door and ushered her in.

Have done.

Amelia lifted her skirt to step onto the mud-streaked veranda and into a grimy kitchen lacking natural light. She saw Mrs. Dennis was in the midst of washing a staggering pile of dirty dishes.

Amelia gasped as she nearly stepped on a baby. The child began to wail. Amelia's cheeks warmed when she realized the baby was naked.

"Sorry, you caught me at cleaning time. Do you mind?"

Amelia set the bag of books down and picked up the baby. Upon closer inspection, when the little one stopped crying and stuck her thumb in her mouth, Amelia realized she was a pretty little girl, with blue eyes and curly hair that reminded Amelia of Polly. Mrs. Dennis tossed her a clean diaper.

She set the baby down on the table, seeing no alternative, and diapered her. Mrs. Dennis put the water on to boil and set a coffeecake on the table. The baby seemed content to remain on Amelia's lap and stare at her, and Mrs. Dennis did not reach for her, so Amelia snuggled her close.

"So, what's my Polly done? That girl will be the death of me, if her brothers aren't first."

"She's done nothing, Mrs. Dennis." As the words left her mouth, Amelia recalled, only a few hours earlier, watching Polly sneak a garter snake into the crack of the outhouse door and bursting into laughter when a young boy came flying out, barely covered. Amelia cleared her throat.

"Polly is a smart girl. She has... spirit. But I'm not here because she is in trouble."

Mrs. Dennis seemed relieved, and perhaps a little proud. The dark circles under her eyes brightened. "I always thought Polly was as smart as a steel trap."

"Of course. I stopped by because I learned that your husband was troubled by a conversation that Polly and I had recently. I wanted to make sure that you understood what I told her."

The woman said nothing, sticking her fork in her cake.

"Polly asked about the doctrine of hell, and I tried to give her an answer founded in the truth of Scripture. I explained that God must punish sin, but that God's love shown through Christ is stronger. I would like to know how you feel about my answer, so we can find some common ground."

Amelia noticed the other woman had become uncomfortable. "Someone told you what my husband said at that meeting, huh? That man of mine, he can get wrathy over just about anything. Best to stay out of his way. Polly needs to learn to hold her tongue. I fear the girl is just like him."

"Polly has expressed interest in the Bible. I would like to help meet her spiritual needs if I can."

Mrs. Dennis shrugged and waved her off. "I'm sure she'll figure it out. Now you eat up every bit of that cake so you have the strength to make that long walk back to town. Especially with all them books you're carrying!"

Amelia smiled. "I didn't realize the distance. I should have left my things at school. I enjoyed the walk, anyway." The baby in her arms whimpered and Amelia handed her to her mother. "The cake is delicious, but I'm afraid my stomach has trouble with rich foods."

Mrs. Dennis nodded and stood to see her out. "I have a sour stomach, too. Used to have more trouble with it, but I got a tonic at the general store. It helped quite a heap."

Amelia picked up her books. "What do you take? Bismuth

powder?"

"Nah, that stuff never did anything except make me feel like I was chewing on chalk. I got the Pemberton tonic just like I saw in the newspaper. Nothing like it. Something about that coca leaf – a huckleberry above a persimmon, I say. Cures my ills."

"I wonder if Mr. Hagaman might have any more to sell." Amelia had not considered the possibility of finding a remedy that the doctor had not prescribed for her. Mrs. Dennis went to the cupboard.

"I got a whole case. They say to only take one glass at a time, but I find my stomach needs two or three to really start feeling right again." She held out a bottle of amber liquid. "Considering you were so nice to come all the way out, why don't you take a bottle as my gift?"

Amelia took it and thanked her, touched by her generosity. Medicine must be precious in such a large family.

When she arrived home, she hid the bottle in the drawer of her desk. She didn't want anyone to see it and misunderstand, especially when she saw the name of the tonic was *Pemberton's Wine of Coca.*

TEN

Gwendolyn looked on as he approached, tall and strong on his horse, gun slung against his hip, Stetson pulled low over his eyes.

He gave her a hard stare, handsome and rugged and thoroughly intimidating. Was he more dangerous than the outlaws chasing her? She was terrified until he reached down, horse in motion, and grabbed her firmly around the waist. He pulled her up into the saddle and to safety, as he shot his gun at the men who pursued them –

"Don't you think, Miss Farnsworth?" Jon's voice interrupted her daydream.

Amelia sat up quickly, glancing around the dinner table. "I, uh... why, yes, of course."

Jon chuckled. "I'm glad you agree."

Amelia hoped she *did* agree with whatever he had said.

"Tell us about your home, Amelia," Amy said as she helped Kathleen cut her meat.

"There isn't much to tell," Amelia said. "It's a small mining community. Most of my father's parishioners are miners or farmers."

"What was it like to grow up in the home of a clergyman? I can't imagine it." Jon eyed her with curiosity.

Amelia smiled wistfully. "I never wished for anything else,

though it wasn't always easy. In any congregation there are those who cannot see the vision of their leader or mean to cause trouble. There were times of turmoil."

"Is that why you decided to come east?" Amy asked.

"No. My father suggested it." As Amelia spoke, she discovered she had changed her mind about the conversation with her father. She still intended to head straight home at the end of her appointment, but now she could see the value.

"And what did your mother think?" Amy asked. Amelia couldn't answer right away.

"I think she agreed. But my mother is ill. She lives in an institution."

She did not elaborate, and Amy did not press for an explanation. The fried chicken she had been enjoying now felt heavy in Amelia's stomach. She took a deep breath, hoping the angry churning would cease. She felt Jon's eyes on her.

"You're pale, Miss Farnsworth. Perhaps you should retire."

"Go right ahead," Amy said in agreement.

Amelia said goodnight, relieved to be excused.

In her room, she changed into her nightgown and got in bed with a book. She read for hours, until the sun had set and the house stilled.

The pain in her stomach intensified, and she got up to move around. She paced until the old trunk caught her attention. As she stood in the middle of the dim room, with lamplight casting deep shadows in every corner, she sensed another's presence. She could almost see the letter-writer at the desk, channeling his broken heart through his pen. She could feel him, as tangible as the breeze that began to blow through the curtains.

She shivered, afraid to move. In the whisper of the wind, she thought she heard a voice. A man's voice, heaving a sob as he threw down the pen and pushed the papers aside. It wasn't enough to write them down. *She* wouldn't be able to read it. He had to make her understand that he had repented. He had changed. But she was gone, forever removed from him by the impenetrable wall of death.

Amelia felt a chill wrap around her like a blanket of ice. She sat at the desk, feeling the grooves in the wood. She opened the drawer, almost expecting to find some new clue to his identity, when the forgotten bottle of tonic rolled into view.

She picked it up, turning it in her hands and studying it. Why did she hesitate to try it? She had never hesitated over the bismuth powder. Why not take a sip and see if it helped?

She felt foolish for hoping that a tonic from the general store would hold any astounding powers to heal. And yet she wouldn't know until she tried.

She pulled out the bottle with sudden resolve and removed the cap. Before she could change her mind, she held it to her lips and took a swallow. Her throat seemed to ignite, sending flames into her nose and setting off a fit of coughing she feared would wake the household.

She looked back at the bottle. Her stomach still churned. But hadn't Mrs. Dennis said she needed two or three glasses to feel right? Amelia wondered what size glass she meant. Perhaps she had not taken enough to cause any effect.

She carried the bottle down to the kitchen where she found a glass tumbler. She went out to the back door and sat on the steps overlooking the garden, making sure to remain in the shadow of the forsythia bush.

She loved the outdoors at night. The world seemed more in focus when the distraction of light faded away. The tree swing swayed in the breeze, giving the effect of a ghostly visitor to the old maple tree. It was an immense tree that covered the garden with huge fingers of rustling leaves, growing brittle as they gave up their summer vitality.

She poured a glassful and drank it quickly, like she took the bismuth. Twice more she filled the cup and drank it down, and then she waited.

She found it strange when several moments later her eyes would not focus. They felt heavy, as if she hadn't slept for days. And the old maple tree that had been rooted to its spot minutes ago now seemed ready to spin around the yard as if in a childish fit of frenzy.

She thought maybe a walk would help. She cast off her shawl, feeling too warm for the restriction, and headed for the swing. It was quite a task to find it, since there were suddenly three of them. When she managed to grasp hands on the ropes and ease herself onto the seat, she didn't care what was wrong with her anymore. She would rather enjoy a nice swing.

It seemed only reasonable that, as she swung, she should sing.

I know not when the day shall be,
I know not when our eyes shall meet,
What welcome you may give to me,
Or will your words be sad or sweet?
It may not be till years have passed,
Till eyes are dim and tresses gray,
The world is wide, but love at last,
Our hearts must meet some day.

Somewhere in the back of Amelia's mind it occurred to her that she should worry someone might hear her. She found the voice dull because she thought she sounded quite nice and so should everyone else. It was a lovely song, after all.

She twisted the swing around and around until there was no rope left, and let go, launching into a spin that made her feel as if she was soaring over a mountaintop. Her eyes caught the shadow of a man standing next to the garden. Watching her.

She didn't think to be afraid.

ELEVEN

William knew what kept him awake that evening. The same thing that had kept him awake on many other quiet nights like this one.

If he was an imaginative sort of man, he would close his eyes and conjure her up. He'd smell her lavender lotion and see the long strands of blonde hair brushing his arm as she whispered to him.

Clara.

He only allowed his mind to go there for a moment. Long enough to catch a glimpse of her stunning features and her mysterious smile. Only long enough to remember that her stubbornness had gotten her killed.

He shook off the memory as one might a bee that landed on his arm. Regrets would do no good. No amount of penance on his part would bring her back from the grave.

He pushed his hands deep into his pockets and walked down Main Street. Turned on Ash. He took the route he always took in the dark, when sleep was a stranger. He came to stand before the familiar house.

He expected to see it dark at this hour, but the attic room spilled light. And now that he was thinking about it, he could hear something. Singing. Good singing, for that matter.

He followed the sound, and found the schoolteacher in the backyard, swinging and singing her heart out. Her hair was down, falling in waves to the middle of her back. William stared in surprise. He could hardly imagine her as a schoolteacher at the moment. Or as a young girl. He hadn't given much consideration to her beauty. She made it easy to avoid, always dressed so prudishly, with her hair tied away in a firm knot.

She had seemed so orderly that he'd adopted the notion she must be a tangled mess within. He didn't need to deal with that. Not that he had any plans to deal with her. Or look at her.

Like he was doing now.

Her nightgown hinted that she didn't lack a woman's curves. She was petite, and on the thin side, but her features possessed an artistic grace. Her mouth was turned up in a secretive smile, and it got him wondering what secret Miss Farnsworth could possibly be hiding.

He heard the words of her song and felt his throat constrict with unwanted emotion. He hated love songs.

He had been content to stand by the garden and watch her with curiosity akin to watching a sword-swallower at the circus, but now he approached her, only wanting that song to cease. He stumbled over something in the grass. Reaching down and picking it up, he held it close to make out the writing.

It didn't take long to connect the dots when he saw it was a half-empty wine bottle. He looked back at her with a chuckle. Could it be? She who'd acted so high and mighty about his presence in the saloon?

He put his hands on top of hers and swung her around. She didn't seem alarmed. In fact, she giggled.

"What have you been drinking, little girl?" He smirked.

She didn't cower in shame. Instead, her lips parted in delighted surprise and her hands went to either side of his face.

"Oh, William, you look like a different person when you smile."

He shook his head. How did she know his name? He hadn't given it to her.

She took her hands off the ropes to hold his face, but did not possess the balance to remain seated without holding on, and so began a slow tumble off the swing.

He caught her and swung her up in his arms. "I'm only smiling at a ridiculous girl who got drunk on snake oil." He nodded toward the bottle. She gasped.

"I would never get drunk! I'm the pastor of a daughter, you know. I mean *the daughter of a pastor*." She laughed with glee.

"I know drunk. You're dead drunk, preacher's daughter. Not only that, you've got caffeine and cocaine in your system. I bet you're flying pretty high right now."

She squealed and kicked her legs. "I do feel like I'm flying! It's wonderful!"

William started toward the house, enjoying the feeling of being close to a woman again. She snuggled up against his chest, and he didn't complain a bit.

"You do realize you were performing your little spectacle for the entire neighborhood in your nightgown." He was sorely tempted to bury his nose in her hair for a moment. She gave a contented sigh that caused an uncomfortable knot in his stomach.

"I like nightclothes. Corsets are so tight and itchy." Her words slurred together as she closed her eyes.

William shook his head with another short laugh. "You better hope you don't remember this tomorrow, Schoolmarm."

"I'm only being honest." She pouted. "You should try them and see."

"No, thanks."

He deposited her on the porch swing and knocked on the door. A few moments later Amy opened it.

"William?" She seemed surprised. Her eyes widened even further when she saw Amelia on the swing, humming and waving at her.

"What's going on?"

Amy's eyes met William's and he saw the doubt there. Would she ever believe he had changed for good?

"I found her in the backyard with a half-gone bottle of Pemberton's. She's lucky I heard her serenade before the neighbors did."

"Oh, dear." Amy put a hand over her mouth, trying to hide a smile. Amelia giggled.

55

"We better keep this our secret. Bring her up to her bed?" Amy asked, holding the door open and standing back.

William nodded and went to retrieve the schoolteacher. She insisted she could walk on her own, and did – for exactly two steps. Then her legs turned to jelly and she fell into his arms. He carried her inside.

She was barely conscious by the time he carried her up the last flight of stairs and set her down on her bed.

"You are going to have one devil of a headache in the morning, Schoolmarm. Until then, enjoy your drunken slumber."

He tried to disengage her arms from around his neck. She held on, smiling dreamily, her eyes closed. Catching him completely off his guard, she lifted her face to his and pressed her lips against the corner of his mouth. He quickly let her go and stepped back.

Amy stood by, trying to hide her snickering. William took one last look at the expression on Miss Farnsworth's face and determined it was well past time to say goodbye.

TWELVE

Sunlight assaulted Amelia's face with rays she would cherish on any other day. Her head pounded like an internal drumbeat announcing her unspeakable sin.

"I'm a drunk." She turned away from the light and would have sobbed if not for the pain in her head.

Amy came up the stairs with a tray, wearing an expression of pity.

"I brought you some tea and toast."

"How can you even look at me after what I've done?"

Amy set the tray down and sat on the edge of the bed. "We all make mistakes. I'm sure you're receiving all the punishment you need right now. I refuse to add to it." She hesitated. "Amelia, where did you get that tonic?"

Amelia fell back on her pillow and held her aching head. "Mrs. Dennis. She said it helped her stomach ailment, and I was hoping it would do the same for me."

"Coca wine has a great deal of alcohol. Didn't you know that?"

"I wasn't thinking. I just trusted her without asking questions. I was hopeful that I might have found something that would work," Amelia moaned. "I'd give anything to take it back now."

Amy nodded. "I know you would. And I know you prefer to think the best of everyone, but I wouldn't take any more medical advice from Mrs. Dennis. She has somewhat of a reputation. I should have mentioned it."

Amelia whimpered. "I'm such a coot."

Amy laughed. "I don't think it's as bad as all that."

"How can you laugh? This could ruin me. The parents of my students don't trust me as it is."

Amy patted her hand. "Who says anyone will find out? I told Jon you were ill, and he's taking care of your students. No one needs to know what happened."

Amelia had the feeling someone else had been there. Yes, someone had carried her to bed. Had it been Jon? Was Mr. Able home from his trip?

"What about –" She felt as if she should know the identity of the person who had rescued her.

Amy didn't speak for a moment, but she smiled in a manner that suggested she wasn't concerned about it. "Your secret is safe."

She stayed in bed until dinnertime. Jon pulled out her chair as she entered the dining room.

"Em, I'm glad to see you up and about. Your students were concerned."

"I'm fine now, thank you." Amelia hid her shaking hands under the table and tried not to grimace at the smell of the food.

"There are new things you can try for stomach ulcers. I could write my mother and see if she has any advice."

Amelia gave him a grateful smile. "I would appreciate that."

"I'm sure Amelia can rule out one or two cures already," Amy said with a surreptitious glance as she served the turkey. Amelia's face warmed. Jon squeezed her arm lightly.

"There's no need to be embarrassed. It's not your fault you were ill."

She gulped and quickly changed the subject.

Amelia spent the following weeks attempting to prove to whoever might be paying attention that she was a competent and industrious worker. She plunged into her teaching, arranging special outings and projects for the girls as well as spending long hours of instruction and tutoring with those who required extra help. She spent time with each of her students, getting to know them.

The Spencer family concerned her. Laura Spencer told her that their father had died in a factory accident earlier that year. Mrs. Spencer had been doing odd jobs since then, taking in laundry and working in the hotel restaurant on weekends when Laura could stay with the little ones. They had many mouths to feed and the farm was falling apart.

"Mama tries hard, Miss Farnsworth, but we're sinking," Laura said in a tired voice a child should never have cause to use. "I told her I'd quit school and find a job like my brother, but she won't hear of it. She knows how much I love reading, and she's got her heart set on me becoming a teacher."

"You have a wise mother." Amelia hesitated. She wanted to help, but she was unsure if her offer would cause offense. "If I came Saturday to spend the day helping you and your mother, do you think it would make her feel badly?"

Laura smiled. "She'd be so grateful. She's been beside herself trying to get everything done."

"I'll ask Mr. Hastings if he will come as well. I'm sure there are some chores that would be more suited for a man."

"Thank you, Miss Farnsworth." Laura took the hand of her four-year-old sister Ellen and set off toward home. Amelia noticed with a breaking heart that both of them had boots that were falling apart and dresses so thin from wear that they would provide little warmth in the coming cooler months.

Amelia went home and looked through her clothes, finding a skirt and shirtwaist that might fit Laura with a little tailoring. She also took her spare boots and set them with the clothes. She asked Amy if Kathleen might have any extra clothes she could spare for Ellen. Amy found two dresses and some shoes that had been given to Jennifer but never worn.

"I can't imagine Kathleen without winter shoes. It hurts me to think about it."

Amelia nodded. She couldn't bear the thought of Kathleen in

need, either, and she wasn't her mother.

Jon agreed to go. They met on the front porch early Saturday morning, dressed in work clothes. Their feet crunched on the leaves covering the path out of town.

"Are you going home for Thanksgiving?" Amelia asked, awkward in the silence. Jon nodded and shoved his hands in his pockets.

"You?"

"No. But my family might visit for Christmas."

"At least you won't miss the dance," Jon said.

"Dance?"

"You haven't heard about the Thanksgiving dance? It's a tradition. All the women make a feast at the Lutheran church and afterward the young people have a dance. You better plan on going. It's considered impolite for a young, unmarried citizen to be absent." He gave her a teasing glance.

"You're missing it," she reminded him with a grimace.

He chuckled. "I don't think I've ever met a girl who didn't want to go to a dance."

"Well, now you have."

"Why not? Are you of the mind that dancing is inappropriate?"

She sighed. "That would make my abstention nobler, but no, that's not it."

"If you can't dance, I'd be happy to teach you."

Her cheeks warmed at his suggestion. "I can dance. But knowing how doesn't make it enjoyable."

She felt his eyes on her, and her intuition told her he thought her odd, but he didn't comment.

The Spencers were hard at work with a laundry pot boiling over a fire in the front yard of a small log cabin. Jon and Amelia were greeted by a variety of children and animals. A weary woman looked up from the fire.

"It's not washing day, but we have to do what needs doing when we have a spare minute. I'm due at the hotel in an hour."

"I understand." Amelia took a pile of wet clothes to the wringer. Mrs. Spencer asked Jon to patch a hole in the roof and told one of the children to show him where he could find the tools. She turned back to her task and gave Amelia a brief smile.

Mrs. Spencer held a supporting hand to her back as she stirred the water. "I hear tell of contraptions that wash your clothes for you these days."

Amelia didn't answer. She couldn't take her eyes off the older woman, marveling at such courage in the midst of her circumstances.

After a heavy moment of silence, Mrs. Spencer looked up and caught Amelia watching her.

"I'll be praying for you," Amelia said quietly.

Vulnerability flashed in the other woman's eyes for a moment. Amelia imagined the images – holding fatherless babies and wondering how to feed them. Sending her teenaged boy off to the same factory where his father had been killed. Looking at the worn clothes of her children and knowing the chill of winter was just around the corner.

"Thank you," was all Mrs. Spencer managed to say in response.

That evening at dinner, Amelia had trouble swallowing every delicious bite of the pot roast, green beans from the garden, and bread still warm from the oven. She felt tears sting her eyes when Amy set a thick piece of apple pie in front of her.

"Are you ill again?" Amy asked in concern.

"No. I just don't understand why I have so much and others have so little." Amelia's voice wavered.

Although she imagined Amy and Jon agreed, the rest of dinner was rather sober because of her words. Jon finally sat back and smiled.

"Aunt Amy, do you think Em can possibly avoid the Thanksgiving dance?"

Amy was dismayed. "Why in the world would you not attend? Everyone will be there."

"So I hear," Amelia said in a grim voice.

"Oh, you'll be going," Amy said with an authoritative tone. "It's a shame Jon won't be here to escort you."

Amelia agreed it was most unfortunate. It would have made the prospect more tolerable.

Thirteen

It was as common an occurrence to her existence as the rising and setting sun, but Amelia could not sleep. She'd been trying to read one of her favorites, *Journey to the Center of the Earth*. Now, while the rest of the house slept, she stared into the shadows of the room.

It's just a social gathering. I'm being silly.

But questions rolled across her mind like headlines on a newspaper. What would they think of her? Would she make a fool of herself? Would she look ridiculous standing by herself because no one wanted to talk to her? It was such a risk. The kind of risk that usually made her stay home and read.

Bring into captivity every thought to the obedience of Christ.

The verse from Corinthians admonished her. "Help me, Lord. My mind won't stop racing unless you intervene."

She blew out the lamp and settled on the bed, pulling the quilt up to her chin. She was close to sleep when a noise jarred her to consciousness. She sat up. The sound had not come from downstairs. It had been in the room.

Her first thought was mice. She had not seen any evidence in the house, likely due to the presence of a cat that roamed the yard on a regular basis, exchanging extermination services for a plate of cream and a scratch behind the ear from Amy. It didn't sound like an animal, anyway. It could have been her imagination, but it sounded like a soft sigh.

It was not uncommon for Amelia to see flashes out of the corner of her eye or hear unexplained sounds in the darkness. She generally blamed her imagination.

One experience she had at the age of nine served as an exception. While spending the night in her grandparents' house, she'd awoke near midnight to see her grandmother standing in the dark hallway, looking into the room Amelia shared with her sister. At first, she had thought nothing of it, since Grandmother had trouble sleeping and would often check on the girls when they were staying with her. But as she drifted back to sleep, she remembered her grandmother had died, and they were there for the funeral. When Amelia looked back at the doorway, it was empty.

Now, motionless in the little attic room, Amelia sensed sadness. But when had she known a happier family than this one?

Faint crying followed the sensation. A man? She sat up, her skin covered in goose bumps, though she did not feel fear, only a heightened awareness. The image she had created of the letter writer came to mind. She tried not to move or breathe as she listened to a noise so quiet it was overcome by the ringing in her ears.

Eventually she fell into a restless sleep, and dreamed of the man. He sat on a rock in a monumental cave, weeping with his face in his hands. Behind him, a fire-breathing dinosaur crashed toward him. She waved frantically and tried to call out a warning, but her voice would only squeak.

A child screamed.

Amelia woke, realizing the scream had been real. She heard childish crying, insistent and hysterical. One of the girls.

She ran down the stairs in her bare feet, reaching the girls' room just after Amy. Jennifer sat on Kathleen's bed trying to calm her. Amy picked her up and spoke in a soothing voice.

"Kathleen, it was just a dream. Come now."

Neither Jennifer nor Amy seemed surprised. It must have happened before. Kathleen did not open her eyes, but she quieted and snuggled against Amy.

"Does this happen often?" Amelia reached out and smoothed sweaty hair back from the girl's face.

"For the last few months. The doctor said some children get them.

He called them night terrors. I'm sorry she woke you up."

"Not at all." Amelia leaned over to press a kiss against Kathleen's cheek.

Amelia stared at the reflection in the small mirror. She had pinned her hair back in her usual fashion, and her good dress was smooth and warm from the iron.

As Amy came up the stairs, Amelia glanced at her with a nervous expression.

"I don't know why you're so flustered." Amy reached up and fixed a stray strand of hair. "It's just a dance. It's supposed to be fun."

"I only hope I look like I belong. And that I can think of something to say."

"Just be yourself."

"I try, but I never seem to fit in," Amelia chuckled in embarrassment at her admission. "The other girls always talk about hairstyles and dresses – or young men. I'm not very interested in clothes, and I find talking to men awkward."

"You talk to Jon all the time."

Amelia shrugged. "Men I don't know."

Amy shook her head. "I don't think you give people enough credit. There are other young women in the world who love to read and think about things other than clothes and men."

"I'm sure you're right." Amelia felt ashamed.

She left the house, determined not to shrink away from her duty as a young unmarried woman. But when she arrived and attempted to assimilate herself into a conversation, she immediately felt the same old frustration.

"What do you think, girls? Are Mary Hagaman and Henry Milford sparking?"

"Never! His mama won't have anything to do with the Hagamans because they go to the Methodist church on Market Street."

"The Milfords are Methodist. They go to the Methodist church on Main."

"Why do you think there are two Methodist Churches? The feud between the Hagamans and the Milfords goes back almost as far as the town."

"They seem awful friendly, don't they?"

The whispers continued around Amelia until her head began to ache. She watched the couples dancing in the center of the room and almost wished she were there instead of here, subjected to wallflower gossip.

"Miss Farnsworth, why aren't you dancing? Do you have a beau back in Illinois?"

With difficulty, Amelia held back the urge to tell her that the *s* in *Illinois* was silent.

"No," she said. They exchanged glances with each other and walked as a pack toward the refreshment table, resuming their conversation with arms linked and heads bowed inward.

As wearisome as they had been, Amelia was more uncomfortable standing by herself. She might as well just get up and announce she was socially inept, and they should remain as far from her as possible.

As she shrank back into the shadows, a beautiful girl entered the room. She paused in the doorway and waited for everyone to turn and acknowledge her presence. Several younger girls surrounded her. Amelia supposed they must be in awe of her extravagant dress or the dark, shiny curls piled on top of her head.

The woman scanned the room until her gaze found Amelia. She walked with purpose toward her.

"Miss Farnsworth, do allow me to introduce myself. I'm Rebecca Sapp. It's so lovely to have you at our little dance." Her words seemed friendly, but overly so.

"Thank you, Miss Sapp." Amelia shifted uneasily.

"Do tell me, dear, where is the delightful Mr. Hastings this evening? Did you see him come in?"

"He's visiting his mother over the holiday." Amelia watched Miss Sapp's eyes flash for a moment.

"Of course he is." Her tone was mild, but forced. "And who has already snagged you for a dance? I'm sure you're only taking a rest. They must be lining up to get a turn with the new schoolteacher. Tell us what ungraceful oafs to avoid for fear of our toes."

"I'm not much of a dancer."

Rebecca giggled, and the sound was like tinkling crystal. "Well, we can't be good at everything, now can we?"

Amelia didn't answer.

"Oh, you mustn't mind me. I don't mean to tease." Miss Sapp looked at the girls around her and they laughed on cue. "It wouldn't be fair for you to be brilliant and dazzle all our young men at the same time."

Amelia was relieved when Miss Sapp marched off. Unable to remain in the stifling atmosphere any longer, Amelia slipped up the stairs and out the open doors of the old stone church.

What would Gwendolyn have said to Rebecca Sapp? Surely she would have said nothing, because Matthew – Amelia had changed his name from Richard – would have stepped in and whisked her away.

She set off for the Ables' home. She took her time, hoping to avoid a lecture from Amy. Fictional Matthew smiled and offered his arm.

Shall I see you home, dearest Gwendolyn?

Amelia pretended to accept his arm and allow him to lead her down the deserted street.

My dear, you simply look angelic tonight. A light shines from within you. How could I not have seen it when we first met?

Amelia smiled. Matthew and Gwendolyn weren't friends in the early days of their acquaintance. Little had he known she would become his everything – when he came to understand her.

Perhaps what you see wasn't there before you loved me.

No, my dearest Gwen, you are beautiful, not merely your form, but the beauty that begins within.

Amelia sighed with pleasure. *Oh, Richard – er – Matthew, you do go on.*

A sudden realization caused Amelia's playacting to cease. The way that she longed to be loved by a man was the way her Savior had loved her all along. She felt foolish for her daydreaming.

Follow me, and I will make you into the woman I created you to be. I promise you will find where you belong.

"Then let me always follow you." Amelia whispered into the stillness of the evening, feeling her words expand to the stars and fly to worlds unknown.

Amelia recognized she was standing in the middle of Main Street and appeared in need of a sanitarium.

She did a quick survey to make sure she was alone. Satisfied, she walked down the pebbled street, peering into the windows of the darkened stores.

She came to the window of the cabinetmaker. By the light of the street lamp, she could see several chairs and a table standing in the display window. They were clearly well-crafted. She wondered who had made them.

A hope chest made of oak caught her eye. It was beautifully carved with intricate flourishes accenting the wood on every side. She stepped back and looked at the sign that hung over the door.

Morehouse Carpentry and Cabinetmaking.

"Whoever this Mr. Morehouse is, he has a gift," she murmured to herself. She leaned closer to the window to get a clearer view of the chest in the dim light. She pictured it at the end of her bed, keeping her story safely hidden under sheets and dishes and other nonsense meant to fill a hope chest.

"I can see the wheels turning. Who's the lucky fellow?"

Amelia jumped and prayed she was not about to be assaulted. When she turned, she saw William. She turned back to the window, relieved. If he hadn't attacked her by now, she supposed she was safe enough.

"Do you not have anything better to do than harass women in the street?"

"I was afraid you might steal something. It's my shop, after all."

Amelia was surprised, but also mortified he had seen her ogling his chest.

Hope chest.

"Thank you for the compliment. I can continue my craft in

validation." His voice carried a satirical tone.

"Just because you can carve out a nice chest doesn't mean you have manners. Talent does not equal finesse." Amelia huffed.

"Finesse." He repeated the word with his irritating half-smirk, half-frown. She wondered if a good slap might erase the expression from his face.

His rugged, stubbly face.

Traitorous thoughts!

"Why aren't you at the dance with all the other people your age?" He sat down on the bench outside the door of his shop and pulled out a small figure and a whittling tool.

"My age? Does that make you elderly?"

"I wouldn't guess you're a day over eighteen," he said with a shrug.

"I'm twenty-one, but I believe I've already mentioned that." She folded her arms across her chest. "How old are you, aged one?"

"Old enough to know a naïve child when I see her, no matter what year she was born."

"You are the most frustrating man!" Amelia fumed.

"You lose control of yourself quick, don't you?" He scraped his knife against the soft wood.

"Quickly!" She shot back.

"Quickly what?" He smiled, and she was almost certain he knew exactly what she meant.

"Quickly! You lose control 'quickly,' not 'quick.'"

"I don't lose control at all," he said with another shrug.

When Amelia arrived home, after receiving the expected chiding about not having stayed long enough, she asked Amy if she had any idea of the age of William Morehouse.

Amy raised an eyebrow as she returned to scrubbing a pan in the sink. "You and Mr. Morehouse are acquaintances?"

"I wouldn't say that."

Amy hesitated. "He's a couple years shy of thirty, I believe."

Amelia had the sense the other woman was holding back and

wondered if Amy knew more than she wanted to reveal. However, she felt exultant that she had been right.

"I knew he couldn't be that old."

"It sounds like you had an interesting night. I'm surprised Mr. Morehouse attended the dance," Amy said.

"He didn't. I ran into him on my way home." Amelia heaved a frustrated sigh. "He is the most arrogant man I have ever met! How does anyone put up with his endless mocking?"

An amused glint appeared in Amy's eyes. "Did he tease you about your age?"

Amelia nodded, pacing the kitchen.

"Maybe he feels he is older in life experience," Amy said, returning to her dishes. "Mr. Morehouse has had a hard road... if I understand it right. Truthfully, Amelia, I've never known him to give any woman a second look in all the years he's lived here. I would think having a conversation with him shows you have caught his attention."

Amelia didn't know what to say. If he was so reclusive, how had Amy come upon the information? Gossip? Amy must have had the same thought.

"I would assume, anyway. One hears stories," she said, clearing her throat.

"If he finds me interesting, he has an odd way of showing it." Amelia stopped.

"Well, Amelia, you're different. In a good way. Like you were saying before the dance, you think on a deeper level than many young women. You feel things intensely and understand ideas. Add that to your pretty face and your innocence, and it's a sure combination to catch any good man's eye." She fidgeted with the dish towel as she spoke the quiet words. "If Mr. Morehouse does indeed have a darker past, he may find your purity a stunning contrast."

Amelia was speechless. How had she not garnered this information by her intuition, which rarely failed her? And why was Amy so sheepish? Was she trying to lead her in a certain direction? Playing matchmaker?

The thought filled her with panic.

FOURTEEN

William thought about the funny little schoolteacher marching away long after the encounter. He loved a woman easy to rile.

He'd riled Clara good some days.

He had imagined Miss Farnsworth was younger than twenty-one, but she was still much younger than his twenty-eight years. And the life he'd lived would shock the prudent socks right off the young schoolmarm.

She was a puzzle, though, and he couldn't deny it. When he thought he had her figured out, she did something that didn't fit. Like her correcting his grammar even in her flustered state.

And he'd watched her in church, peeking at the rest of the congregation, almost as if she didn't know how to act, though she said she was a preacher's daughter. He'd seen her hold the pew as if she was trying to restrain herself from swaying to the music. And she'd stared at her communion bread and wiped away tears before anyone noticed them.

She read books like *Anna Karenina* and didn't hesitate to speak of the more delicate aspects of the plot.

And she got drunk. Not just drunk, but happy, interesting, unrestrained drunk.

With very soft lips.

He hadn't counted on being back in this place again. Not ever. He'd been content to welcome solitude the rest of his days. He had purposely avoided looking at any woman in Little Sicily since the moment he decided to stay. The plan was to stay in his shop and read books. He'd done enough drinking and carousing in earlier days, and he didn't intend to give himself any reason to return to that life.

Not only was he underserving of the attention of a woman like Amelia, it carried too much risk. It didn't matter how much fun she was to tease or what kind of thoughts she kindled in his mind when she surprised him with that kiss. She didn't have all the facts. He was sure she would never speak to him again if she knew the whole truth. He would protect her from what he wasn't willing to tell her.

He had avoided females this long. Surely he could stay away from one little lady who was proving to be as tempting as a cold glass of lemonade on a hot summer day.

Since lemonade – or any other beverage – was not on the menu, William ended up in the billiard hall that evening. As he listened to the conversations around him, he aimed his cue at the ball.

Mustaches twitched. Cigars billowed smoke around their heads. William knocked the desired ball into the pocket.

A voice at the next table caught his attention. William stood back to prepare for his move while he sharpened his cue and considered his strategy.

"I tell you, gents, she was a beauty, promenading down the hall with lace flouncing everywhere and curls smartly arranged in all the right places."

William glanced at the speaker and confirmed it was the young schoolteacher, Jon Hastings. He wondered which young lady he meant. The new teacher, perhaps?

He dismissed the idea. She didn't wear lace and wouldn't know how to flounce to save her life.

"Miss Sapp's a pretty one," said one of Hastings' friends.

William missed the ball. He stood back while the next man came forward to take his turn. He waited for one of Hastings' friends to tell Jon the truth about Rebecca Sapp. Sure, she was beautiful. Beautiful and off her chump. He hoped for Hastings' sake he realized it sooner rather than later.

"It's too bad we're forced by decency to choose one of them. Even old Jacob in the Bible had a stash of females." Jon laughed as he took his turn and sent a ball cleanly into the pocket.

William made a face. What version of the Bible had Hastings been reading? Because William didn't remember Jacob's decision to make himself a harem to ever work in his favor.

One female was more than enough. Especially if Hastings were thinking of going after the craziest woman William had ever had the misfortune of being acquainted with.

FIFTEEN

Polly Dennis was in a rush to get somewhere. She had looked at the clock on the wall at least three times in the last minute.

"Miss Dennis, do you have something more important than our discussion of British literature?"

The eleven-year-old with the pixie face gave Amelia an innocent look. "Nope."

"Then I'd appreciate it if you'd pay attention and stop willing that clock to move faster.'

"Sorry."

Ten minutes later she dismissed the girls for the day. Amelia called Polly to the desk before she could dash out. She heaved a loud sigh and stomped up the aisle to Amelia's desk.

"Polly, where are you going?" Amelia asked as she stacked papers.

"Ice cream parlor."

"I see. I didn't realize you spent much time in town, with your chores and your home so far out," Amelia said.

Polly scratched her head and looked out the window. "Someone asked me to meet her. Said she buy me an ice cream if I'd tell her a few stories."

Amelia frowned. "Stories about what?"

"School."

"Who is interested in your stories about school?" Amelia said uneasily.

"She said it was a secret. I think she wants to make sure you are teaching us the right stuff."

"Please don't say *stuff*. And I hope you will tell her we are enjoying all the usual school subjects."

Polly shrugged. "I'm just going for the ice cream."

Amelia was plagued by curiosity after Polly left. She decided to take her work home. By way of the ice cream parlor.

The parlor was new in Little Sicily and a busy place on sunny afternoons. Both children and adults crowded the counter, anxious for a tasty treat. Amelia had visited once with Jon, but the richness of the dessert irritated her stomach and the crowd made her nervous, so she hadn't returned. This, however, seemed as good a night as any to give it another chance.

She stepped up to the counter amid the laughter and talking. Someone played a lively tune on the piano, dismantling her thoughts so she found it hard to focus on the task of finding a dime in her reticule. The atmosphere almost reminded her of the unfortunate night in the saloon, and the thought made her blush.

She eyed Polly, tossing her books on the counter and hopping up on a tall stool. No one was with her; she seemed to be waiting.

The clerk handed Amelia a bowl of fluffy white cream and a spoon. She paid her ten cents and looked for a seat. There were none available, but, to her relief, she saw Jon sitting with two other young men. He waved her over and scooted down on his bench so there would be room for her.

"Miss Farnsworth, what a nice surprise," he said. "I didn't think you cared for the ice cream parlor."

She smiled briefly at the other gentlemen and took a bite. "It seemed like a nice day for it."

The men returned to their conversation while she watched Polly out of the corner of her eye. Finally, someone pushed through the crowd and claimed the barstool next to the girl.

Rebecca Sapp.

"Caught you," Amelia mumbled.

"Pardon?" Jon said. "Did you see someone you know?"

"Just thinking out loud. Pardon me."

Amelia watched as Rebecca and Polly sat close together and talked. What were they saying? Why would Rebecca bribe Polly for stories about the school?

Only one reason made sense. She must be trying to find something to implicate Amelia. She wanted the teaching position she felt Amelia didn't deserve to have.

Amelia stirred her ice cream, her stomach churning with apprehension. Was there anything Polly could tell her?

Did Polly know about the coca wine?

Amelia pushed back her bowl with a sick feeling. Jon turned his attention to her.

"Not feeling well?"

"I don't know what I was thinking. The ice cream doesn't agree with me this time either."

"Well, no one can blame you for giving it another try." He grinned. "Can I see you home?"

"Oh, you needn't do that, Mr. Hastings. Finish your treat and your conversation."

"Nonsense." He stood up and took his hat from the table, bidding his friends farewell as he picked up Amelia's books and his own. They walked out the door. As Amelia turned to look back, she saw Rebecca Sapp staring at her, a dark scowl muddying her features.

Though she couldn't quite account for why, a chill crept up the back of Amelia's neck.

At that moment she missed the threshold and tripped, falling hard against Jon's chest. He caught her with a chuckle, offering her his arm to prevent further mishap. When they passed by the window, Amelia noticed Rebecca standing in the aisle, her fists balled at her sides. Menace was written on her face. Amelia quickly looked away, but not before a cold feeling of dread squeezed her chest.

Sixteen

Amelia wrote furiously in her journal. She saw most of the congregation had left the church when she finally looked up. She stood and hurried to greet Pastor Bertram at the door.

"What were you working on?" He nodded toward her journal.

"I'm sorry. I find if don't write my thoughts down, they're gone forever."

"Those must be important thoughts." The pastor smiled.

She shrugged, embarrassed. "I suppose one never knows."

She moved to leave, but he held up a hand to stop her.

"I'm glad I have you here, Miss Farnsworth. I was hoping to speak to you."

She gulped, hoping she was not about to endure another lecture about her teaching methods.

"I wanted to ask if you might be willing to play the piano for us," he said. "I've noticed that you sing well and I wondered if you were musically inclined."

Amelia nodded, trying not to show how flattered she was by his words. "I love to sing and play the piano. I took lessons as a child, but I'm afraid my playing is mostly by ear now."

"All we need is someone to play the hymns. You never need the hymnbook, so you must know them well."

"But Mrs. Doughty plays the piano."

"She does. And at the end of every service, she reminds me how much it aggravates her rheumatism."

Part of her still hesitated, but he was waiting for an answer, and she could think of no other reason to decline.

"I suppose I could help."

"Thank you, dear. You don't know how you've eased my mind."

She said goodbye. As she walked down the path to the road, she felt unease. Though it seemed silly, she wondered if she should have insisted on praying about it first.

She forgot her hesitation by Monday afternoon, when she stood in Hagaman's Store and surveyed the variety of sheet music available.

"You play?" Mr. Hagaman took her dollar and gave her change. She nodded, but she felt guilty, as if she was not being quite honest. She only used the music to assign a key to the song and learn the words and melody. She had not mastered the skill of sightreading very well, especially considering the lessons her parents had sacrificed for her to have. She had spent her practice time composing music in her head. She recalled the admonishment of her teacher.

"Amelia, you must put your head into the process. You have an ear for music, but what good is that if you never develop your ability? The Bible says *to whom much is given, much is required.*"

What might have happened had Amelia applied herself to the scholarship of music instead of the creative outlet it provided? She could have been a world-famous pianist. She sighed with regret.

The white clapboards of the small church seemed to glow in the light of dusk. Amelia lit the lantern outside and practically skipped to the piano, remorse forsaken and replaced with excitement. She sank onto the bench and allowed her fingers happy freedom with the keys. Her remorse faded. Who would want to resign themselves to staring at someone else's harsh little notes on a page when they could play with abandon from the notes in their head?

She played through a few hymns for the next service. The melodies transported her back to childhood, standing on the pew next to her mother and singing her heart out. She did the same now, her voice echoing in the empty room.

She set the sheet music on the stand and read through the song she had chosen. The title said it was a German melody.

> *How can I leave thee, Queen of my loving heart?*
> *Dearer to me thou art, than light and life.*
> *This heart and soul of mine, so close are knit to thine*
> *That I can sooner life than thee resign.*

Amelia brushed away tears. She had the maddening desire that the words be something tangible she might touch. She thought of Gwendolyn. Did her sweetheart give his life for her?

She was captured by the thought. What would it be like to be loved like that? So much that someone was willing to give his life for her well-being? That kind of love would put any other to shame.

A love like Mine.

Of course. She was loved that way even if that man never came along. One had already loved her all the way to death, and back to life again. She had to use both palms to wipe away the tears in order to see the words and notes on the page.

The last notes of the piano echoed off the furthest wall. Amelia closed her eyes and breathed deeply of the peace of the moment. She could almost feel the warmth of the Savior's hands on her own and feel his whisper in her ear.

"What do you think you're doing?"

Amelia considered screaming in terror, but recognized William's voice and only yelped in surprise. She squinted against the darkness to see him in the doorway, his hands on his hips, clearly angry.

"I was playing the piano," she said. "Now I'm trying to convince my heart to start beating again."

He made his way to the piano and reached over her to grab the music. She watched in disbelief as he crumpled it and dropped it on the floor. For a moment she sat there, stunned, but then indignation took over.

"What do you think *you're* doing, Mr. Morehouse? That cost me ninety cents."

He ignored her. "Last time I checked this was a church, not a saloon."

Amelia fidgeted, guilty. She had considered the same. The church might not be the place for love songs. But she looked at the crumpled paper again and became suspicious. "Why does it matter to you? Are you so devout?"

He made a sound of disgust and waved at her as if she wasn't worth his time. "Foolish girl."

"I take it your answer is no," she said with a certain measure of triumph.

He scoffed before he turned and walked out.

She stared at the crumpled paper on the floor, feeling his strong emotions and compelled by them. She wondered if she should be offended by his ungentlemanly actions, but she wasn't. Not at all.

She had the sense they had nothing to do with her.

SEVENTEEN

Amelia Farnsworth must have some secret window into his soul. William was sure she intended to drive him crazy. Why else would the woman choose the one song that was like digging up the grave and prying open the coffin?

He had the familiar urge to head past his door and down to the saloon. He might have, had he not been convinced it would only rip the wound open further.

A roar of frustration escaped him as he entered his empty shop. He slammed his fist into the rough boards of the dresser he'd been carving, giving himself scraped knuckles and quite a sliver. He leaned back against the wall and slid to the floor, giving up the fight, surrendering to the memories. He let the vision of her invade his mind.

Her hair glowed like streams of sunlight around her face, and dangerously deep eyes hidden under the shadow of the old Stetson she always wore. Her smile overflowed with mystery, driving him and every other man in the city wild. He pictured her leaning across the piano in the Black Eagle Tavern in Indianapolis. A crowd gathered around as she sang the words to the German song. She'd sing them in German first, then in English, until the whole roomful of troublemakers stilled.

Her eyes were on him. Only on him. As if she was sending him a message. As if she knew her days were numbered.

"Clara," he said in a whisper. Pain tore at his chest in the agonizing reality of her absence. Her absence that was neither beautiful nor hopeful as the song suggested.

"She was playing your song, Clara."

William woke in his chair with a book of Robert Browning poems on his lap. He rubbed his eyes and reached for his pocket watch. It was nearly one in the morning.

He yawned and stood to put the book away. He was a fool for resorting to poetry as solace for his melancholy, but it had helped.

He heard a noise at the door and turned. It opened a crack and a face peered at him.

"Who's there?" He pulled on the door and Rebecca Sapp stumbled forth.

She was fully dressed, despite the hour. Her strange brown eyes stared up at him, beautiful until William looked closer and saw the cracked sensibilities hiding beneath the surface.

"Can I help you, Miss Sapp?"

"You had an argument with Amelia Farnsworth."

He stood in front of the doorway so she couldn't enter. "You felt the need to come over here and tell me about my private business in the middle of the night?"

Her expression remained dark. "What did you fight about?"

William shrugged. "Can't see how that's any of your concern."

"She's not all she pretends to be. Jon must understand that."

William was more convinced than ever that the girl was crazy as a loon.

"Sure, Miss Sapp, whatever you say. Now go home and let a man get a decent night's sleep."

He nudged her foot out of the way of the door and closed and locked it.

He peered out the window, making sure she headed in the right direction. He hoped this wasn't the beginning of a new round of trouble in Little Sicily.

There were some troubles he wasn't keen to face again.

When Amelia arrived home after encountering William in the church, she found Amy in the parlor, mending.

"While I was practicing at the church..." Amelia wondered how to put the strange conversation into words. "Mr. Morehouse came in."

She had Amy's full attention.

"He was quite upset with me. He crumpled the music I was playing."

"Did he say why?"

"He gave me a lecture on how church wasn't the place for love songs."

Amelia noticed the flash of recognition in Amy's eyes, followed by a guarded blankness.

"Is there something you aren't telling me?" Amelia sat down on the settee.

Amy looked back at her mending. "It's not mine to share, Amelia."

"I wasn't aware that you knew William beyond a neighborly acquaintance," Amelia said. Amy didn't answer.

"Am I correct in assuming that he wasn't really concerned about my playing love songs in church?" Amelia continued.

"If you must know his story, you will have to ask him."

Amelia watched for clues Amy might forget to shield. "Would you recommend I do that?"

She breathed a humorless laugh. "If you're up for a fight."

Amelia huffed. "Where Mr. Morehouse is concerned, it seems a fight is all we're good for."

Amy sat back in her chair and allowed a small smile.

"I have a feeling the way he acts toward you is not based on his opinion of you."

"Meaning?"

Amy studied her folded hands in her lap. "When I was a little girl, I remember once coming across a dog, caught in one of my brother's traps. When I reached toward it so I might help, it snarled and tried to bite me."

Amelia nodded, hoping Amy would go on, but she didn't. She

picked up her mending and stood, avoiding Amelia's inquisitive gaze. Amelia understood what the other woman wouldn't say.

If she wanted to know more, it would have to come from William.

Amelia had the immediate sense that people were talking about her as she entered the church. Just a few people, but enough that she noticed. She swallowed hard and tried to hold her head up as she went to her seat.

When Pastor Bertram motioned her to the piano, she gave an inward sigh, perhaps something like the sigh expressed by Anne Bolin as she marched forward to an unjust execution.

She could admit it was an overly dramatic comparison.

Amelia felt William's critical eyes on her. Would he come forward and tell the whole room what Amelia had done to desecrate their instrument of worship?

Her time at the piano passed without incident and she returned to her seat. She tried to refocus her mind on the sermon, hungry for encouragement or instruction.

The sermon was on the subject of temperance. In recent years, in many Midwestern cities, certain groups had been militant about the need for regulation of alcohol. Wives and mothers marched to protect the homes threatened by drunkard husbands or sons, or both. Clergy like Pastor Bertram called for the eradication of the drink that caused so much pain in families, and claimed that God's Word said as much.

She was ashamed that she should dare to disagree with those suffering on account of strong drink. Of course, Amelia also felt guilt when she realized she had done exactly what he was preaching against. To allow herself to become inebriated was wrong, no matter how she tried to justify it.

On the other hand, it bothered her that he was taking Scripture out of context. If what he said was true, Jesus would have sinned when he turned water into wine at the wedding feast. That was one step from calling God a liar for saying Jesus was sinless. And besides, she feared making alcohol illegal might only cause people to crave it even more.

She peeked around the room, feeling foolish when she saw that no one else seemed bothered. A few nodded their support of his call for prohibition. A few were asleep. She chided herself for becoming so engrossed with details that no one else seemed to notice.

She left as quickly as she could after the benediction. When she stepped out into the December air, she imagined taking a full breath after being underwater for a time. She wrapped her cape around herself and headed in the direction of home.

"You might as well just wear a sign that says you are disgruntled."

William. She sighed and pretended she hadn't heard him, walking faster.

"You don't hide your feelings well," he said bluntly.

Amelia gave him a look she hoped might deter him from speaking to her, but he only smiled when he saw it. She pondered the strange twinge of excitement she felt at hearing his voice. Apparently, after avoiding conflict her entire life, she now anticipated it. She stopped and turned to face him.

"Meaning?"

When he grinned, she glared at him and resumed her walking.

"I enjoyed your playing." He fell in step beside her. "It was a refreshing change."

"I find your opinion interesting considering your feelings about my playing the other night."

He grabbed her arm to stop her, making her turn to face him. She kept her eyes on the ground, clutching her Bible to her chest.

"I was wrong for the way I acted."

She wanted to look at him. His voice almost sounded gentle. She fought the inclination until his finger caught her chin briefly and forced her gaze up to meet his.

"I mean it. I'm sorry. It didn't have anything to do with you."

She pressed her lips together and nodded, now unable to look away from his face. Were there clues written there? He dug into his pocket and held out a silver dollar.

"That's not necessary, Mr. Morehouse."

"I ruined your music and I owe you this." He took her hand, forcing it open and placing the coin on her palm.

His fingers lingered on hers and his eyes met hers, registering surprise. What would he be surprised about? He seemed to recognize something she did not. As if he was awed by the glimpse of an old friend he thought was long gone. Amelia felt her face flush and pulled her hand back.

He shoved his hands in his pockets. Having no idea what to do, since all the things that occurred to Amelia surprised her, she turned again for home. He walked beside her. She assumed he was going the same way.

"What bothered you about the service this morning?" His voice sounded distracted.

She sighed with resignation. "I… disagreed."

He looked at her again, amused. If she wasn't mistaken, she also saw a bit of admiration.

"What did you disagree with?"

"I don't know. I'm probably just being silly. What he was saying seemed more based on his opinion – what he wanted to be true – rather than what the Bible really says about it. It makes me uncomfortable when I hear people use the Bible to fit their agenda. We shouldn't try to make it conform to our needs; we should mold ourselves to its teachings. You must be willing to take it as a whole or not at all."

Amelia prepared for the odd expression on his face she was accustomed to receiving from people when she spoke her true thoughts. He would most likely change the subject. Or worse, he would take offense, given what he had been doing the night she first arrived in town. But, instead, she only saw humor in his expression.

She felt the need to further explain. "I'm not saying I approve of drinking. I know the dangers of abusing alcohol, but that's not the point. I'm concerned the pastor felt the need to add to God's Word for larger effect."

"Never thought about it that way. But I suppose you're right." He grinned at her. She had the sudden thought that he looked like a different person when he smiled. Unfortunately, she watched him too long and tripped over a dip in the road. He caught her arm.

"I've been drunk before. Plenty of times," he said easily. "As you know. Though the time you heard about was the only time I've been in a saloon in years."

She wasn't sure how to respond. It shouldn't shock her, knowing he had a darker past, but he seemed so comfortable with his admission.

"I've also seen the chaos that can erupt when a roomful of men have a few under their belts."

Amelia was quiet, not understanding his point though she was sure he was attempting to make one.

"How about you, Amelia? Ever downed a few tumblerfuls?"

Amelia understood then, and humiliation seeped into every part of her being.

Eighteen

William had to bite his lip to keep from laughing at her tortured expression. "It's alright if you'd rather not say. As you know, I'm hardly in a place to judge."

He'd no idea a woman's face could get that red. Her voice faltered when she finally spoke. "I'm the daughter of a clergyman. What would people think?"

"That doesn't really answer the question."

She stopped. They were standing in front of the Able home. He expected her to mumble a goodbye and run. Instead, she took a deep breath and gave him a direct look.

"I have been inebriated, Mr. Morehouse. So completely I don't even know who carried me inside. I didn't mean for it to happen, but it was only because of my stupidity."

Something wrenched inside him to see her so contrite. He had only been teasing her, and she was making a humble confession. To him, whom she didn't seem to trust or like. He had to resist the sudden urge to reach for her.

"It was me," he said before he thought better of it.

She was confused.

"I was the one who carried you to bed."

Her mouth formed an "oh" and fear lit in her eyes.

He didn't enjoy her unease. "I'm not judging you. And you can put your doubts to rest because I will not tell anyone your secret. You drank on accident. I set out to get drunk with the first sip. I still have that urge every time I pass the saloon."

She seemed affected by his words. She took the first step up to the porch, but seemed torn between saying goodbye and lingering.

"I'm not sorry for being there that night," he said with a shrug. "Not at all. I enjoyed it."

"You enjoyed my humiliation?"

"No." He stepped toward her, eyeing the curve of her waist where he had held her that night. She must have noticed it because he saw pink flood her cheeks yet again. "I enjoyed your inhibition. That spirit of yours you never let get out of hand even though it wants to be."

"You think you have me all figured out," she said in a quiet voice.

"Oh, come on, Schoolmarm. You have me figured out as well." William pushed his hands into his pockets.

"I thought I did."

"You thought I was a low-life outlaw who takes his pleasure shooting men in the kneecaps, ripping up piano music, and making innocent schoolmarms feel like they should be sorry for being innocent?"

"I suppose." The hint of a smile pulled at her lips.

"That's all still true," he said.

She hesitated, glancing back at the house. "I should go in." But she made no move toward the door. Her gaze met his once again. "Outlaw?"

She seemed frightened by the notion, but if William wasn't imagining it, which he wasn't prone to do, she seemed a little excited by the thought as well.

"Oh, no, Miss Farnsworth. If I were to tell you everything, what in the world would I hold over you? I can't just let you have it. You have to *earn* knowing my story."

He was teasing her, but he made sure enough warning came through that she got the message.

"You don't know me as well as you think, either." She folded her arms across her chest in a contrary way. He was doubtful, but he raised an eyebrow in invitation for her to continue.

"I didn't mean to get drunk, but it does sound like something I would do. My family most likely wouldn't be surprised."

He narrowed his eyes. "I doubt it, preacher's daughter."

"I am forever trying to find something to make me feel better," she said, avoiding his gaze.

"Why?" He realized he was quite captured by her expression.

"I've always been delicate, and it plagues me. I have this idea, that if I search long and hard enough, I will find something to cure me. But the cure is always just out of my reach."

Worried, he decided to be direct. "Are you sick?"

"Not exactly," she said.

"Then what gave you the idea you're delicate?"

She seemed caught off guard, as if she hadn't expected the question. He wasn't surprised by her answer.

"I was ill when I was a young child. I had several attacks that almost took my life."

"Did your parents treat you differently? Protect you from anything that might be dangerous?"

She considered his question. "No. They tried to avoid the triggers that caused the episodes, but they didn't hide me away at home. My father was the one who wanted me to come east."

He nodded, allowing the information to shape his opinion of her into a more detailed image.

"You're stronger than you think," he said.

She seemed doubtful. They lapsed into another silence.

"Why did that song upset you?" She finally broke the stillness.

He felt a charge of emotion. Images came to his mind without invitation, a progression of tragedy that mocked him. He couldn't change the outcome. There was no way he could resurrect her from the grave, and it was his fault she was there. He turned to walk away.

"Because of the person who used to sing it."

William muttered a curse when he found the wood box empty.

"Sorry, Lord."

He was anxious to get the day's work done. He only had one order left, a stepstool for Mrs. Hale on First Street. He kept meaning to hire one of the boys running around in the street after school to chop wood for him.

He sighed and grabbed his coat and hat and turned the sign on the window to *Closed*. He took his ax from the shed behind the shop and tossed it onto the wood cart. He pulled it toward the tree line where the town met the forest. There was a nice selection of pine half a mile in.

The day was unseasonably warm for early December. The sun had even made an appearance. Some said it would be a warm winter, and if this kept up, he would believe it.

He examined the trees. As he made his choice, he found his thoughts returning to his conversation with the schoolteacher.

He had dismissed her as naïve and prudish. Those observations had not been disproven, but now she had made herself vulnerable. She had admitted her weakness. It added a layer that caught his attention.

He thought she was still holding something back. Something that pained her too much to talk about. He could press a little further to figure it out. Maybe. As long as she didn't press him for *his* secrets. A chorus of giggles caught his attention.

Peering through the bare trees, he saw a group of girls a ways off, sitting on the ground in a circle around a small fire in front of one of the cave mouths. Younger girls ran around them.

He heard the schoolteacher's voice, soft and dramatic as she read a poem. Her voice echoed in the cave behind her.

> *If thou must love me, let it be for nought*
> *Except for love's sake only. Do not say*
> *'I love her for her smile, her look, her way*
> *Of speaking gently, for a trick of thought*
> *That falls in well with mine, and certes brought*
> *A sense of pleasant ease on such a day.'*
> *For these things in themselves, Beloved, may*
> *Be changed, or change for thee, and love so wrought*
> *May be unwrought so, Neither love me for*
> *Thine own dear pity's wiping my cheeks dry,*

A creature might forget to weep who bore
Thy comfort long, and love thy love thereby
But love me for love's sake, that evermore
Thou mayst love on, through love's eternity.

The girls were quiet, considering the words. William started chopping.

"What's it like to be in love, Miss Farnsworth?" He heard a girl ask after he threw the first log in the cart. He chuckled to himself as he looked for another tree.

"Well, I admit I am not completely sure. I hope it is as nice as Elizabeth Browning suggests."

Nicer than you can imagine, Schoolmarm. More brutal, too.

"I thought it was kissing in the shadows and whispering on the porch swing," one girl said. Some snickered, some made gagging sounds.

William stopped chopping to hear her response.

"Well... I think when love is true, it goes deeper than that. I think you will know you're in love by what you're willing to give up for that person. Just think of Jesus. How do we know of his great love for us?"

"He died for us."

"And don't you think that when we learn to love, we will follow his model?"

William nodded his approval of her answer before he moved to start chopping again. But the next words from one of the students stopped him mid-swing.

"I thought you were in love with Mr. Hastings."

Other girls murmured their agreement. "I think he's in love with you, Teacher!"

A long moment passed in silence.

"Well... I suppose that when love finds me, God will help me know. If you ask him, I'm sure he will do the same for you. Or he will patiently teach us to be satisfied with his love."

William swung the ax again, choosing to disregard the slight relief her words offered him.

93

Nineteen

Amelia hoped that whatever eavesdropping soul had been chopping wood out in the woods had approved of her faltering answers.

She spied Jon on the way back to town after school and tried to catch up to him, wanting to ask him about plans for the Christmas season. She was hoping they could put on a small program at the school, allowing the children to read passages of Scripture and sing songs for their parents in celebration of the holiday.

She stopped pursuing him when he stopped and stuck his head into William's shop. She ducked into the millinery shop next door and listened through the open door, pretending to look at a selection of ribbon. She smiled a greeting at Mrs. Hughes, the owner.

"Can I do something for you, Hastings?" She heard William ask.

"I have a desk that needs fixing." There was a pause and Jon sighed. "Don't ask. It involves Dennises."

"Course it does." She could imagine William's deadpan expression as he spoke. "I'll come out in the morning before school and take care of it."

There was a pause, and Amelia wondered if Jon had left. She leaned closer to the window. William was bringing freshly chopped wood from his wagon and throwing it in the box outside his shop. He motioned for Jon to help him.

"I couldn't help but notice you walked Miss Farnsworth home from church Sunday," she heard Jon say.

Amelia gasped, receiving a glance of disapproval from Mrs. Hughes. Amelia smiled and held up a length of ribbon.

"Are you her guardian now?" William replied in a voice so low Amelia could barely hear him.

Jon chuckled. "Not in the least. I was just toying with the idea of courting her, so I wanted to know if there was any competition."

Amelia initially felt flattered, then chafed. Was she an animal at a stock sale? She almost went out and asked if they'd like to check her teeth first. But she was interested in his answer. For curiosity's sake, of course.

William had taken quite a long pause.

"Why would I care what you do with her?" He sounded irritated. She had no idea what to make of her own response to his words. The emotion felt strangely like disappointment.

"Well, good." Jon wiped his hands of wood dust and started to walk away.

"Are your intentions honorable?" William spoke after him without looking up from his task.

"Of course." Jon stopped and turned around. "I haven't decided to pursue it, but if I do, I won't compromise her, if that's what you mean."

William stood up. Amelia noticed he was a good two inches taller than Jon.

"Why wouldn't you pursue it? Do you think something's wrong with her?"

Amelia found she did not care to hear the rest of the conversation, but she was stuck unless she bought some ribbon, and she certainly had no need for ribbon. She gulped.

"She's pretty," Jon said. "Though she tries to hide it. She says odd things sometimes, and she's very religious, but she's quiet and honest. I guess I'm just thinking it through."

"There are plenty of other girls in town." William sounded indifferent, but his voice was lower than usual.

"True. I think Rebecca Sapp might be interested. Quite a peach."

William didn't answer. Jon's smile faded and he left. Amelia waited until William had gone back into his shop before she said good day to Mrs. Hughes.

She was reminded why eavesdropping wasn't a good idea. All her faults had been on display as the two men sized her up in the street for anyone to overhear. And both of them had been apathetic at best in their interest.

Amelia had grown quite tired of Polly's sneer. She would have liked to turn the child's desk around and let her sneer at the wall. There couldn't be a more willful child in all of the state of Ohio.

"Polly, you will do the sums, and you will do them correctly, or you will stay after school and do them again."

"I can't. I've got chores."

"Then your only choice is to do them right. Now."

Her leering grin irked Amelia, but she chose to ignore it and move on with practice for the Christmas pageant.

"All the girls who have speaking parts, come forward and we will rehearse."

The girls put down their pencils and came to the front with excitement. She was thankful for their enthusiasm. She would have been quite discouraged if no one had seen her vision for the small program. She could tell Jon thought the idea was rather silly, even if he went along with it.

"We only have one week left. Don't forget to invite all your family and friends. And let's pray that God will use our efforts for his glory."

She also prayed the affair would not result in any more ruffled feathers or scandalous accusations. Those seemed common in the town of Little Sicily. One couldn't always predict an outbreak.

That was not the only thing Amelia could not have predicted.

Twenty

The day of the program, the sky was heavy with snow. It held off, and Friday evening, the boys' side of the schoolhouse filled to overflowing with parents and neighbors.

Jon had the boys recite some Scripture and sing a song, which they did with a great deal of shuffling feet and embarrassed scowls. Halfway through, one of the Dennis boys sneezed into another boy's hair, nearly causing a fistfight. Everyone was relieved when it was the girls turn to climb onto the makeshift stage, which was decorated with pine boughs and paper stars.

As the girls delivered their lines, a hushed silence fell over the crowd. The magic of the evening deepened as Wanda Hubble stepped forward in her costume with her baby brother and sang the words of the Christmas hymn "Thou Didst Leave Thy Throne."

Amelia was thrilled to see tears being wiped from eyes. This was Christmas. Forget presents and dinners and even loved ones. Jesus was Christmas. Jesus was everything.

She hugged her students afterwards. Even Polly. She tried to squirm away but Amelia thought she saw the hint of a smile. Then they were gone, dancing off into freshly falling snow. Jon and Amelia stood side by side at the door until the last family had faded from view.

"You did great, Em." Jon reached for her hand. "Your students love you."

"I love them." She felt warm at the praise. He reached a finger to trace her jaw.

"You're radiant. Your cheeks are flushed, and your eyes are lit up like stars," he said in a hushed voice.

She couldn't speak. After a long moment, he let her go so he could extinguish the lamps and shut the door behind them. They walked out into the snow. He retrieved her hand as they made their way down the path.

"How beautiful." She breathed in the smell, noticing the difference in the cadence of the air. The snow buffered the sounds of the town and caused a cozy silence to descend. She wished she could speak the words to capture the mysterious stillness of the night.

Oh, for pencil and paper!

Her heart began to hammer as they approached the Ables' porch. She turned to face him when they reached the door, noting he had not let go of her hand, even when she gave it a gentle tug.

"Will you come in?" Her voice was breathless as it sliced through the crisp air.

He didn't answer. With his free hand he traced the outline of her arm through her cape, reaching up to pull back her hood. He smoothed back her hair and let his palm come to rest on her cheek.

She leaned against the heat of his hand, trying to smile but fighting inhibition. It confused her, because until this moment the night had been the closest thing to perfect. Now, the only thoughts that occurred to her were odd questions.

What now? Should I pull away? Lean forward? Am I supposed to close my eyes? Are my lips too dry? I hope my breath is not repugnant.

Repugnant. What an awful word.

She had the most inappropriate urge to giggle. She stifled it, but at the same moment he leaned in to kiss her. Their mouths met in what she could only describe as…

Awkward. The kiss lasted only a moment, but involved more moisture and nose-bumping than she had anticipated. It was not the moment she had dreamed of. Her heart sank with a resounding thud on the floor of her aspirations for a romantic life well-spent.

Was that all?

Jon didn't seem disappointed. He smiled and squeezed her hand before he stepped off the porch and made his way into the night. She stared after him, feeling entirely disenchanted. Why could nothing ever compare to her imagination?

She went to her room, trying to be positive. Ella would be glad to hear she had finally been kissed, but Amelia would immediately have to describe it. In detail.

Amelia changed into her nightgown and buried herself under the quilts on her bed.

Perhaps she was just incapable of passion. Maybe God only meant for her to spend her days as a schoolmarm.

It seemed the strangest moment to think of William, but she had heard him acerbically refer to her as "Schoolmarm" on nearly every occasion they had spoken to each other. Her thoughts went, without her consent, into a fascination with what might be different if she were ever to have a reason – which she did not foresee happening – to share a kiss with him. William, who went into rages at love songs. Who forever had a wrinkle in his brow over his secret thoughts.

She fell asleep with his face in her mind, feeling ashamed over it, yet unable to erase the lines of his form.

When she dreamed, she heard the letter-writer sobbing. He asked one question, over and over, lifting red-rimmed eyes to heaven.

Why?

TWENTY-ONE

Amelia believed nothing quite matched the feeling of waking up on the morning of Christmas Eve.

Especially this Christmas Eve. Her father and sister would arrive on the train that very evening.

She spent the day helping Amy clean the house and decorating the Christmas tree with the girls. Connor and Amy had invited Amelia's family to stay with them during their two-week visit, and they had accepted. Amelia was worried about the expense of the journey, but Ella had written to say the church had given their father a sum of money as a Christmas gift. She also worried about her mother being alone on Christmas but Ella mentioned their mother's sister, a widow, intended to spend the day with her, and mother had insisted they come and see Amelia.

As Amelia held Kathleen up to place her ornament in just the right spot, she pondered the fact that she had not seen Jon since the program. She didn't want to admit it, but she felt a certain relief. She didn't know what to expect. Did the kiss signify a deepening of their relationship? She assumed Ella would know.

As Amy and Jennifer began baking, it grew obvious that Kathleen's "helping" was beginning to wear on Amy's nerves. Amelia offered to take her out to do some Christmas shopping until the train arrived.

Kathleen narrowed her eyes, as if suspicious that Amelia was trying to trick her, but a trip to the store proved too tempting.

They pulled on their coats and set out on their adventure.

They talked about bugs.

They skipped.

They made up a story about a polar bear named Albert who came south to spend Christmas in Ohio with his cousin Grizzly.

They rounded the corner and came upon the busy town. In many senses it was business as usual, but a thread of excitement pulsed just beneath the surface.

Kathleen stopped in front of William's shop and pointed at the hope chest in the window.

"It's pretty."

"You're right, it's beautiful. I'm surprised it's still there."

"Can we go in?" Kathleen asked hopefully. Amelia shrugged, not about to tell the little girl that the thought of entering the shop made her heart start to race. She followed Kathleen across the threshold, wondering if Kathleen knew William. How would he react to having a small child underfoot?

Kathleen ran to him and hugged his leg. He picked her up, giving Amelia the answer to her question. He was smiling until he noticed Amelia was with her. His demeanor changed, and he set the child down.

William knew the Ables better than he – or they, for that matter – had ever admitted. Why the secret friendship?

Amelia's thought process might have continued had he not pointed Kathleen toward a box of unfinished wooden toys and come to stand by her.

"Miss Farnsworth."

"Don't you mean *Schoolmarm*?"

"Well, sure, but I was trying my hand at being polite."

She smiled, angling her head while she surmised him. "No. Politeness doesn't work on you. You're more authentic when your manners are atrocious."

"As long as I'm authentic." He chuckled. "So what brings you and Miss Able out this morning?"

"We were in the way. With the family coming, Amy's in a baking frenzy for Christmas dinner. I thought it would be helpful if we found something else to do."

"Family coming?"

"Not hers. Mine. She wrote and asked them to join us for the holiday."

He nodded, folding his arms across his broad chest. "That does sound like Amy Able. She invited me, as well. I suppose it would look pathetic for me to spend Christmas reading alone in my room."

"Don't you have family?" Amelia broached the subject, not surprised when he shifted his weight and looked away. At least the ever-present line in his forehead didn't deepen.

"Sometimes a man makes choices that have consequences."

"All choices have consequences."

He nodded, staring hard at the floor where Kathleen played. He offered no more. Amelia wanted to encourage him to elaborate, but feared stirring his ire.

"So, we get to meet the schoolmarm's family, do we? I hope your folks will tell plenty of tales on you."

"There's not much to tell," Amelia said. "I've led a rather boring life."

"Something tells me you harbor a secret or two." He gave her a pointed look. "I know one of them."

"You know the only one." She gave him her best look of condescension, trying not to blush, but not succeeding. He watched her with amusement and something else she wasn't able to define. She looked down at the ground.

"It's only my father and sister who are coming," she said, her voice quieter.

"What about your mother?"

Amelia hesitated. "She's ill."

"Sorry to hear that." He eyed her with a certain level of curiosity that made her feel exposed.

"Miss Emmy has a secret," Kathleen said in a matter-of-fact tone. She sat Indian-style on the floor in front of a dollhouse. "But I can't tell."

Amelia's blush deepened as William turned back to her, his eyebrows raised in expectation. "Kathleen and me will need to have a chat."

"Kathleen and I." Amelia corrected.

"Confound it, woman! Can't you just let conversation be conversation? I'm not your pupil."

Amelia heard the teasing in his tone and gave him a stern appraisal. As her eyes travelled over his form, she had to agree. "If you were, I've a feeling you'd spend most of your time in the dunce chair."

Kathleen giggled and covered her mouth with her hand. William gave Amelia a smoldering look that threatened to break into a full-fledged smile.

"Well?"

"Shush."

Ella sat on Amelia's bed, leaning against the headboard with ankles crossed. She picked up page after page of Amelia's story as Amelia watched, perched on the chair at the desk.

Amelia observed her sister, noting small changes that had occurred in the time they had been apart.

Ella was even more graceful and stylish now. Her hair was piled in curls on top of her head. Her outfit seemed to come straight out of the Montgomery Ward catalogue, even though Amelia knew most of Ella's clothes came from the donation bin at the church. Amelia had always envied her sister for the air of confidence she possessed. Amelia forever wondered what others thought of her, while Ella never gave it a thought.

"Ella! For goodness' sake, speak to me!"

Ella heaved a dramatic sigh and flipped back through a few pages. "There are two grammatical errors on page thirteen and one on page twenty."

"You would notice."

She made a face. "I think you should explore the idea that love isn't safe."

"Okay," Amelia said. "What about the characters?"

Ella twisted her mouth and shrugged. "Gwendolyn is a dear, but her love interest is an insufferable bore."

"What?" Amelia protested, grabbing the pages away from her sister. "He is not!"

"He is. I can't stand him. He has no depth and no genuine qualities. He acts like a man who lives inside a woman's brain, not an actual man. You feel the same way deep down, Emmy Jo. You don't even get his name right half the time."

Amelia sulked and held the papers against her chest.

"Your love scenes are lacking, too. They need more description and feeling."

Amelia threw her pencil at her. "I should just toss the whole mess in the fireplace."

Ella rolled her eyes. "Don't be so theatrical. If it were worthy of the fire, I would just say it was very nice. It's only because it has potential that I play the part of your worst critic."

"You're hardly the worst one."

Ella raised an eyebrow but didn't ask for an explanation. "Don't you have a beau now?" She gestured as if her point was obvious.

"I thought so," Amelia said. "He kissed me."

"Your first kiss!" Ella clapped in excitement. "Tell me. Don't leave anything out or so help me, Amelia Josephine..."

"It wasn't anything like I expected. It was awkward. I guess kissing is only romantic in books."

Ella laughed. "Maybe you were just kissing the wrong person."

"And who else should I be kissing?"

"Why don't you try your worst critic?" Ella said with a devilish grin. "I assume you are speaking of this William person you have been writing about in your letters so ferociously. Maybe he'd teach you a thing or two about kissing."

"Ella Farnsworth! If kissing a friend, whom I hope will be more, was strange, what would kissing my truest enemy be like?"

She smirked. "You'll never know unless you try. Ask him to kiss you. Or just kiss him without permission; he won't complain. And when you do, make sure you write everything down so you can describe it later in your love scenes. Catalogue it in your library of feelings."

"And how exactly would that go? 'Pardon me, William. I know you basically despise everything about me, but do you think you might spare a kiss for the schoolmarm, for the sake of research?'"

Ella laughed loudly, and Amelia couldn't help joining her.

"Oh, Emmy Jo, you have so much to learn!" When her laughter died down, Ella continued in a more thoughtful tone. "And yet, you don't seem to be quite the porcelain doll you were. Maybe you are discovering a bit of confidence out here in Ohio. I guess we'll have to see what happens."

Amelia barely heard the hesitant knock on the door over the noise of the people inside. When she opened it, William gave her his familiar frown in greeting. She noticed the book he carried under his arm.

"You stole my book." She gestured to the worn copy of *Uncle Tom's Cabin* that, last she knew, had been sitting on her shelf at the school.

"I fixed a desk. It was my payment." He shrugged and moved past her, greeting Amy with a commendation on her dress.

Amelia looked down at what she had thought was a festive choice of dress for the occasion. Apparently, it was not worth a compliment.

"Thank you, William." Amy took his hat and coat. "I'm glad you came. I wasn't sure you would."

He nodded, but Amelia didn't miss the unspoken words that passed between them. Why *had* he come? What was she missing?

The house had become segregated. The women sat in the parlor chatting and drinking cinnamon tea, while the men stood around the dining room table with cups of coffee, discussing politics. Amelia listened covertly as William introduced himself to her father and the two shook hands.

"Please to meet you, Reverend Farnsworth. Thank you for loaning us your daughter. She's doing a good job."

"Of course." Amelia's father raised an eyebrow and caught

Amelia's eyes. She didn't miss the curious wink.

William cleared his throat and took a long sip of coffee.

TWENTY-TWO

William did his best to fade into the wallpaper. He was surrounded by family togetherness and warmth, and it made him uncomfortable. He answered direct questions evasively or asked questions in return. He kept his eyes down on the turkey and cornbread dressing that tasted just like his grandmother's recipe. He felt Amy's eyes on him often, so he tried to reassure her by loosening his frown now and then.

What he seemed unable to do was keep his eyes from straying to Amelia Farnsworth.

She was across from him and one seat to his right. She was quiet, as usual, but it was a contented sort of introversion. She didn't seem as uncomfortable or conflicted as usual. Her sister sat next to her, and they shared quite a few private jokes. He found her secret giggles to be the most appealing. He wondered what Amelia had told her sister about him. Judging by the way the younger sister kept eyeing him, he assumed none of it was positive.

Jon was on the other side of Amelia, quite attentive. He whispered close to her ear and placed his arm on the back of her chair in a possessive manner. William could tell the relationship had taken steps since Jon had approached him on the subject.

Panic surprised him.

"Is he good for her?" Amelia's father, sitting next to him, leaned over and asked in a quiet voice. William searched for words.

"She could do worse."

"But could she do better?"

William thought about the conversation he'd had with Jon. He could see a line of progression that might occur if they made a match. He figured there wasn't much of a chance Amelia would survive without wounds. Jon disliked the very things that William admired in Amelia. Her spirit. The ways she was different than other women — more genuine, more unpredictable. Thoughtful and intuitive.

She could do better than Jon. More than that, she *needed* better than Jon.

Reverend Farnsworth sat back and gave a dramatic sigh of satisfaction. "Mrs. Able, there are few women on earth that can cook a better meal than you have. Thank you." Amy smiled and nodded.

"Please excuse me; I feel the need for a stroll to let this glorious food digest."

As the conversation returned to the former noise level, he stood and caught William's eye. William felt apprehension when the older man nodded toward the door. He reluctantly set down his napkin and followed the imposing man outside.

They crunched through the remains of the snow.

"What is your connection to the family?" Reverend Farnsworth asked. His hands were folded behind his back; his handlebar moustache twitched in consideration.

"A friend."

"Hmm."

William thought he heard incredulity. If this was going to be an interview about his past, he would need an escape. He prepared his excuses. But the other man seemed to let it go.

"I was sorry to hear your wife is ill," William said.

Reverend Farnsworth considered him at length. "Has Amelia shared with you the nature of her illness?"

"No, sir. She only said she couldn't make the trip because she was ill."

The man suddenly seemed much older. He nodded, his gaze fixed on the path in front of them.

"My wife has been ill for quite some time. She lives in an

institution where she can be cared for."

"Consumption?" William guessed, feeling a pang of empathy for Amelia. Suddenly so many things about her made more sense.

"Yes."

William didn't know what else to say. He knew that tuberculosis was a slow and ruthless killer. He knew this family was enduring a heartache that wouldn't end well.

The reverend seemed to rally his control. "Tell me something, Mr. Morehouse. If this Mr. Hastings was to ask for my daughter's hand, as I suspect he might do at some point, why should my wife and I allow it?"

William wondered why Amelia's father thought he had the answer to that question.

"None of my business."

"I see."

They walked in silence again, until William could no longer hold back. "Miss Farnsworth and I can barely have a conversation without arguing. As far as I can tell, Mr. Hastings has been nothing but a gentleman in her presence. Why are you asking me?"

The reverend's tone was casual. "You watched them. At dinner. I wondered if you might disapprove. Perhaps I have misread the situation."

He'll take everything right about Amelia and dry up her spirit like a desert. He'll be polite, respectful, but he'll be distant. And when the house is dark, he'll sneak away and get his fill elsewhere. I've seen his kind. He'll break her heart.

To Amelia's father he said nothing. He couldn't. He had no proof, and to get more involved would put his secrets in jeopardy.

"You must consider me overprotective. But Amelia is unbolted and honest. Wonderful qualities, yet it makes her vulnerable. If she was betrayed by someone she thought loved her, it would wound her in a way that wouldn't heal easily."

He stopped, and his narrowed eyes fell on William's face. "I just want her safe. She's my little girl. Will you watch out for her for me?"

The older man's words compelled him, and there was only one

answer William could give. "I won't let her get hurt, if it's in my power to stop it."

TWENTY-THREE

There had been many times in her life Amelia had been disappointed. In fact, it was by far her most familiar emotion. But something about that Christmas day was enchanting.

She tried to decide what it was. Having her family there was part of it, but it was more. It wasn't really Jon, she had to admit. It was nice having a man stay close to her and be attentive in a way she wasn't used to, but she avoided being alone with him. He tried several times to get her into a hallway or out in the yard for a stolen moment, but she was too afraid of repeating the kiss that had gone so wrong, or to chance her father seeing them together. She sensed he wasn't sold on the idea of Jon as her beau.

If she was being honest, neither was she.

There was a voice in the back of her mind hinting at where the hum of pleasant tension came from. She was not ready to accept the notion, and she couldn't see how it would be true. She liked to be able to tell herself that she had a grasp of relationships around her. She didn't care for something not to make sense. And it didn't make sense to her how she could derive so much satisfaction from being close to William.

But as the day went on, her doubt faded. It was true. William had met her gaze so many times that day that she had memorized every detail of his green eyes. He still wore his frown, but somehow it seemed to have more to do with Jon's arm being around her or Jon's knee touching hers than disapproval of Amelia.

She resisted it. It was her imagination. It must be.

111

Gifts were exchanged. She received a new leather-bound journal from her family, and a fancy pen from Connor and Amy. Jon presented her with a set of turtle shell hair combs. The personal nature of the gift made her uncomfortable, and she had no idea where she would wear them. She mumbled her thanks and set them aside, out of sight.

She tried not to look around at the faces of her loved ones as they opened the embroidered handkerchiefs she had made, though they acted as if they were perfect. She was never sure what to give for gifts. She was too afraid of disappointing everyone.

When Kathleen's turn came, the biggest gift under the tree was presented to her. She didn't dance around the room with her sister, but her eyes shone with such a light that no one supposed she was unhappy to receive it. She pulled away the wrapping and her eyes widened in awe. It was a beautiful hand-carved Noah's Ark, complete with two of every animal.

"Pretty!" Jennifer squealed and kneeled next to her as they pulled out each unique animal.

Amelia studied the gift. Hadn't William been carving a small animal the night of the Thanksgiving dance? She looked over at him, meeting his eyes. If he had done it, he did not give himself away. She supposed Amy and Connor could have secured his services.

When the gifts were cleared away, Amy announced they would be playing parlor games. Amelia tried not to grimace. She was a miserable failure at parlor games.

They played her least favorite. Only one person was allowed to smile. They could do anything to make the next person smile. When Jon leaned in her face and crossed his eyes, she immediately lost, not because she found it funny, only because it made her uncomfortable and she wanted it to be over. And so, it was her turn to coax a smile from –

She looked next to her on the floor where Kathleen had been playing with her new toy, but she was gone. The next person was William, sitting in an armchair and staring her down with a severe frown. She heard titters of laughter from around the room.

There was no way he would ever crack a smile, and she refused to make a fool of herself trying.

"Can I forfeit?" Her voice squeaked.

"No way, Emmy Jo!" Ella laughed with glee. "And ruin the best entertainment of the day?"

When Amelia reluctantly looked back at William, he wasn't looking at her anymore. In fact, his face had turned somewhat pale, and he was staring at Ella.

"What did you call her?"

"Emmy Jo. Short for Amelia Josephine."

Amelia watched William with curiosity. What about her sister's nickname for her was so startling?

She lost the game, inelegantly, as she expected. A half-hour later neither William nor Ella had faltered. It was declared a tie when everyone tired of watching them stare each other down.

When evening shadows started to fall, Jon said his farewells. Amelia wondered where he could be headed on Christmas day, but she didn't say anything as he kissed her cheek and squeezed her hand at the front door.

The girls went to bed, and Connor and her father retired to the study to continue a discussion on political party strategies, as if their talking over the matter would make some sort of difference in the way things were done. Amy, Ella and Amelia had been playing a tournament of checkers, but Amy forfeited so she could put the girls to bed, and Amelia was no match for Ella's determination. She was distracted by the man sitting in the armchair, reading her book.

"I don't recall you asking permission to borrow that," she said, crossing to the settee and sitting down. He grunted and looked up as if she had pulled him from another world.

"I didn't ask."

"Well, what do you think? Is it shocking enough material for impressionable young minds?"

"Very shocking." He began to read again. Amelia thought the conversation was over, but after he turned the page another time, he spoke again.

"I like Eva."

Amelia was surprised yet again. "So do I. She's my favorite character."

He looked at her as if he was trying to decide something. "You're like her."

"I am?"

"I like this part," he said as he looked down and began to read aloud. "*But, of old, there was One whose suffering changed an instrument of torture, degradation and shame, into a symbol of glory, honor, and immortal life; and, where His spirit is, neither degrading stripes, nor blood, nor insults, can make the Christian's last struggle less than glorious.*"

Amelia's heart stirred and she felt a gentle ache in her chest. *Jesus.*

They were all quiet in contemplation.

After a moment, she spoke her thoughts, refined over many years of considering the meaning behind the controversial book dealing with the issue of slavery. "Death means more when it happens as a sacrifice. It changes people."

Ella nodded in objective agreement, but William just watched her. She wondered if he agreed or not.

He stood. "Walk me home."

Amelia laughed, thinking he was joking.

"Come on." He nodded toward the door. What could she do?

As she went to grab her wrap, Ella made a snorting sound. Amelia thought it might be a not-so-subtle cough of the word "catalogue."

The snow was not as beautiful as it had been the night of the program. It was mostly melted and dirty, clumping at the sides of the road. But the air was crisp and alive as if it marveled along with the world at the magic of the holiday.

"It was a good day." William's pleasant words were dissonant with his voice, short and petulant as ever. She nodded, not feeling a need to respond. She held her hands behind her and wondered again why he had wanted her to join him on his walk home. He didn't say anything else until they were standing at the door of his shop. She gave him an expectant look. Should she turn around now and walk home by herself?

He opened the door and lit the lamp on the table inside. "Come in."

She narrowed her eyes. "Mr. Morehouse, this is not proper."

"Says who? I don't see anyone watching. Get in here."

Amelia crossed her arms and gave him a stubborn stare. He sighed.

"I promise not to ravish you. Is that what you wanted to hear?"

The heat from her cheeks was a stark contrast to the winter chill. She didn't know why, but a sudden obstinacy made her walk inside and allow him to close the door behind her.

"There, was that so bad?" He gave her a smug expression. "May I take your wrap?"

"No." She pulled it more tightly around herself. "This is highly reprehensible."

"No need for fancy language around here, Schoolmarm." He said the words in a drawl as he went behind the counter and pushed something large from behind. It was wrapped in newspaper.

"What's this?" She watched him with apprehension. Had he gotten her a gift? Why would he do that? Had she misunderstood the casual nature of their relationship? Should she have something for him?

"Don't get all flustered. I can't seem to find a buyer for it, and I need the space in my window. You liked it, so you get it."

She gulped back the hard lump that sat in her throat, realizing what was under the wrapping. She didn't want to, but she reached out a hand and pulled back the paper to confirm her suspicion. It was the hope chest, now stained a rich maple color. It was breathtaking.

And Amelia was tongue-tied.

They stood for a long time as she gulped back tears, both in appreciation of the beautiful gift and his willingness to give it to her. But she didn't want him to see the way it affected her, so she fought back the emotional response and cleared her throat.

"William," she said in a mixture of wonder and reproof. "What do you want me to say?"

He sighed again, shifting his feet. It occurred to Amelia that he was also embarrassed. She had never seen him show self-doubt before.

"As I said, I'm just trying to get rid of it. You can say 'Thanks, Morehouse, I think I'll take it off your hands,' or you can say 'no' and proclaim me 'highly reprehensible' or some other nonsense if you'd rather."

"Thank you. I'd be honored to take it," she said in a meek tone.

"Done."

"But you're reprehensible either way."

He leaned against the counter, making no move to see her out now that their business was cared for.

"You're a puzzle, Schoolmarm."

"I can't imagine why. Of the two of us I'd say you are the mysterious one."

"I'm mysterious for a reason. You're a puzzle because I can't seem to categorize you. I can't dismiss you like I thought at first." He took a step closer to her, and she felt goose bumps on her arms.

"Maybe you've changed since you came," he said, his voice quiet.

She decided this might be as good a moment as any to pursue his mystery. "Since you seem to understand me so well, perhaps it's time to tell your secrets. You can start by explaining why a scholar such as yourself uses poor grammar on occasion." Her voice held a breathless quality that seemed to affect him.

"I like vexing you, of course," he said, but he was distracted as he spoke.

She dared to push further. "Will you tell me about your past?"

He mulled over his reply for a long time. "There are things a nice girl like you shouldn't hear."

"I don't believe you could have done anything that would shock me."

It wasn't true. She was easily shocked, and both of them knew it. He smirked at her.

"You might shock me, but I would get over it. I admit I am naïve, but I don't judge. At least not in the way most others do."

He remained incredulous.

"If we are to have some kind of acquaintance between us, I must understand you. I have to know why you are the way you are. Why you treat me with disdain when you seem to... appreciate being near me."

Had she said the words aloud? She caught his rare look of surprise. His expression became thoughtful.

"I do believe you wouldn't judge. But your opinion of me would change. And for some reason..." He took another step closer and put a finger lightly under her chin. "That matters to me."

She could feel his breath on her face. She unconsciously leaned forward a tiny bit.

His hand dropped. "Time to get you home, little girl." His voice was thick.

He stepped out of the shop, motioning her to follow, and they headed back to the house at a brisk pace.

"You know, William," she said as she caught up to him. Had she called him William twice during their conversation? She decided not to draw attention to that fact. "If my opinion of you is not based in truth, what good is it – to you or to me?"

He didn't answer. He seemed determined not to interact. Something had happened. She wasn't sure what it was, but she sensed it was an amendment from which they could not return.

Ella was waiting up for her. "Did he kiss you?"

Amelia made a face as she undressed and pulled her nightgown over her head. "He gave me a gift. For Christmas."

Ella looked around the room. "Well, where is it?"

"He'll have to bring it discreetly. It's a hope chest."

Ella laughed loudly, and then clapped her hand over her mouth. "Oops. Why in the world would he give you a hope chest?"

"I admired it in his window some time back. He needed to get rid of it, so he asked if I wanted it."

"I doubt it. Why didn't you get him to kiss you? It was the opportune moment."

"Because we were alone in his shop, Ella. That's hardly proper. And anyway, I refuse to force a man to kiss me. That's not romantic."

Ella scoffed.

"And I have a beau. Sort of. I shouldn't be running around town kissing every man I see," Amelia added.

"I did not get the impression that Mr. Morehouse was a random person walking about town. Did you see the way man stared at you today? He's smitten!"

"He is not." Amelia tried her best to scoff back at her sister. She got in bed and pulled the covers up to her chin, trying not to touch Ella with her feet. Her sister was repulsed by feet.

"You're just saying what a sister is supposed to say," Amelia huffed.

Ella sighed with dramatic flair.

Amelia lay awake for a few minutes, her thoughts inevitably returning to the sweet agony of being so close to William.

"Say hello to Grandma if you see her tonight," Ella mumbled.

They both giggled.

TWENTY-FOUR

The morning of New Year's Day, William tried to work, but he kept thinking about Amelia Farnsworth.

Which made him think of Clara. Which made him crazy with longing.

His eyes fell to Amelia's copy of *Uncle Tom's Cabin* on his desk, giving him an excuse to pay a call on the schoolmarm. He threw down his hammer in a fit of decision and left the shop before he could change his mind.

The day was warm for the first of January, so he wasn't surprised to see Amelia sitting with her sister on the porch. They both stared him curiously. Ella appeared smug. Amelia seemed welcoming, though he thought he glimpsed the sheen of recent tears in her eyes. Had her sister been giving her an update on her mother's health?

"Good morning, Mr. Morehouse," Ella said as she gestured to the middle of the swing, as it was the only available seat. He acquiesced and sat between Amelia and her sister.

If he wasn't imagining things, Ella leaned his way slightly to force him to sit closer to Amelia.

"Many happy returns in the new year." Ella continued, her manner taunting. "What brings you out this morning?"

William handed Amelia the book. "Just returning this."

"That's all?" Ella shot him a dubious look.

He shrugged.

She gave a disdainful sniff. "It seems like you could have just given it to her the next time you saw her."

Amelia glared at her sister. "Thank you for your thoughtfulness, Mr. Morehouse. Have you been busy in the shop since Christmas?"

He had taken off his hat and was holding it in his lap. He twisted the edge. "Nope. Slow time of year."

"How did you come to be a carpenter? Did you learn the trade from your father?" Ella asked. He could see the resemblance between the sisters. They both had the same shade of blonde hair, though Ella's was styled in a more modern fashion. He wondered if they both favored their mother. He pictured her as an older version of the girls, with wizened eyes and an altruistic smile. It made him think of his own mother, and how sad her life had been.

He should have lightened her load. He wished she hadn't died before he made his peace with God.

"I learned the trade awhile back when I was living in Indianapolis."

He knew his answer was hardly informative. But he saw no reason to say any more. He definitely did not wish to discuss his father.

"I'm cold. I'm going in for a cup of tea." Ella stood and went to the door, bidding him a quick goodbye before she disappeared into the house.

He didn't know what to say when they were alone. He wished they could reclaim the spark from Christmas night.

He knew it was possible. He even had a few ideas how to go about it. But he also knew it wasn't a good idea, for reasons more important than his present satisfaction.

"Have you enjoyed the time with your family?" He turned to look at her. He didn't move away though there was plenty of room since Ella had left. Her face was pink as she stared at her hands.

"More than I can say. It has made me miss home."

He didn't like the sound of her tone. "But you're staying."

She smiled. "That didn't sound like a question."

"It wasn't."

She chuckled and bit her lower lip. It could have been July for all the warmth he felt.

"What are you thinking?" she asked.

He shook his head. There was no way he would admit those thoughts.

After a moment of silence, he cleared his throat. "Do you and Hastings have an understanding?"

"I suppose." Her shrug told him she wasn't certain of anything.

William wanted to ask her if she thought Jon was a good man, but he knew she would say he was. Amelia had trouble recognizing people's faults. He also wanted to ask if she thought Jon would make a good husband, but he didn't. It wasn't his business.

He had no right to judge Jon Hastings, after all.

William heard a feminine laugh as he turned the corner, heading home to the carpentry shop. He saw Jon standing on the porch of the Sapp house across the street.

"You're such a darling!" Rebecca gushed, inching closer.

William made a quick decision. He picked up a newspaper from a bench and pretended to read as he eyed the couple over the page.

"I've had a nice time this afternoon," Jon said. "Thank you for inviting me."

"It was my pleasure, Mr. Hastings. And you were such a dear to see me home. With the first snowfall, walking gets awfully treacherous in these high-heeled boots."

"I can imagine," he said.

"Maybe next Sunday you could rent a horse and carriage and pick me up." She reached for his hand. "Yes, that would be perfect! I'll look forward to it all week."

As William cringed at her enthusiasm, Jon only smiled.

"So will I. Thank you for the tea and cookies, Miss Sapp."

Jon put his hand over hers for a moment before he turned to leave. William glared daggers into Hastings' back as he retreated and walked down Main Street toward the school.

He'd promised Amelia's father he would try to keep her from getting hurt. Jon was not going to make it easy to uphold his word.

121

TWENTY-FIVE

Amelia saw her family off at the train station and returned to school the same morning. Jon caught up with her as she walked by the stables. He smiled and caught her arm and tucked it under his own.

"Why were you at the livery?" Amelia peeked inside the barn and saw the horses stamping, impatient in their stalls.

"Nothing important. Wanted to rent a carriage for something. Did your family leave?"

She sighed. "They did. I miss them."

He made a sympathetic expression. "It must be hard to be so far away. I miss my mother, and I still see her fairly often."

Amelia nodded. They continued in silence toward the schoolhouse. When they arrived, he gave her a quick kiss on the forehead. "See you at lunch."

The snickers from her class made her blush. He smiled as he went into his classroom. She caught a glimpse of two boys standing on their chairs and throwing an inkwell back and forth, laughing as ink splattered across the desks.

Her face was still warm when she got to her stool in the front of the room. She was setting down her books and calling the class to order when she heard a loud gasp from Laura Spencer. In fact, the entire class was staring at the chalkboard with whispers and wide eyes.

She turned around and saw the scrawled message.

You never know what might happen to the schoolteacher when she isn't paying attention. There are so many ways to bring her harm! She better keep an eye open in every direction, and be ever ready to send off the alarm.

She couldn't believe the words. She read it again to be sure she wasn't seeing things.

"Who would have written such a thing?" Laura sounded as if she might cry. Amelia swallowed her own fear and set to work erasing the evidence of the message from the chalkboard. Her stomach rolled.

"I'm sure it was just a silly prank." Amelia tried to make her tone match her words. But Laura ran from the room. A moment later, she returned with Jon, explaining what they had seen. He studied the chalkboard, though Amelia had already erased the message. He returned to the door of his classroom and addressed the boys in a loud voice.

"Did any of you boys leave a message on the girls' chalkboard for Miss Farnsworth? I want the truth this instant."

Amelia had never heard him sound so stern. None of the boys made a sound.

"If this is just a childish trick, your punishment will be lighter if you confess."

The silence continued. Jon turned back to Amelia.

"I can't think of anyone who would threaten you. Can you?"

Only one person came to mind. Amelia eyed Polly, noting that she was flipping through a book while the other girls all stared ahead with terrified expressions. But Amelia couldn't accuse her without knowing for sure.

"It was just a joke," she said softly.

"We will get to the bottom of this."

Word had spread. Amy had already heard about the incident before Amelia walked through the door. She must have also told William, for he stood there with his arms folded across his chest,

123

his expression harder than usual.

"What exactly did the message say?"

Amelia sighed, wishing she could leave the whole humiliating mess behind her. She told him the words that were burned into her memory.

"And none of the students wrote it?"

"None admitted to it." She took off her hat and gloves and Amy took her coat. She wanted to take off her muddy boots to keep from tracking the mess all over Amy's floor, but William would be witness. She wrestled with impropriety, but decided if it bothered him he could look away. She reached down to unfasten them and pull them off, leaning against the door for support. He watched her without shame. She threw her boots in the corner, hoping he'd enjoyed the full view of her ankle.

"What should be done?" Amy addressed William. He stared at Amelia.

"I'll be watching. I won't let anything happen to you."

His words were delivered in the usual stiff manner, but she felt warmth behind them. Even if she didn't care to be the center of attention, and enjoyed even less the idea of having an unknown enemy capable of such a threat, still William's tenderness touched her.

When she was by herself in her room later that night, she felt the gravity of the hostile message. She looked out the dark window into the night. Someone might be staring at her right at that moment and she wouldn't know it with the mask of shadows to hide them.

Someone wanted to hurt her. Or at least wanted her to be afraid. Wasn't this proof she should have stayed at home, where she was safe?

Her hands felt like ice when she covered her face.

TWENTY-SIX

William didn't go to church. Ian Durey at the train station had sent him a message. He'd seen a suspicious character hanging around the depot, and the description of the man bothered William. Stringy hair, gun belt. But Durey hadn't said anything about the man having a limp. William sat by the window of his bedroom and kept an eye on the comings and goings as he sipped coffee and read Jules Verne.

The adventures of Phileas Fogg got him wondering if Amelia had read any of Verne's novels. He thought she would like them. They were imaginative enough to catch her attention.

Just as she was imaginative enough to catch his.

William had always been a reader. When he was a boy and they were struggling to keep food on the table, he read anything the teacher would loan him from her bookshelf at the school. He even invented a wooden holder to keep a book open while he was doing the milking.

He read more during his time in the gang. Every night, whether by lamplight or firelight, he read whatever he could get his hands on, be it thick expositions on the law or popular fiction. He liked the feeling of a new adventure calling. He never knew where he might end up, but he could be assured that wherever it was, it would mean something, even if his life seemed pointless.

Once or twice a fellow had mocked him for his pastime. He'd

made sure they never did again.

He supposed it was partly why he couldn't stop thinking about Amelia. They shared a love – a passion – for books. They both had an insatiable drive to learn more or experience other lives through a world crafted by words. He downplayed his interest in books around her, but he had the feeling she knew because she recognized that love. She had it as well, and he'd be hard-pressed to avoid any woman that loved books as much as he did.

He'd read to Clara. She wasn't a strong reader since her pa didn't send her to school and would come home swinging his fists if she didn't get her chores done. But she loved to listen to William read, and she'd been carried away by the stories they read together.

Now he put down his book, overcome by the memories and regrets that remained, as familiar as breathing. When would his mind or his heart accept she was gone? When would he stop looking for her next to him the minute he woke up? When would he stop seeing a pile of bright blonde hair atop some woman's head and feel his heart jump in that split-second before he remembered it couldn't be her?

His eyes fell on the hope chest waiting by the door. Maybe it was a good time to take it over and leave it in Amelia's room. She wouldn't be back from church for another half-hour. He needed a distraction or he might find himself heading in the direction of the saloon again.

On the way home after making his delivery – and perhaps lingering overlong in Amelia's room, and perhaps catching a peek of paper sticking out of her dresser drawer, and perhaps suspecting that the hand-written missive might be a story she was writing – he saw Jon and Rebecca again.

There was no doubt he was guilty of spying this time. He remembered Jon's promise about a carriage ride and kept an eye on them standing in front of the livery as he walked home.

"I think she is just the dearest little thing, don't misunderstand, but I do wish she would give thought to the way she presents herself. For her sake, of course; I'm only thinking of her. She had on such a plain little blouse and that ugly black and gold rose brooch. And that twill skirt with the brown coat hanging open – why, I don't believe I even own a twill skirt."

Rebecca laughed as William passed them. He fought the urge to stop and give Miss Flouncy Pants a piece of his mind.

"Anyway, I don't know why she doesn't like me. Maybe she is jealous of you and me."

William waited for Jon to make some sort of defense on Amelia's behalf, but the lout just stood there, looking uncomfortable.

"She lacks basic comportment," Rebecca continued. "I wish she would ask me to help her. I suppose it's not her fault. She is from a mining town, after all."

Jon cleared his throat as William entered the shop and stayed at the doorway to continue eavesdropping.

"Miss Sapp, I've been honored to spend time with you. You're a peach, just like I always say. But I—"

Apparently Rebecca didn't wish to hear more. She reached up on tiptoes in full view of the ice cream parlor and the livery and kissed him on the mouth.

He resisted at first. But then he pulled her into the small space between buildings. A moment later they came out again, both breathless.

William glowered, straining to see them in the shadows. Jon glanced around as if he was worried someone had seen them.

Someone had.

William stepped out to the front of his shop so he could see them. He couldn't hear what they were saying, but Jon appeared to be apologizing. Rebecca reacted with anger at whatever he said, but quickly replaced the rage with a seductive expression. Her hand ran up his chest. William watched as Jon's resolve faded. He grabbed her, pushing her back against the brick wall and leaning against her as he kissed her again.

William was disappointed in the younger man. But he was also glad he'd been a witness to the lapse. It confirmed a truth he had suspected.

Jon finally grew embarrassed enough to let her go. He stumbled from the alley with a red face and hurried away.

Rebecca emerged with an exultant smile, as if she had just reeled him in.

Twenty-Seven

Amelia half-expected everything to change following the threatening message on the chalkboard. But routine resumed, and no one at school mentioned the incident again.

Amy still worried for her, and reminded Amelia often that William would be close if she needed him. But when two full weeks went by and no one had tried to murder her, she began to relax. It must have been a cruel joke.

Meanwhile, her relationships with certain women in her church continued to deteriorate.

Mrs. Doughty apparently believed Amelia usurped her position as piano player on purpose because she thought she could do better. Amelia wondered if she should approach her, but she had not gathered the courage.

She would need to summon some nerve soon. Pastor Bertram couldn't understand why half his congregation refused to sing anymore.

Amelia received a letter from Ella, with news of their mother. She wasn't doing well. They had been walking through this trial for so long that Amelia did not panic, but the ache within her grew stronger.

One evening, Amelia said she was going for a walk to clear her head. Amy was concerned, but Amelia promised she would only walk to the church and back, and she would mention it to William on her way.

She did see him inside his shop, and he opened the door. Their eyes met briefly, and she knew he would be watching, so she felt no need to speak. The street was deserted. She longed for the long, warm days of spring and summer to arrive, but knew they were still months away.

The chill and the gray reminded her of her mother's existence. How did she ever find reason to be joyful? And yet every time Amelia had visited her, she had been at peace. She had smiled. Her worn Bible had always been nearby. What was her secret? Maybe it was the time she had to pray. She must receive her strength from the Lord.

Amelia could pray.

She lit the lantern and went inside the church that had become so familiar, so dear to her. She played the piano, allowing the words of the hymns to speak on her behalf.

After a time, she stopped playing and closed her eyes. "Dear Father, I don't know what to do. I don't know why someone wants to hurt me or intimidate me. Help me see the path you want me to walk. Please grant me peace and protection. If this is your way to test me and refine me, let my belief in you never be shaken. I don't dread hardship, Lord, but I beg for your wisdom. I hate not knowing what to do."

She couldn't deny that some of her trouble was her own fault. "I was wrong to let pride govern my decisions. Help me be considerate of others. Help me make amends. And dear Lord, please be especially close to Mother."

Her voice caught and she took a deep breath, feeling release. It made way for hope to invade her spirit like a windstorm, sweeping away discouragement.

Before she looked up and saw him, she knew William was standing at the back of the room.

He stood in the doorway, his hands in his pockets under his leather work apron. He watched her. He didn't say anything, so she waited at the piano. Eventually he walked down the aisle and came to stand next to her. Another long moment passed as he said nothing, staring at the floor.

"Her name was Clara."

She stifled all response, hoping not to spook him.

"I always thought she took my soul with her when she died. I'm still not sure she didn't. But I got her killed. I'm not safe." He lifted his eyes to meet hers, and she saw the raw injury the words caused him. "I don't want to hurt anyone else."

His look softened as he watched her. Did he wonder if she understood his deeper meaning? When she didn't say anything, he shifted his weight. He gestured toward the piano, where he had found her praying.

"If God can forgive this rotten sinner, your requests are not too big for him," he said.

She could only nod.

"It's going to be alright. You'll see."

She almost said the same to him as he grabbed the lantern and motioned for her to follow him out.

They were almost back to the house. William knew he needed to say it. "Amelia, I'm sorry about your mother."

She looked up uneasily. "What do you mean?"

"Your father told me. At Christmas."

She nodded, but her expression was troubled. Did she not want him to know something so painful and personal?

"I'm sorry. It's just so hard to think about. Talking about it would…" Her voice died away.

"You don't have to say anything. Just know that I understand how hard it is to lose a mother. And even more to watch your mother face hardship she doesn't deserve."

He saw her push back the emotion, fighting back tears and swallowing with difficulty. He wanted to tell her she could confide in him. He wanted to take the poor girl in his arms, if he was being honest. She was facing one of life's deepest hurts, and he ached for her.

William saw her home, his thoughts unnerving him. When had he started feeling so strongly about the schoolteacher? Part of him

131

felt it as a betrayal. His devotion lay beneath the earth in a grave, marked only by the name "Clara."

Even if he were to somehow push aside that obstacle, there was no guarantee Amelia would meet a better end than Clara. He wasn't safe. Those he loved ended up in danger or dead, and he wouldn't let that happen again.

He felt her presence. Amelia hadn't spoken a word, but he felt her empathy for his loss as if she had spent an hour describing it. She was making it impossible not to care for her. He hadn't been able to keep her out of his mind, not since Christmas when he'd heard Amelia's sister say those words that had changed everything. Transposed everything into a different key.

Maybe time itself paused in that moment Ella spoke, just so he would catch it. So he would hear her voice, calling from the past and from the grave, guiding him, urging him to reconsider everything. It was important. The quiet little schoolteacher was important.

Emmy Jo.

TWENTY-EIGHT

The day whispered rumors of spring. Amelia let the girls go a few minutes early to enjoy the sunshine. She followed them out, but her mood was dampened when she saw the frill and lace on the bench by the maple tree.

Rebecca Sapp straightened her blue gingham over many layers of petticoats, smoothed her ruffled apron, and centered her flowered bonnet on her head and patted her brown curls. She made herself appear busy by holding a book in front of her face. It seemed to Amelia she was putting on a show for someone. And that someone had to be Jon.

He stepped out of the school. "Sunshine! No wonder I couldn't get those boys to focus on anything."

As he spoke, Rebecca stood and waved with her handkerchief. "Jon!"

He raised his eyebrows, surveying her outfit. "Miss Sapp?"

"Isn't it a little cold to be out without a coat?" Amelia asked her.

"I suppose it's a little chilly." She spoke in a sweet voice, but Amelia didn't miss Rebecca's momentary cold stare. "Maybe I can borrow Mr. Hastings' jacket."

Jon appeared indecisive. Amelia shrugged at him, and Rebecca watched the exchange.

"Oh, my, I'm afraid I've caught you off guard. I do apologize. I was hoping we could take a walk, Jon. Perhaps another time."

Jon took off his jacket and draped it around her shoulders. "Of course not, Miss Sapp. Let me see you home."

He avoided looking Amelia in the eye. "Do you mind, Em?"

"Em?" Rebecca stared at Amelia with distaste. "Why, that's improper. Jon, You disrespect Miss Farnsworth by speaking with such familiarity."

Jon seemed uncomfortable. "Do forgive me, Miss Farnsworth. I'll see you tomorrow."

Amelia couldn't answer. She watched them walk away.

"What's wrong?" William's voice broke the long silence and made Amelia jump.

They sat together in the parlor after dinner, books in their hands. She was reading *The Scarlet Letter* at his request, and he was reading *Frankenstein* at hers. Though she wasn't reading anything at the moment. She was staring out the large picture window.

He waited for her response, eyeing her with scrutiny.

"What are you looking at? Is there something wrong with me?" She looked down at her dress. Her hand went to her hair to smooth it down, and flitted across the buttons on her blouse to ensure they were all buttoned properly.

He shrugged. "I was trying to figure out what color your eyes are."

She was speechless at his admission.

He smiled at her pink cheeks. "I'd say blue, though green is the more obvious answer. With specks of brown. And when the sunlight hits them, they glow. Did you know that?"

She shook her head and lowered her gaze. "I think you are mocking me."

"I'm not."

"What did Clara look like?" she asked, testing the waters, but also hoping to deflect his original question. He leaned back in his chair.

"Long blonde hair, so blonde it was almost white. She was beautiful, like you rarely see. Her eyes were something, too.

Fathomless."

Amelia imagined Clara through his description, adding small particulars she sensed through her intuition until she came up with a rather detailed picture in her mind.

"She always wore her hair down, free and reaching to the middle of her back. Unlike you, wearing your hair as if you are afraid it might run away from you if you allow it any freedom."

Her hand went to her hair again. "There's nothing wrong with wearing my hair up. That's what most women do. Amy does."

"You try to give the impression of orderliness, but don't think you can fool me," he said. "I know there is a wild, free part of you in there that will never be tamed completely."

"Honestly." She shook her head, flustered by his close observance.

"You still haven't told me what's wrong," William reminded her. He noticed her anxiety when he pressed her. He knew he'd been fairly harsh with her in the past. She didn't understand that things were different now. Knowing what he knew. But how could she understand it? He hadn't told her. Not yet.

"It's okay to talk to me, Amelia." His voice sounded impatient and he knew it. Not with her, but with himself for building walls so hard to tear down. She looked away; out the window. He figured he'd lost her to her thoughts.

"I suppose I am trying to figure out where I belong."

"What do you mean?"

She shrugged. And didn't answer for a very long moment. "Well, I was under the impression Jon was interested in me." She hesitated. "And yet he walked Rebecca Sapp home today. I noticed he also drove her home from church several weeks ago."

Selfish lout. "Did you ask him his intentions?"

"I'm afraid he'll be upset. Or laugh at me."

"So what? Shows you what kind of man he is if he does. Better to know now than when he's sneaking out at night to cavort with an adventuress."

She gasped. "William! Your language! What if one of the girls heard?"

He wasn't sorry he said it. It was important she realized what some men were capable of. It was difficult for Amelia to see the weaknesses in others. She was always thinking the best and assuming people meant what they said. After all, she had developed a relationship with him, hadn't she?

She wasn't through with her lecture, and it seemed like she had been reading his mind. "Why do you always suppose the worst of people? What happened that made you think everyone and everything was determined to disappoint you?"

He felt a spark of irritation at the intrusion. Why did *she* always suppose he should tell her about his past with all the ugly details? She couldn't handle it. He *was* the sort of man who would cavort with an adventuress. Once upon a time.

"I have my reasons."

She shook her head and slapped her book down on the side table. "Not a good enough answer. If you're going to come and sit in this parlor and be sour and closed up, you better give me a reason to allow it." She waited for him to say something. When he didn't, she continued. "Did it have something to do with your parents?"

"How could it be? My father didn't stay long enough to hear my first word, and my mother worked so hard to provide for us, she was never home. My older sister was the closest thing to a parent I had most of the time."

He saw Amy's face turn in his direction from the kitchen where she and Jennifer were washing dishes. Her jaw clenched.

"I'm sorry," Amelia said meekly. "But I'm glad you told me."

He shrugged. "We did okay. I had my sisters. One to take care of me and one to take care of." He didn't know why he kept talking. She was a confounded good listener. "I didn't want to be like my pa. But I was. I could never seem to stay out of trouble. By the time I was eighteen I'd already been in two gunfights. Started one of them."

A troubled look passed across her face. Was she shocked? Done hearing his story? She kept listening, so he risked continuing. He sensed a cleansing in speaking the words.

"I was headstrong. Thought I was invincible. I joined a gang and we robbed a bank. Spent some time in jail. After that I spent more time in saloons. I earned a name for myself, more than I deserved. Men trying to prove something would call me out for the sheer adventure. I was always the one who walked away."

He couldn't take the disillusionment in her gaze any longer. He got up to leave.

"I've never seen a gunfight," she said in a small voice, stopping him in his tracks.

"I'm glad of that. It's no place for an innocent young lady."

"What does it feel like? To stare down the barrel of a gun?"

He chuckled in surprise, but he answered her question. "In a way, you feel like you're on top of the world. It's exciting. Makes you feel alive. On the other hand, you dread what you won't admit – that you might die."

"That's how I imagined it might be." She leaned her chin on her fist and stared thoughtfully out the window.

"I guess you have a good imagination." He reached for his hat. "Goodnight."

"Goodnight, William." She said the words with a level of distraction that told him she was off in a gun battle somewhere in the adventures of her mind.

He hoped her imaginings were better than his memories.

Twenty-Nine

Amelia plunked the last chord rather loudly on the piano, and the sound echoed through the small church. She returned to her seat, petulant. Not only did no one sing anymore, Pastor Bertram acted as if he didn't notice.

She sat down in a huff. What good did pretending away problems do for a group of people who were supposed to think of themselves as family? Had her prayers accomplished so little?

And why in the world did some people in town dislike her so much? What had happened to those three teachers? There was at least one piece missing from the puzzle.

She didn't hear the sermon. By the benediction she was settled on her course of action. She marched back to the pastor standing at the door. He smiled and held out his hand, irritating her further by continuing the pretense.

"I can no longer play the piano." She tried to say the words with more gentleness than she felt. She didn't wish to make a scene.

"But you've done so well. Is it interfering with your school duties?"

She almost agreed, but she couldn't lie. "I feel it is causing discord within the church. I never should have said I would do it in the first place."

A crowd gathered around them, causing her stomach to clench with dread.

"I'm sorry, Miss Farnsworth. I had no idea you felt this way."

His eyes darted to the people closing in.

"You didn't?" She wanted to believe him. She couldn't read dishonesty in his expression. "I think things should just go back to the way they were. Mrs. Doughty, would you be willing to continue your service to us?" Amelia turned and tried to smile politely.

The woman sniffed. "After we've all heard how talented you are? Why should I wear my aching fingers to the bone?"

Murmuring erupted all around them. Amelia closed her eyes and wished she was anywhere else.

"You are a natural musician. You shouldn't stop playing over feelings you presume others to have," Mrs. Hubble chided. The women around her nodded.

"But no one is singing! No one smiles or enjoys the hymns. They are for worship, so we can turn our hearts to Jesus, but no one is thinking about him."

The murmuring intensified. They were offended by her accusation. She felt lost within the din as the mumbling grew noisier.

"They didn't sing, smile or worship before you started playing, either." William's voice rose above the disgruntled chorus.

"I beg your pardon?" Mrs. Doughty huffed at him.

William took a step into the circle so that he stood at Amelia's side. He put a hand on her arm. "The problem is not Amelia, and you know it. Stop acting like it's her fault just because she cares."

"Just who do you think you are, accusing us?" Mr. Doughty spoke to William. "It's no secret that no other church in this town would have you. Just because we showed a sinner mercy does not mean we will allow you to insult us."

Amelia gasped in surprise at the spiteful words. She glared in expectation around the circle, but no one came to William's defense. Just how petty could people be? William didn't seem surprised. He stared at Mr. Doughty with an even expression.

"I have it on good information that Miss Farnsworth usurped the position of pianist because she wanted to control the songs we sing," Mrs. Doughty said. "I also heard she was using her practice time to sing love songs better fitted to a bawdy house."

"Now, now –" Pastor Bertram said in a feeble voice.

"In the church?" Mrs. Hubble gasped in distress. Amelia glanced at William, wondering if he had spread the information.

"I'm sure all of this is just a misunderstanding," the pastor said, holding up his hands. William grabbed Amelia's arm more firmly and directed her out of the circle as the cascade of disapproval grew louder. The pastor would have to sort out the ruffled feathers.

When they were a good distance away, she turned to him, grateful.

"Thank you," she started to say, but he interrupted.

"As for you," he said in obvious disapproval. "What do you think you're accomplishing when you just give up? You don't solve problems by avoiding them. That makes you no better than them."

"I never said I was better than them." Her voice was small but insistent.

He scoffed. "You getting all high and mighty and refusing to use the talent God gave you because you don't approve of what people do with it, well, that doesn't solve anything. It just makes you a quitter."

Tears stung her eyes, but she fought them back. She wanted to go home. Stay in her room for a week. Better yet, she wanted to go back to Illinois where nothing had ever been this complicated.

I am a quitter.

When she dared to look back at William, shame wouldn't allow her to voice a response. He must have taken her silence as obstinacy, because he waved her off and turned away in the direction of his shop.

She hardly spoke the rest of the day. She had no patience to act pleasant in Jon's company, so she used her churning stomach as an excuse to retire to her room. She berated herself for being so easily overwhelmed by conflict. Shouldn't a woman living on her own be able to weather the stresses of life better than this? How would she manage if something truly devastating was to occur?

If Mother dies…

The consideration brought tears and a dreadful pain in her stomach. She grew desperate for something else to think about. The stack of papers hiding in her dresser called to her, promising a satisfying escape from troubling reality. She longed for the joy of losing herself in a story.

But then she remembered Ella's criticism. How would she fix her story? She gave a cry of frustration and threw herself on her bed.

Her sleep was troubled, and several hours later she ended up in the kitchen looking for something to nibble on to drive away the pain in her stomach. She found Amy in the kitchen with a cup of tea.

"You couldn't sleep, either?" Amy asked as she took a sip.

"I'm sorry, Amy. I hope I didn't wake you with my wanderings."

"I was awake. Kathleen had another dream. I don't want to go back to bed until I'm sure she's settled."

Amelia sat down and reached for a cookie. "She has so many. I wonder why."

Amelia thought Amy already had an idea, and she hoped her words would encourage her to share.

Amy was hesitant. "Kathleen... had an ordeal. Something that was out of our control. I'm sure she revisits it by dreaming, though she doesn't remember it. She was so young when it happened."

Amy's explanation only served to make Amelia more curious. Her question must have registered on her face, but Amy did not elaborate. She wondered what could have happened that would be so painful to explain.

After a long silence, Amy spoke again with a forced cheerfulness. "Jon tells me you two are getting along fine. He's quite taken with you."

It was Amelia's turn to be uncomfortable. She shrugged. "I guess."

"Do you not agree?"

"Jon is nice. I guess I just expected to feel more of a spark for the person I would consider spending my life with."

"What do you mean?"

Amelia hesitated. "Jon kissed me. After the Christmas program. I thought it would be different."

"Different than what?"

"I thought it would be more like it is in novels. Romantic and exciting, and all the proof I needed to know he was the one."

141

Amy smiled. "I would venture to guess that most people recall their first kiss as being somewhat awkward. How was the next one?"

Amelia shrugged. "There hasn't been another. I've been avoiding it, because I'm afraid things may not improve."

Amy nodded. "From my experience, love has moments that are like a storybook, but that's not the way it usually is. Eventually dishes need to be washed and socks darned."

Amelia must have appeared confused, because Amy continued. "What I mean is, even if love begins with an emotional upheaval, the goal is to be a family. To belong with someone."

Amelia considered her words and nodded. She definitely wished to belong. "But you and Mr. Able seem like peaceful people. I don't think I've ever heard you argue. What if I'm not that sort of person?"

"Do you mean you wonder if you'd be content with a quiet relationship?"

Amelia wasn't sure what she'd meant.

Amy shrugged. "I don't pretend to know all about romantic love. Maybe in the end it is simply that God gives you the freedom to choose whom you will spend your life with. He'll guide you if you ask him, but I think you have the fairytale notion that the right person will fall out of the sky and you will be sure of everything from the first moment. I don't think there's necessarily one right choice."

Amelia didn't know if Amy was right, but the words didn't sit well. She had always thought of love as one mysterious right choice. She held a sacred duty to discover it.

Amy saw her furrowed brow and continued. "You're right. Mr. Able and I have always had an easy relationship. Our love came quietly. But that's what I needed. I came from a troubled home. I didn't need another person to fight with; I needed peace. That might not be what you need. Maybe you need someone to awaken what has been too safe an existence."

Amelia thought of William. "But wouldn't two zealous individuals only fight all the time and make each other miserable? How could they be together?"

Amy took a sip of tea as she mulled over Amelia's words. "Perhaps the question is – how could they not?"

THIRTY

Amy stood in the middle of Amelia's classroom, her chest heaving as if she had run all the way from home. Amelia set down her book, fear causing her stomach to tighten.

"Have you seen Kathleen?" Amy asked between breaths.

"Not since last night. We took a walk into the woods. What's wrong?"

"After lunch she was out in the garden while I washed dishes. When I went to get her, she was gone. Connor left this morning for Columbus, and I don't know what to do! I looked everywhere I could think."

Amy's words were interrupted by gasps for breath. Amelia felt the chill of panic. Little Kathleen was out there, alone.

Or worse.

When Jon and Amelia had dismissed the students, he turned to his aunt. "Did you see her walk out of the yard?"

Amy fought her tears. "I told her to stay there until I was done. I was talking to her through the screen door. She answered me a few times, but I stopped to scrub a stubborn spot and when I went to the door to check on her, she wasn't in the yard. Oh, Jon, what if someone took her?"

Jon put his arm around her. "Now, now, let's be reasonable. Who would take her? She is a smart girl. I'm sure she's just sitting somewhere nearby waiting for us to get her."

143

He looked at Amelia. "I heard you say you took her into the woods. Did you notice anything that might have caught her attention? Something she might have wanted to see again?"

Amelia considered his question. "We did come across a cave entrance. We were making up a story, and we used the cave as our setting. She seemed rather fascinated by it, but I warned her never to go into caves by herself."

Her words seemed to trouble him. "Amy, go home and wait for her in case she comes back. Em, go to the livery and have Ed get a few horses saddled. Tell him it's an emergency and that I sent you. I'm going to get help and then I'll be there within a half hour." He turned back to Amy. "Don't worry. We'll find her."

He was gone, running down the path to the street that led to town. Amelia grabbed her cape and Amy's hand and closed her eyes.

"Jesus, even though we can't see where Kathleen is, you know. Please protect her. Guide her to a safe place and watch over her with angels until we can find her. Lord, please lead us to her! And give Amy your perfect peace which surpasses understanding."

Amelia kissed Amy's tear-stained cheek before she ran for town.

Main Street was busy. Amelia saw Pastor Bertram walking down the boardwalk, apparently on his way to Hagaman's store. Amelia waved a frantic hand to stop him.

"Miss Farnsworth, what's happened?" he asked.

"It's Kathleen Able! She's missing, and she's only four. Will you spread the word so everyone can keep their eyes open for her?"

"Of course." He patted her arm in reassurance. Amelia ran across the street toward the livery, but she turned back to him as she ran.

"Please pray!"

He nodded, his features twisted with concern. "I won't stop until she's found."

She nodded her thanks and ran inside the livery.

After she had given Mr. Bishop the message from Jon, she could do nothing else but wait. She stood outside, pacing and wringing her hands. William stuck his head out of his shop several doors down.

"Since when do you ride?" He called to her, a wry grin

144

stretching across his face.

She ran to him, her hands grasping his arms. "Kathleen is missing."

The look of terror that passed over his face surprised her, even knowing he was close to the family. It was as if a thousand possibilities tormented him in the space of a moment. His fingers grabbed her arm so tightly she winced.

"Why didn't you tell me?"

His voice was harsh, and he pushed passed her, running in the direction of the train station.

Fifteen minutes later when the search party had assembled, Jon told the men to search around town while he rode into the woods by the cave. William had returned from the station and he swung up on his bay, jerking the reigns sharply to the right.

"I'm going with you, Hastings. I just need to talk to Amy first, so I'll catch up."

He was gone, without a word of explanation.

Amelia looked up at Jon, who was tying a lantern and rope to the saddle before he mounted.

"I'm going as well," she insisted.

"No, you're not." Jon shook his head. "I admire your courage, but you're more useful here, letting people know to look for her and comforting Amy."

"Pastor Bertram will do that. We're wasting time arguing about it. My instinct says she is in that cave, and she's going to be frightened. Not to mention it's my fault she's there! I'm going."

Amelia grabbed hold of the nearest empty horse and managed to swing up without making a fool of herself. Jon sighed and shrugged. He set off toward the woods outside the Ables' neighborhood and Amelia convinced her horse to follow, not allowing her mind to consider what she was doing.

She had the greater fight on her hands when they met William outside the cave mouth. She eased out of the saddle and slid down, managing not to fall on her face or end up with her skirts over her head.

William caught hold of her wrist, his face red with irritation.

"You are not going in there. Do you know how many people have gotten hurt or killed in these caves?"

"I *am* going." Amelia knew there was only one way she would get past them. As Jon untied the supplies, she walked up to the edge and eyed the cave opening. There appeared to be a steep slope down to the floor.

"Be reasonable." She turned around and narrowed her eyes at William. "I want to help her. It's my fault, and she'll need someone with more maternal instincts than you two oafs."

Jon walked past them toward the cave. "You might as well let her, Morehouse. She's determined, and she has a point."

The moment she felt William's grip lighten, she took the opportunity to twist her arm free and run to the cave mouth. She meant to sit down and ease herself along the slope into the dark cavern, but in her haste, she slipped on the smooth rock and fell, sliding rather ungracefully into a small pool of water at the bottom of the slope.

"Confound it, woman, if you killed yourself –" William ended his sentence with a curse. Jon carefully made his way down the slope toward her and helped her up. She dusted off, her cheeks aflame.

"You okay?"

"I'm fine," she said quickly, though pain radiated from her tailbone. William reached the bottom of the slope, his face red. She presumed he was ready for a fight, and she would oblige. She poked him in the chest.

"I'll thank you to watch your language. Just because you can't have your way doesn't mean you should be allowed to assault us with filthy words."

"You are going to get us all killed. Get back up there or I swear I will tie you up and leave you right here for the snakes."

"Just try it!" Her voice echoed through the chamber. He stepped closer, so close their noses almost touched.

"Don't assume I won't."

"Stop it, both of you." Jon walked down the dark tunnel, his lantern casting eerie shadows on the walls. "You're wasting time we could be using to find my cousin."

"You're right." Amelia pushed past William and followed Jon, determined to pretend the other man wasn't there.

She ventured in, stepping carefully and staying in the center of the path. It quickly became blacker than night as they made their way inside.

She heard William mutter a few more choice phrases. He hit the wall with his fist.

She hoped it hurt.

William cursed again when he slammed his fist into the rock wall, and he blamed every bit of the pain on the stubborn little woman without a lick of good sense. He hoped she'd heard his language, and that it shocked the socks right off her prudish little toes.

As he followed them down the cool, damp path, he had to admit his anger had far more to do with the stress of the situation than anything else. He mentally retraced his steps to the train station, and reviewed his conversation with the steward and the clerk. No one matching the description he provided had exited the train that morning, or anytime in recent days. Amy had noticed nothing unusual, nobody lurking.

Surely the child had just wandered away. They would find her.

He'd been too careful to miss anything.

Even so, he prayed fiercely that they might turn the next corner and see her perched there on a rock, waiting for them, safe and sound.

As he walked on behind the others, his mind insisted on revisiting another time. *Her* face easily appeared in the darkness of the cave. He hadn't been able to keep her safe, either.

William thought back to the time he was living with Clara in an old farmhouse near a tiny town in Indiana called Sage. One dismal day he came across the field carrying a rabbit he'd found in a trap and saw her.

She was dirty from scrubbing laundry and weeding the small garden she had started. She looked exhausted, but she managed to

147

produce a genuine smile as he approached.

"Well, now, aren't we living just like the pioneers?" She pushed back the damp blond strands from her face.

"That's one way to look at it."

She tried to keep up the smile even though he didn't return it. His eyes fell to the thin dress that hung around her frame, causing him to curse in shame. She had lost weight. She wasn't getting enough to eat, and he was to blame.

She must have read his mind, because she gestured to the stoop where he saw three small carrots, mostly greenery. "I got the first of the carrots today. I'm sure there'll be plenty more."

"It's not enough. We need more food."

Her smile wavered and he saw fear flicker in her eyes. "I don't want to go back."

"And I don't want you dying because I couldn't take care of you. How is that better than where you were?"

She came to him and touched his arm. He saw her words written in her eyes before she said them. "Have you been drinking, Will?"

He had. And he had no excuse.

"Where'd you get the money for whiskey?" Her tone was sad.

"I didn't," he said, trying to sound clearer than he was. "I took moonshine off a back porch when I was hunting."

Clara sighed and touched her fingers to her forehead. "This ain't working."

William set down the rabbit and reached for her. She came to him, but not with eagerness as he hoped. He rested his chin on her head and held her slight body close to his.

"Maybe some farmers nearby need some help with planting," she said, her optimism reviving as he held her.

"I already asked. The first man recognized me from an old wanted poster and wouldn't talk to me. He'd spread the word before I made it to the next farm."

She didn't answer. It broke his heart. At least she'd never been hungry back at the bordello with Clint. He thought about her now, exhausted, starving and shivering in his arms every night. He had thought their love could conquer anything, but it was obvious he hadn't solved the problem. And as their circumstances continued to deteriorate, he could also see the part of her that always had longed for more was only growing more famished by the day.

"Will you read to me tonight?"

"Of course," he replied quietly.

"I love to hear you read, Will. It gives me hope."

He kissed her head. "We need hope."

After a few minutes of walking through the dark, narrow tunnel, Amelia's stomach began to burn with anxiety.

She didn't know what she had expected when she threw all good sense to the wind and jumped into that cavern. She suspected part of her motivation was to irk William. But it didn't help her now, as the walls closed in and she started to breathe faster, imagining the ceiling caving in on her, the mammoth stalactites that hung above her head falling and impaling her. Her lungs felt starved of air.

She whimpered. Both men looked at her. In the dim light, she thought she saw sympathy in Jon's eyes, but William only regarded her with impatience.

There was no use lying to them. "I'm afraid of close spaces."

Jon patted her arm, nodding in understanding, though she thought she saw a twinge of annoyance. She didn't blame him.

"I didn't expect it would take so long. I thought we would walk down the tunnel and find her waiting."

Jon nodded as he kept moving. "Hopefully we'll find her soon."

William gave a loud sigh. "You should have listened, foolish woman."

"Morehouse." Jon sounded like a weary parent tired of children squabbling.

Amelia glared at William. "I just want her to be safe."

"Then you should have stayed where I told you."

"Let's just keep moving." Jon's voice had a hard edge.

"I'm not sure I can." Amelia felt the weight of the walls of rock closing in. Dizziness set in, and her hand went to her chest, trying to force air into her lungs. Jon helped her sit down.

"Take deep breaths. It should pass," he encouraged.

"Move." William pushed Jon aside and pulled her to her feet. He shook her. "Get a hold of yourself! It's all in your infernal imagination. I'll slap you across the face. If that don't work, I'll leave you here to faint away. You're being selfish."

She felt her wits returning. She would regain control, even if it was only to spite William Morehouse.

"Doesn't," she managed as she breathed deeply.

"Doesn't what?"

"If it *doesn't* work."

Jon chuckled. William let her go, not moving to help her when she nearly fell off her seat.

"She's fine. Let's move."

Amelia stood to follow, pretending she was in a spacious meadow filled with light and fresh air. She stared hard at William's back and followed on.

"I'd like to see you try to slap me, you horrid man," she whispered.

"I'd like to see you try to stop me."

"There's no shame in being delicate, Em," Jon said. "What you have is claustrophobia. My mother treated a miner with it. He went crazy down in the mine, attacking folks and hyperventilating. Needless to say, he had to find a new job."

Amelia felt the skepticism from William.

"She sure got it together when her pride was on the line."

"I'd hardly call you threatening her with bodily harm a matter of pride," Jon said, his tone icy.

Amelia thought she heard William mutter something under his breath. She was curious what he said, until a little voice captured everyone's attention.

Singing.

Kathleen was sitting in a small alcove. Her eyes were closed, her hands pressed against her ears as she rocked back and forth.

"Thank you, Lord," William murmured. He must truly care for

the little girl. Amelia almost felt sorry for quarreling with him.

Amelia went to the child, kneeled in front of her and touched her hand. "Kathleen."

Her frantic eyes flew open. "Miss Emmy!" She began to sob, grabbing Amelia around the neck. Amelia stood with the child in her arms.

"It's alright. You're safe now."

The reunion was interrupted by an unsettling rumbling. It seemed a kind of foreboding – a reminder that they were in a dangerous place and it was time to get out before everything became much worse.

"This cave is near the lake," William said, eyeing the walls.

"It is," Jon agreed.

"How was the weather when we came in?"

Amelia thought back to the day, before they were enveloped in cave darkness. "It was cloudy. I think we were due for a rain shower. Why?"

Jon and William wordlessly communicated something Amelia did not understand.

"We need to get to higher ground."

William grabbed Kathleen, Jon reached for Amelia's hand, and the two men scrambled up the nearest pathway. After running for several minutes, the group heard a crashing sound behind them.

Water.

The path opened into a huge cavern, and Jon and William hauled them up the side until they were perched on a high ledge looking out over the expanse of the room. In the dim light of the lantern, Amelia watched as waves of water invaded the tunnel they had just exited.

In a frenzied moment, water overtook everything, filling the room with a rush that seemed to defy the imagination. Jon pulled her back and they shrunk into the corner of their tiny shelter from the sea that now splashed at their feet.

They were all quiet.

"How are we going to get out?" Kathleen's voice finally broke the silence.

"Even if we swam, there are no tunnel openings up here."

Amelia felt the need to point out the obvious. Jon and William both seemed to be calculating. Or perhaps they had lost all hope.

Panic began to rise in her chest again, but she caught a look of challenge from William. She swallowed her fears and refused to lose control.

"There might be some entrances that travel upward and are not completely submerged," Jon mused.

"But there's no way Kathleen could swim all that way," Amelia protested. Jon sighed and shrugged as if he had no better option.

"She's right. We'll just have to wait until the water recedes and hope that there's a way out," William said.

They sat in silence for a long time, watching the water as if the force of their will might convince it to regress. As the waves lapped a taunting rhythm at the side of their rock, a chill settled in the air. The lamp sputtered, letting them know it wouldn't be long before the kerosene ran out.

"Where are you from?" Jon asked William, his voice a surprise in the deceiving stillness of the dark.

"Indianapolis." William's voice held a guarded tone Jon didn't seem to catch.

"Interesting. My mother lives on the edge of Indianapolis."

"My grandparents were from Indianapolis," Amelia added, thinking of her feisty little Grandma and all the memorable times they had shared. It occurred to her that she might be seeing her dear face again, much sooner than she had expected. The chill that hung in the air and caused her to shiver in her damp clothes seemed to confirm her suspicion.

"Ever been there?" Jon asked her. She nodded.

"We went on the train to see her a few times before she died. I spent a summer taking care of her after she became ill."

After a time of silence, she renewed the conversation by launching a literature discussion. She asked if either had read *Jane Eyre* or *Wuthering Heights*. Jon shook his head, but William said he'd read both and asked her opinion.

"I find the Bronte sisters a little raw, but I enjoy them, if I am taken by the right mood," Amelia said. "I believe I would have told their stories differently, but an author writes in a tone that marks their own personality and experiences."

William looked at her with a curious expression. "You realize you just categorized yourself as an author?"

Amelia would have kicked herself if it had been possible to do so.

It was not Kathleen who couldn't keep her secret.

"*If* I were a writer, I would have written them differently."

"That's not what you said."

"Honestly, I don't know what you're getting at. Who hasn't jotted down a story or two for amusement?"

"I haven't," Jon shook his head.

"Can't say that I have, either." William grabbed her right hand and unceremoniously dunked it in the water, wiping away the dirt with his shirtsleeve.

"Excuse me!" Amelia tried to pull her hand away, but he held on as he examined it in the lamplight.

"Just as I thought. You're a writer."

"You can tell that from my fingers?" Amelia attempted to sound dubious.

"Calloused third finger. And an ink stain."

"I'm a teacher," she huffed, pulling her hand away.

"And a writer."

She sniffed and wrapped her arms back around Kathleen, who giggled.

"Do I get to read it?" he asked.

"Read what?"

"Whatever you're working on." He shrugged, leaning back and folding his hands across his chest.

"Just let it go, please." She mumbled the words.

"I wouldn't mind reading what you've written, Em," Jon said, but his voice lacked the persuasion William's held. They both stared at her, waiting for her answer.

"Let's just focus on getting out of here."

153

"Not much we can do about that," William said. That brought their attention back to the waters still hovering. Amelia wondered, indeed, if she would ever write again.

Thirty-One

They all became irritable as the hours wore on and the water seemed every bit as high. Kathleen dozed for a time and woke, crying with hunger. Amelia held her close and tried to distract her.

"Kathleen, do you remember when I told you never to go into the cave? That it was dangerous?"

"Yes."

"Why did you leave your mother and go inside?"

She twisted her dirty dress and squirmed. "The lady in the woods came in the garden. She told me to follow her."

"Someone told you to go into the cave?"

She nodded. "But I only went because I wanted to see if the gopher really lived there."

"The gopher?"

"From the story we made up. I know you said he was pretend, but I wanted to make sure. Since the cave is dangerous."

Amelia felt terrible. The story had been make-believe to her, but to a four-year-old, it would seem real.

"I'm sorry, Kathleen. I should have been clearer. But you must never listen to strangers. Can you tell me who the lady was?"

Kathleen shook her head. "She wore a veil. She said she was the lady of the woods, and that I must go in the cave and find the gopher for her."

A chill not completely related to the temperature in the cave crept along Amelia's back. Who would do such a thing? And for what purpose?

Kathleen stuck out her lower lip. "I didn't mean to go all the way in. I leaned over the edge and called him, and when I put my ear down to hear, I fell down."

"I'm sorry, Kathleen." Amelia hugged her.

"I walked in the dark because it was too slippery to climb back up."

"I'm glad God was watching over you." Amelia's eyes brimmed with tears.

Kathleen was quiet for a long time. Finally, she looked up at Amelia with a miserable expression.

"I didn't just want to find the gopher, Miss Emmy. I wanted to be bad."

Amelia felt dismay but held it back. "Why?"

"Sometimes I feel like doing what I shouldn't do."

Amelia held her for a few minutes until she fell asleep. She was troubled by the girl's words, though she was affected by her honesty. Couldn't she say the same? Couldn't anyone?

As Amelia worried over the conversation with Kathleen, the lantern flickered and the tiny flame died away. Complete darkness settled over the cave. The only sound was the slap of the water against the rocks.

They were sitting close together due to the size of the rock, but now they crept even closer, William and Jon on the ends. Amelia trembled as her eyes tried to make sense of the blackness.

For one moment she fought against overwhelming panic. Then a large hand gripped hers. At first, she thought it was Jon, but she remembered Jon was sitting on her left, and her right hand was being held.

William pulled her closer with Kathleen nestled between them. Amelia knew him by the smell of pine, by his fierce embrace. She knew by the reaction of her racing heart.

"If we die, we'll do it together." She heard the whispered words in her ear, so softly spoken Jon would not overhear.

"I don't suppose you could just promise we'll be okay?" She spoke next to his ear, his whiskers tickling her face.

He didn't answer. In a way, Amelia appreciated his honesty. After a few minutes, Jon's even breathing told her he was asleep.

"Are you still awake?" William's deep voice vibrated in his chest where her head still rested, just above his steady heartbeat.

"I don't sleep well away from home." *Or when I am going to die.*

"William, do you think we stand a chance of escaping?"

He was quiet for a long moment. Too long. "If the Almighty wants us home, that's where we'll end up. If not, we'll find a way out."

His perspective gave her comfort.

"You sound like you know what you're talking about," she said.

"I do."

Amelia barely remembered the times she almost died from illness as a young child. She was curious. "Is being near death a fearsome thing?"

"It was for me. Because I would have died without God's mercy. But he gave me another chance."

I asked him for another chance. I knew I was out of them, but I asked him anyway. I said if he'd let me live, I'd promise to find out why he gave me life. And what I could do about the rotten mess I'd made of it so far.

Amelia sat up in surprise, looking in William's direction though she could see nothing. How had she not seen the connection?

"What?" He must have sensed her surprise.

"I just realized something. Something that was a puzzle."

"You mind sharing?" He sounded dark. As if he suspected what puzzle she had solved and wasn't happy about it. She decided not to tell him she knew of his letter to Clara that had somehow ended up buried deep in the old trunk in her room.

"Never mind. It's nothing. Tell me about your second chance."

She squeezed his hand as she spoke, and wondered at the irony. She should be terrified at their circumstances. Wasn't this experience proof she had been right to worry about leaving home?

157

And yet now that she was here, she felt peaceful. Calm. As if, for the first time in her life, she was where she belonged.

It startled her to think it, since she had always felt so different, so out of place. A puzzle piece that didn't quite fit anywhere.

"I already told you I was in a gang. I wasn't the type to care much about anyone or anything else. I cared about my sisters, but I distanced myself from them, so I could live the way I wanted."

His voice was thoughtful. Musing. Amelia had the feeling he wouldn't be saying these things or holding her if he thought there was a chance they would get out of the cave alive. She tried not to dwell on that fact.

"When I was at my worst, I walked into a brothel and met Clara."

"She was a...?" Amelia gulped.

"I was taken with her from the first moment. She had a survivor's spirit, even if she'd been forced into a rotten life. I didn't mean to, but I fell for her.

"Clara wasn't given a choice. I don't know if good folks like you realize this, Amelia, but plenty of prostitutes are sold like cattle, just as cruelly as the slaves we fought a war to free. Her father was a lousy excuse for a man, and when she was twelve, he sold her to the man who owned the brothel just so he could buy more whiskey."

Amelia felt sick. She'd had no idea that such things happened. She had been given the impression prostitutes were evil women with no morals who flaunted their bodies to get what they wanted. The picture William painted was contrary to her beliefs. Could it be true? Were children forced into that life? She thought of Kathleen sleeping at her side. A lump grew in her throat at the thought that someone could do something so cruel to a helpless child.

"You wouldn't have thought she'd had such a life to be with her. She could find the bright side of anything. No matter how many men came through that hell-hole and used her for their pleasure, she had this ability to rise above it. Imagine herself elsewhere."

Amelia heard a smile in his voice. "Kind of like you and your imagination. If we live, I want to see what kind of story comes out of that head of yours."

She blushed. And held her breath. She could feel him considering her.

"I suppose you are shocked by the life I lived."

She heard uneasiness in his tone. She would never have expected to see William Morehouse feeling awkward over someone else's opinion of him.

"I'm more accepting than you give me credit for. I've seen what God can do with broken souls. My parents taught me that it was our entire purpose here on earth to love the ones who have been caught in sin. I confess I had no idea that children were forced into such a life, though. It makes me want to do something to stop it."

He nodded. "Me too. And I tried."

He didn't elaborate. He let go of her hand and threaded his fingers through her hair that had fallen out of its knot and was loose around her shoulders. He twisted the ends around his fingers. The moment felt intimate. Part of her was on edge, wondering if she should establish boundaries. But it felt nice to be held. If they might die this night, didn't they deserve comfort?

"You are quite a girl."

"I'm a woman," she reminded him, letting her head relax against his chest. He chuckled.

"You are. A young woman, but a woman indeed. I've noticed."

She felt her cheeks grow warm again.

"Tell me what you are writing."

She chewed her lip. Showing William her secret craft would be opening herself to his honest appraisal. Ella was truthful, but in a loyal, sisterly way. What if he read it and thought it was foolishness? She knew he wouldn't hesitate to tell her so.

The possibility he might think it was good was more frightening. Then she would be required to do something about it, something she had never done before.

"It's just a silly novel. The only one who knows is Ella. Unless you count Kathleen."

"I always count Kathleen."

She smiled. "Me too."

"What's it about?"

"You wouldn't believe me if I told you." She considered the

parallels her story had taken after she found his letter.

"I guess you will have to show me. When we get out of here."

She didn't answer for a few moments. "Okay."

THIRTY-TWO

Amelia fell asleep against him, and William took the opportunity to brush a light kiss against her temple.

"Emmy Jo, indeed," he whispered.

He realized he was treading on dangerous ground, holding her in such a way. He was surprised she allowed it. But how could he deny the urge to be close to her? He was a man, after all, and he had been alone too long. But as he breathed deeply of her alluring scent, he felt guilty. A girl as sheltered and unstained as Amelia needed a man who would only add more light to her life, not one who dragged the darkness behind him.

On top of everything else, he had confirmed his suspicion that she was a writer. It made sense. Considering his love of books, the thought that she loved them enough to write them was just as enthralling to him as her graceful features and curves. He couldn't wait to get his hands on that manuscript she was working on and see what came out of that perceptive mind.

He supposed they would have to get out alive first. He wished for light. He was sure there was a way out, but how would they ever find it in the dark?

"Jesus, you're light. Show me how to get these girls out alive."

His whisper was swallowed up by the water-filled cavern. It reminded him how small he was. He used to think he was invincible. He used to like danger, because he could prove how strong he was when he walked away and left the other man on the ground. It had taken his inability to save Clara to show him his grave error.

161

The thought stirred up the fear. He was holding treasure in his arms tonight. What if he let himself get closer, but lost her, too?

He really shouldn't let himself fall for her. Even as he admonished himself, he knew it was probably too late.

You are not going to die today, Amelia.

The voice, whether audible or not, woke her up. She adjusted herself against William's shoulder. When she reached for Kathleen, she realized the child had crawled up and nestled in the crook of his other arm.

What would it be like to wake up like this every morning, only with sunshine spilling through the bedroom window rather than the total blackness of a cave?

Her movement caused William to stir. Not yet awake, his arm tightened around her.

"Clara," he whispered. His sleep-induced mistake disheartened her. Was sleeping next to her for hours nothing but a reminder of the one he longed to hold? She pushed back and tried to make sense of the darkness.

She noticed something above their heads. A muted shade of light?

"Is there another cave opening up there?" She said aloud, causing both the men to stir.

"Where?"

"There!"

"In case you didn't notice, Schoolmarm, it's pitch black in here. You can't just point," William growled. She took advantage of the darkness to make her rudest face at him.

"Up to the right. Just behind our heads. Unless I'm imagining it, I see light. And put your hand in the air! I feel air moving toward it."

"She's right," Jon said. "But it's going to be nearly impossible to climb up there without a light of our own."

"Hold Kathleen." William shifted the girl's weight and set her on Amelia's lap, ensuring she had a firm grip before he let go. He felt around behind them on the rock until he found the rope they had brought, and then shuffled around on the rock for a few minutes.

"What are you doing?" Amelia asked.

"Tying the rope to something strong." He spoke in a tone that suggested she should have known. She felt his body warmth lift away from her and heard the complaint of the rope as he stressed it with his weight.

"Please don't fall on us." Amelia scooted closer to Jon.

"If I did, it wouldn't be intentional." He sounded annoyed.

A few grunts and muttered oaths later, he spoke again. "I can see it. The opening is small, but I think we could squeeze through."

"How do we get Kathleen up?"

"I'll attach her to my back." Jon took her and began making a harness with the rope to keep Kathleen against him while he climbed. Amelia waited, feeling more uneasy as Jon and Kathleen climbed up into the tunnel.

Would she have to climb it by herself? Would her arms be strong enough? Would her boots provide any traction against the rope?

She didn't know if she could do it. But she must. Somehow, she must.

The rope was tossed back down when Jon and Kathleen were safely in the tunnel. She took several deep breaths, wiping her palms on her skirt to dry off the sweat.

A thud next to her made her squeal in surprise.

"I'm here."

It was William. His arms slid under hers as he moved his body close behind her.

"Grab hold and do your best to pull yourself up." His hands were on hers, guiding her to the rope. "I'll do the rest."

She did as he told her. She was surprised by the burst of strength that lifted her into the air.

"See?" he said in her ear when they had almost reached the top. "You're stronger than you think."

They carefully crawled over the rock into the entrance of the small tunnel. William's words stayed with her. The tiny crevice they would crawl through was barely bigger than a coffin, but the light was so faint, she could pretend she was in a vast expanse, her mind fooled.

"I'm going to lead the way," Jon said in the darkness. "Kathleen, you stay behind me. Miss Em is right behind you."

Kathleen agreed with a small voice.

It seemed like hours that they eased their bodies through the tunnel, sometimes flat on their stomachs and inch by inch. But with every length they traveled, the light grew stronger and the tunnel bigger.

The rocks gave way to woods. The cool spring morning signaled the end of their journey. They were free. Dirty, hungry, thirsty and weary, but free.

They met the rescue party in the woods and delivered Kathleen to her immensely thankful parents.

When Jon and William said their goodbyes, Amelia felt a strange disappointment. She searched the faces of the two men, but she couldn't sense the closeness they had shared anymore. She missed the bond that had joined them all as they worked together in order to survive.

"Goodness, Amelia, you seem rather dejected for one whose life has just been spared," Amy teased before she gave her a big hug.

When they arrived home, Amy drew a bath for Kathleen. After the child was clean and tucked in for a long nap, Amelia took her turn in the water closet, starting to feel right again as she soaked away the dirt in the porcelain claw foot tub. Her tailbone still ached and it seemed every inch of her skin was covered with scratches and bruises, but she would recover.

As she relaxed in the warm water, she considered the conversation with William the previous night. She wanted to know what would happen. She wanted to hear the rest of the story. If her life was a book, she might peek ahead to the final chapter for just an instant to see if his name was written anywhere in the last paragraph.

At least she could talk to one who already knew her future. He was already there.

"Lord," she began a bit sheepishly. "I guess you know where my thoughts keep going."

It seemed monumental to acknowledge. She peeked around the

room to verify her privacy.

"It's pointless to deny it. I can't stop thinking about him. I want to be close to him. I wish he would kiss me, as much as I wish Jon would stop trying. And I want to know every last secret. Everything he's hiding."

She inhaled deeply of the lavender-scented water and sorted her thoughts. "It seems dishonest to speak like this, because I am involved in some sort of courtship with Jon. Help me know what you want. Even if I have to tear out my heart to do it, I will."

She meant it. And she felt a peace settle over her as her spirit heard the answer.

Wait.

THIRTY-THREE

The town took on a cheerful atmosphere as spring warmed and flowers bloomed. The word spread about Kathleen's rescue. Connor and Amy's church hosted a picnic in honor of all the brave men who had helped to find her. Amy insisted that Amelia was included. And that she should come to such an event with a new dress.

Amelia did not agree, but she went with Amy to the dressmaker's and the millinery, and she had to admit, the final result was lovely. Amelia chose a dress of delicate blue lawn, with a lace collar, a gathered waist and puffed sleeves. The night of the picnic, Amy dressed Amelia's hair in a loose twist and curled the wisps around her face with tongs heated on the stove. She used the combs Jon had given Amelia as a Christmas gift to complete the style. Amelia donned her new bonnet with a large floral decoration and a thick white ribbon tied under her chin.

"Charming." Amy stood back and nodded with approval. "He'll love it."

Amelia started to ask to which "he" she was referring, but she guessed she should already know the answer.

She felt most conspicuous when she arrived on the lawn of the Presbyterian Church. Many pairs of eyes looked up.

"They hardly recognize you," Amy murmured close to her ear, sounding rather triumphant, if Amelia didn't miss her guess.

William and Jon both began to walk toward her, but when William saw Jon approaching, he stopped. He watched her with

166

interest as he reached for a cup of punch.

"Em, you look divine!" Jon took her gloved hand and kissed it. "I'll be the envy of every man in town."

He wrapped her arm around his. As they went to the refreshment table, William caught her gaze. When he was sure she was looking at him, he gave her entire person a slow perusal. His eyes returned to hers with a devilish grin.

"Well, Em, what do you think of that?"

It occurred to Amelia that Jon had been talking for the past few moments and she had not heard a word he said. He saw her blank expression and followed it to where William had been standing. Fortunately, William had moved away, and was standing with Amy and Connor.

"I'm sorry, Jon. I was thinking about something else." She smiled around her guilt and tried to give him her full attention.

She enjoyed herself that evening, even if social functions were not high on her list of favorite activities. But every time she turned around, Rebecca Sapp glared at her or tried to capture Jon's attention. Amelia had come to understand she had not only taken the job Rebecca wanted, but the man she was interested in as well. She felt momentary pity along with a measure of guilt, since she had no idea whether she even desired to be linked with Jon.

It was a relief when sunset tinged the bright sky, and Jon asked if she would allow him to escort her home.

William had left earlier, and when Amelia and Jon came from the church to the road, she saw him on his bench, whittling. For reasons she didn't try to understand, she pretended not to see him. She allowed Jon to take her hand as they traveled the other side of the wide street in full view of Morehouse Carpentry and Cabinetmaking. When she stole a glance at William, she saw he was frowning. She couldn't tell if it was his usual frown or if he might be jealous. To her shame, she realized she was hoping for the latter.

Jon was helpful to that end. He pulled her into a shadow between two buildings and wrapped an arm around her waist, pulling her close for another kiss.

She giggled. She did not find the kiss any more exciting than the last. In fact, she found it more unpleasant, but she had become an actress on the stage, performing for the reaction of her audience.

When she stole another glance toward the bench, she saw that William was no longer sitting there, and the door to the carpentry shop had been closed.

"Atheists are dull, who cannot sense God's presence out of sight."

Amelia quoted the Browning poem in front of her class as she peeked behind the curtain to see spring's dark rain clouds hovering over the canopy of trees that surrounded the school. Thunder grumbled in the distance, warning of the coming storm.

"Just like the storm is like a picture of God for us to look at, even though we can't see him." Laura answered. Amelia smiled.

"That's true in all creation. From the tiniest insects to the heavens above."

It was a thoughtful group of girls that left the schoolhouse a few minutes later; before the sky spilled forth the rain it had been holding back. Amelia watched the storm from inside the classroom until she heard heavy boots on the floor behind her. Expecting to see Jon, she turned with a courteous smile.

"Hello." William leaned against the doorjamb, his hands shoved in his pockets under the apron. He was dripping wet.

Amelia's heart thumped hard. "Good afternoon, Mr. Morehouse."

She cleared her throat and busied herself with gathering her books. She hoped he wouldn't see how excited she was to see him. It had been several days.

"Have you been busy?" She asked, trying to make her voice casual. He narrowed his eyes at her as if he were sizing her up.

"Yep."

"Well, that's good, I suppose." Amelia cleared her throat again.

"That and I didn't appreciate your childish display the night of the picnic."

Amelia was horrified. "I beg your pardon? I have no idea what you are talking about."

He only smirked at her before he reached for her books and lunch pail.

"I see we're reading Jane Austen again today."

Amelia decided it would be better not to reveal that she had read *Mansfield Park* so many times she could quote large portions.

"I don't know how you put up with her," he said with a shrug. "She uses way too many words. And I can never quite tell whether she's making fun of her characters."

"I love her characters! Sometimes the only place in the world I feel at home is inside one of her novels." She felt embarrassed at her admission, especially when he didn't respond. It was not her day to impress him. "But they are not intended for the tastes of men."

They went to the front door as she peeked into Jon's room. He was at his desk and one of the Dennis boys was at the chalkboard writing sentences.

I will not put dead frogs in my classmates' boots.

Jon gave her a sigh and signaled he would not be leaving anytime soon. She smiled and waved goodbye before she rejoined William on the steps. She surveyed the mud with a sigh of her own.

"I have nothing against romance." William's voice was smug. He held out a hand to help her down the stairs and around the mud puddles. "Or at least what follows it."

"You mean marriage and family?" Amelia was surprised at his sentimental thought. He snickered.

"Uh... sure."

Her cheeks flamed. Would he ever think of her as anything but naïve if she could not stop blushing at every innuendo that came from his mouth?

But then, her innocence wasn't a secret to either of them. She couldn't even attempt to evoke a jealous response without him seeing straight through to her motives.

She gave him a surmising glance as he opened the gate. She saw his strong forehead and ever-present crease where suspiciously arched brows met. Shadows marked his gaze, as from a sleepless night or a few too many drinks. It made her wonder about all the secrets she still didn't know.

His mouth turned up in a smile that wasn't really a smile, like the mischievous leer on the face of a difficult child. Framing his mouth, she saw the shadow of a beard he never allowed to grow past the stubble.

"What are you looking at?"

She gulped as if she had been stealing candy. "I guess I was looking at you."

"Like what you see?" He grinned at her, stirring her irritation.

"Do you have one ounce of humility in that inflated head of yours?" She scoffed at him and looked away as they crossed the muddy street.

He was not intimidated. "Sure. But I try to save it for special."

She laughed in spite of herself and slapped his hand lightly. "Did you have a reason for coming to harass me this afternoon or do we owe this entire conversation to your lack of meaningful work to do?"

"I had a reason. And I have plenty of work."

"What could be so important that you might be dragged away?"

"You promised me a story."

"I did nothing of the sort." She felt panic.

He leveled his gaze.

She sighed. "What could you possibly gain from reading a silly woman's secret novel? Don't you have enough to tease me about? Why should I give you more fodder for my persecution?"

He chuckled. "I tease you because you react, Amelia. If you learned to ignore me, I might stop. The key is to hurt my ego."

She wasn't about to tell him she did not have the personality to hurt anyone's ego, even an overbearing tease. She would also not admit that she didn't mind his teasing as much as she claimed.

"I don't let anyone read my stories."

"You let your sister."

"Ella is different. She takes it seriously. She helps me see how it could be better and encourages me to keep trying."

"So, you are willing to take the time to write an entire novel down on paper just so one person can read it?"

She had no response. She did want people to read her stories.

And enjoy them. Perhaps they might even learn something by them or be drawn closer to God. But her writing still seemed so inadequate.

She had spent several nights rewriting it, though. It was better.

"Amelia, I promise I won't tease or be false. I'll tell you what I think as a reader. I read all sorts of books. I realize yours probably has some romance in it, given your preoccupation with Jane Austen. I still want to see it."

She made a face at him for his jab. "How could you know that?"

"Because I know *you*." His voice was softer.

Her cheeks flushed and caught his gaze. He watched her with a combination of curiosity and amusement.

She took a deep breath. "I suppose I could go get it."

THIRTY-FOUR

Her heart beat faster with every step she took up the stairs. Even more when she realized that instead of waiting in the parlor as a gentleman should, William was following her up the stairs.

She stopped on the middle landing. "What are you doing?"

"I didn't think you wanted anyone else to know."

"I think you should wait downstairs," she said in a faltering voice.

He shrugged. "I probably should. Doesn't mean I will."

She could not think of anything else to say, nor did she wish to make a scene and appear even more childish than he had already branded her, so she allowed him to follow, though her conscience was ablaze with protest.

She climbed the remaining stairs to her room and went to the dresser drawer to retrieve her story. He stood at the top of the stairs, not entering. But he took an unhurried look around.

"Very tidy."

"That surprises you?"

"No, but the pile of clothes on the floor confirms my suspicion that there are holes in your orderliness."

She cringed when she saw the nightgown left forgotten on the floor by her bed. She had been in a hurry that morning. Too long daydreaming at the window.

"Go ahead. Tease me for my childish ways." "No, I wasn't thinking of you as childish." He cleared his throat, and it became quiet with awkwardness that hummed in an almost pleasant way.

172

Pleasant, yet dangerous.

He seemed to agree. "I'm going to wait in the parlor."

She couldn't focus on a thing for a few moments after he left. She should have been incensed at his brazen attempt to break the rules and climb not one, but two flights of stairs to her unchaperoned room. She should, at the least, be afraid for her reputation. Yet Amy and the girls were outside in the garden and, even if Amy happened upon them, she would believe Amelia if she said nothing inappropriate happened.

Still, Amelia worried over her apathy. The focus of her life to that point had been to follow the rules and traditions that were in place for her protection. Unconditionally. She had been taught that disregarding boundaries for contact with men was shameful.

So how could one man so quickly rewrite nearly twenty-two years of instruction? And yet, he had. She no longer thought of him as dangerous.

She reached for the bound stack of papers in the drawer, and as she did, the old trunk across the room caught her attention. She went to it, breathing deeply of the musty smell and fingering the cracks that marked the passage of time.

Here were secrets. Here were whispers of mysteries too hard to share, sacrificed to the passage of time because of their burden. Here, beneath a baby quilt, tucked away to forget how quickly a baby becomes a young lady, she found the letter.

She reached under the quilt and felt for it. The crumpled paper sat in its place, bearing testimony to a moment in time. It would wait here as silent witness until it was so old it turned to dust.

She let her fingers touch it. She felt a kinship with the man she had come to call her friend. She had never asked him about the letter, but she didn't need his explanation. She could piece together most of the puzzle of words he had spoken and the letter he had written. Of course, it was meant for Clara.

She was sinking in the sea of his story. And the deeper she sank, the less she cared that she might drown.

She stood up and dusted off her skirt as a wave of anxiety fluttered in her stomach. It meant so much to her that he wanted to read her words. It was a way of sharing herself with him without defying every sense of propriety. She needed for him to know her. As she knew him. It was only fair.

She returned to the parlor. Hesitancy and anticipation mingled as she clutched the papers tied with string.

"You aren't facing a firing squad," he said with a soft chuckle. She held out her offering with trembling hands while she lifted her chin in the air and tried to look confident and unconcerned.

He deliberately let his fingers trail along hers as he took the stack. "Don't give me that nonsense, Schoolmarm. I'm not going to hurt it."

She shivered at his slight touch. He watched her for a moment.

She had expected him to take the book with him and read it on his own, perhaps a chapter here or there. Maybe he would return it to her in a month or two. But he sat back on the settee, pulled the string, and gave her a raised eyebrow, precipitating the scandalous thought that he was pretending that ribbon was somehow attached to her person.

It was, in a sense. A great sense. Her hand went to her collar as she swallowed hard.

He offered one more poised smile, as if he knew what she would think and had intended it. Then he held up the first page and began reading her neatly written – for the most part – lines of prose.

She couldn't help but read over his shoulder. She wanted to experience the same journey of words with him, to feel his response to every character's words and every plot's pathway. He gave her an inquisitive glance, but didn't seem to mind.

And so they read together:

> *In a most sensible irony, Gwendolyn was not the sort of woman that would turn any man's head, this or any day she purposed to cross Main Street.*
>
> *This was not due to any unfortunate lack of beauty. In fact, she took great lengths each day to comb into submission every black curl until each strand was tightly hidden in an unrelenting bun. She placed most unnecessary spectacles on the end of her nose, and wore unremarkable gray and brown*

in plainest of styles over her proportioned figure.

Some might have said, and indeed some did say, that Gwendolyn was attempting to hide her alluring appearance because she had no interest in love. Her aspirations carried her higher than such carnal fancies, and so she must dress accordingly to ward off unwanted attention.

The carefully guarded truth was the opposite. Gwendolyn craved love. Not only love, but oneness of souls she hoped existed in such a disappointing world. She desired it so much the thought kept her awake some nights.

Yet as she went about her duty-filled days, she shunned it, for the simple terror love aroused in her senses.

For indeed, she realized most clearly, love wasn't safe.

Amelia read faster than William. It gave her a perfect opportunity to watch him after every paragraph. She read his body language and expressions, trying to guess his opinion. He grinned at her once, but as he came to the end of the passage, he frowned.

"What is it? What's wrong?" Amelia panicked, staring at the page to find the offending word or faulty punctuation.

He met her gaze, hesitating. He glanced back at it and sat up straight. "Where did you hear the phrase *love wasn't safe?*"

She backed away slightly. "I don't remember. I suppose I thought I made it up."

He took a deep breath. After a moment he seemed to force himself to relax, to let the silent thought go. He nodded. "This is good."

Amelia grimaced. Was he trying to be polite rather than honest?

"I think you have a gift," he assured her. "It could use polishing, but you have the heart. I'm looking forward to reading the rest."

She relaxed, though she knew there was something else he wasn't saying.

After a quiet moment, he spoke. "Is that why you hide?"

She sat back in her chair, folding her hands in her lap. "I'm sure I don't know what you mean."

"I'm sure you do." He leaned closer, shortening the gap that she

175

had placed between them. "I've wondered why you hide your thick, pretty hair in that schoolmarm bun." He extended a hand to touch a loose tendril.

"I *am* a schoolmarm." Her voice wavered.

"And it must be why you wear those dowdy dresses and plain skirts. Never a flounce to be found on your person."

"I find this conversation incongruous."

He smirked at her choice of words, although he didn't mock her as she expected. "All buttoned up to the neck."

She stood, covering her middle with her arms. "I didn't realize it was a crime to be prudent."

He stood up as well. "Only if it's against your nature."

She huffed. "We all have a sin nature. That doesn't mean we should conform to it."

She thought she had won, but still she asked. "What makes you think you know me?"

His eyes bored into hers. "Because Gwendolyn betrays you. She is whispering clues. She says you are afraid of love, Amelia."

She looked away, pretending to be interested in the porch swing swaying gently in the afternoon breeze outside the window. When she looked back, he was still waiting for her response.

"Do I act afraid? I have let Mr. Hastings court me."

He shrugged as if her evidence was invalid. "No depth. Bad match."

"What would you know of it? I think it's time for you to go." She marched to the door and ushered him out. He followed, but stopped in the doorway, close to her.

"Do you deny it?"

She didn't answer. She had no idea what to say. She wasn't prepared to agree with him, as that would put her in an uncomfortable position with Jon. She tried to control the quivering sensation his nearness generated.

He brought his hand to her cheek and gently forced her gaze to his.

"What are you afraid of?"

She sighed in surrender. "I don't know. I suppose if I allowed myself to love with meaning –"

"You mean passion," he corrected in a forbearing tone, nodding for her to go on.

She tried to ignore him. "I'm afraid I would be wounded. I'm not good at doing things with less than my whole heart. And what if I gave all and was rejected? Abandoned? Would I recover?"

His hand fell as understanding lit his eyes. His answer was marked by sadness. "You would. The heart is sturdier than you think. So are you."

"I also fear I would hurt someone else. That would be worse."

He leaned close again, and she felt an alarming ache for him to cover the distance remaining.

"Love has a heavy load of possibilities. You can't have it without some measure of pain. They go together with an inseparable bond in this world. But it's worth it. I promise you, the treasure is worth the pain."

"Just like Jesus showed us."

His gaze found hers and held it. "Our best example. Love isn't safe. Not even for God."

"It must be worth it, or he wouldn't have bothered."

He didn't answer. Her breath seemed to have stolen his attention. She felt risk in the silence, and in the thoughtful look on his face.

"The only safe love is God's love for us," she mused quietly. "It may knock us down, bend us almost to the point of snapping; it may overwhelm and terrify us with its power, but it will never break us. It will only make us stronger."

Her words regained his attention, and he looked at her with eyes that seemed glassy. She wanted to hear his response, the tangible words that would give evidence to her claim by his experience. She wanted to know it was true – she could trust enough to step into deep waters. But the sound of childish laughter broke the spell of the poignant moment.

"Maybe we'll finish this conversation sometime," he said before he left her in the doorway. Seconds before Amy and the girls came around the side of the house, he turned back.

177

He held up the stack of papers. "I think *this* will be enlightening."

She eyed him doubtfully. "Don't drop any of those."

She fretted about that possibility for the rest of the evening. By bedtime she was sure that she should have followed him and picked up any stray papers that flew out of the pile. She went to sleep with the mortifying scene playing out in her mind: Mrs. Hagaman standing in front of the store, reading the contents of Amelia's story to an amused crowd of spectators. They laughed to the point of tears.

It wasn't her most restful night of sleep.

THIRTY-FIVE

Amelia peeked behind her worn copy of Frankenstein.

"Did she leave yet?"

"Not yet." Kathleen peered over her picture book toward the grocer's, her forehead wrinkled in concentration.

They had been sitting on the bench outside William's shop for a half-hour, while he built a frame for a bed. He had walked past twice, muttering about crazy females with too much time on their hands.

The target of their spying mission exited the store as she pinned her voluminous hat in place, peacock feathers fluttering behind her. Mrs. Hilda Hagaman headed toward the First Methodist Church with a purposeful stride.

"There she goes. Off to Women's Christian Temperance Union, which means she won't be back for at least an hour." Amelia glanced at the little girl.

Kathleen nodded her approval. "Let's go!"

They set their books inside the shop on the counter before they walked across the street with careful indifference.

"Well, hello, ladies," Harold Hagaman greeted them from behind the counter where he was recording inventory. He didn't seem surprised to see them. It was common practice among the citizens of Little Sicily to measure the comings and goings of his wife. His busiest times happened to occur during her outings. "Coming in for some penny candy?"

Amelia set Kathleen on the counter where she would have a good view of the candy selection. "That's Miss Able's purpose. My intention is to spend more than a penny."

"Well," he said in surprise. "What can I get for you?"

She cleared her throat. "I've been saving for a bicycle."

"Now that is interesting." He pulled out the thick Sears Roebuck catalog from under the counter. "A velocipede in Little Sicily."

He was exaggerating. She knew she had seen bicycles.

Surely she had?

He hummed as he turned the pages. "What are you looking to spend?"

She forced herself not to consider the controversy. Bicycles could not be the tool of the devil to entice women out of their rightful place. She was certain she would not act and dress in a lewd manner upon making such a purchase.

At least she doubted it.

After looking through the choices, she decided on the White Star. It was supposed to be a high-quality bicycle without the high price. At forty-five dollars, almost fifty with the cost of shipping from Chicago, it seemed extravagant. She had been saving most of her salary, first at the library and now at the school, and it would take most of her savings, but she expected the expense would be worth it.

When the transaction was made, she asked him to keep it between the two of them.

"You have my word," Mr. Hagaman assured her with a knowing smile. "I promise not to tell my wife."

As they walked back to the carpentry shop, she felt William's curious eyes on her. She claimed her book, said a quick goodbye and walked home with Kathleen, wondering what in the world she had just done.

William watched her walk away, wondering what she had just bought at the grocery that had her face as red as beets. She wouldn't even look at him.

Maybe it was a feminine thing. He allowed himself one last look at her pink cheeks before he returned to work.

Carpentry work, when one was used to it, offered much time to think. He pondered Amelia's book, and the eerie way the story reminded him of Clara.

It occurred to him that he hadn't thought about Clara as much in recent days. Before the schoolmarm came to town, he had been in a bad place. His anger over the mistreatment of the saloon girl had not been as noble as he liked to think. He could only see Clara, so he'd pulled out his gun for her sake.

But then Amelia came, and things changed.

Nevertheless, his interest in Amelia left William in a precarious position. If he gave in to the attraction and tried to win her, he'd be responsible to protect her. To preserve her innocence and make sure that his past never – ever – hurt her. Was it realistic to attempt?

He sighed, throwing down the block plane and stretching his neck muscles. His eyes traveled to the desk. He walked over and opened it, sifting through the piles of receipts and invoices until he found what he was looking for.

He pulled out the old letter. It had been creased and softened by the many times he had folded and unfolded it. He avoided his own writing, insistent and hopeful. His eyes jumped to the bottom of the page, to the four little words that had both comforted and confused him for four years. He saw Clara's handwriting, hurried and panicked, yet still as lovely as she had always been.

Take her to Emmy Jo.

"I'm sorry, Jon. I'm afraid my company is not first-rate this evening."

Amelia didn't feel especially sorry. She was irritated with herself that, on this beautiful April evening, she wished she was with William instead of Jon.

He reached for her hand. "You don't have to talk. I like just looking at you. You're beautiful and I'm glad you're mine."

She was not able to recall when they had decided he would take ownership of her.

"I don't belong to anyone but Christ," she said, sounding more contrary than she intended.

181

He dropped her hand and stood up, leaning against the post. "Maybe not now, but I would like to change that."

She panicked, looking for a way of escape. But before she could make her excuses, he pulled her into a standing position, keeping a firm grip on her fingers.

"Marry me, Amelia."

Her stomach cramped and she gasped with the pain. Her face flooded with heat while she tried to form a response. What would he do if she put him off? She didn't want to risk making him angry. After all, wasn't he was a good man who would provide for a family? She would have to alter her ways and learn to be content with a normal life, but she would be looked after.

Still, her spirit cried *no*.

"If you need time to think it over, I'll allow it. I want you to be sure you are ready to become a wife."

She frowned.

"I know you are independent, and you don't like to be told what to do. But you can't be a housewife and a mother if you are always daydreaming and reading. And, of course, you'll have to stop teaching."

She stared hard at the wooden planks of the porch floor, hearing a ringing in her ears.

He put his hands on her shoulders, as if to soften the harsh words. "I know it sounds callous, but I'm just being honest, Em. I want to marry you. You must understand I'm only trying to help you decide if it's what you want."

She had imagined her proposal at great length, and it had gone nothing like this in her head. She'd expected to feel treasured. Even if what he said was true, and she knew it was, why did he feel the need to remind her as if he was stating his terms for a business deal?

But when had anything ever met her expectations? Perhaps she projected too many unrealistic dreams into life.

"I'm sorry – I need to go inside." She pulled away from him and fled to her room.

The school year was drawing to a close.

Amelia would be free. She could climb aboard a train heading home as early as the last day of classes. She could return to her life and pretend this strange year had never happened.

But she knew she wouldn't. She was not the same person who had come to Little Sicily the year before. The people she came to know and her experiences here had changed her, and she knew she could not go back to the way she used to be.

Yet she wasn't sure how to move forward. She suspected Amy was worried about her after Jon's proposal. Amelia had no idea how much until she happened, by accident, upon Amy and William discussing the situation on the front porch.

Amelia was going to walk away when she heard them speaking in low voices, but when she heard her name, her feet wouldn't move from the bottom stair.

"Jon needs a girl who doesn't want to think on her own," Amy insisted. "He's a good man, but he isn't right for Amelia."

"I know he's our nephew, but I think you give him too much credit," William said.

"I keep hoping he'll mature." Amy looked away; her tone resigned. "His father left him with such a heartache, and he hides it away and never speaks of it. Elizabeth was too busy with her own pain and her doctoring…"

"You never know what can happen when you pray. Look at me." William slipped his arm around Amy's shoulders.

Amelia was confused. Why would William embrace a married woman? And what did he mean by *our nephew*?

The words sank in and she gasped. How had she not known they were siblings? Why had they not told her?

William spoke again. "Amelia has to make her own decision. If you try to stop her, you'll just push her toward him. She's a stubborn one."

Amelia huffed.

Amy pulled her shawl around her shoulders. "I had hoped you might give her an alternative. Maybe I misread things."

Amelia started to panic. Her head buzzed as she realized she was

183

about to hear the honest truth about how William felt about her. There was no way she could run fast enough not to hear, and, if she covered her ears and sang loudly, they would know she was eavesdropping. She held on to the banister and gritted her teeth in preparation for whatever he would say in response.

"I would be lying if I didn't admit I want her."

Amelia sat down on the step, covering her mouth with her hands.

"Anyway, we've hardly had a conversation when she's been civil to me. What makes you think she'd even consider an old grouch like me?" He chuckled, and she elbowed him.

"What do I have to offer her, Amy? A dark past always trying to catch up with me."

"And a broken heart," Amy said, holding a hand to his chest. "But Amelia isn't looking for perfection. And something tells me she'd be a patient instrument of healing for you."

"She's wholesome. Unspoiled. I have blackness inside me that won't be washed clean this side of the pearly gates. I don't want her stained with that. Do you?"

"Shouldn't that be her choice?"

"Why would any woman choose that?"

She shrugged with a small sigh. "I know what she would say."

"She'd probably say something about how much Jesus suffered at the hand of his beloved," William said.

Amelia nodded in agreement.

"Maybe I'll talk to her, Amy. But I can't promise anything. I'm not sure I should fight for her. She might be better off with Jon, no matter how wrong he seems now. Don't forget what I've warned you about, what could happen."

"She's better off with the one that loves her the way she is. And life is full of uncertainties, no matter what our past may use against us."

After a long pause, he chuckled. "You know what intrigues me? The dreamer. The woman she tries to hide because she's afraid she won't fit in."

"Jon wants to change that," Amy said softly.

They were quiet for a few moments before he said goodbye and

Amelia heard his boots on the steps. She went to the door to watch him walk away.

There was a part of her that knew he was attracted to her. His words were more confirmation than revelation. But she could see his point. They were so different. How could they ever become one and make a life together? And what had he meant by his ominous warning?

Amelia felt a tingle of anticipation when she wondered what would happen next. She'd felt the same way when she boarded the train to come to Ohio. She'd felt it when she took her first step into the school. She'd felt it that very moment on the stairs, when she had heard William admit he had feelings for her.

What would he do? Whom would she choose? What would the next page of her story reveal?

THIRTY-SIX

William thought about his sister's words. All day. All night.

He'd be a fool to try to deny he loved Amelia. He could recognize it well enough. The quiet assurance that he would happy to alternately squabble over their differences and make love to her for the remainder of his days.

More than that, he knew she could accomplish much if she had someone believing in her, pushing her. He loved the passionate, creative spirit she desperately tried to hide. He would never want to subdue it. It was what made her so beautiful and vibrant.

When he thought about her marrying Jon, he was sure he couldn't allow it. But he chafed at the thought. It was time to make his move. He might not have another chance.

Clara, would you forgive me if I loved another?

William was irked when he saw Jon head into the saloon later that night. He fumed a little before he went in after him.

Hastings was at the bar with a saloon girl draped over his shoulder. His friends stood around him, shouting encouragement as he reached across the polished counter for the shot glass of whiskey.

"What do you think you're doing?" William demanded, causing Jon to spill his drink into his lap. He jumped up, uttering an oath as he reached for a towel.

"What is it to you, Morehouse? You've been here yourself a time or two," Jon said, but he avoided eye contact.

William glared at him. "You propose marriage to the daughter of a reverend. You say you are a Christian man; you attend church. You're supposed to be an example to the boys of Little Sicily."

Jon tried to meet his gaze with defiance, but he faltered and looked away. William could see masked shame.

Good.

"It wasn't Jon's idea to come in," one of Jon's friends said. "We thought it might help him relax. He's never been in here before."

William directed his words to Jon. "So why would you start now? You, of all people, should know what these places do to people. To fathers."

There was a long silence. Jon dropped a coin on the counter and headed for the door.

William followed him out. When they were outside, Jon tried to walk away but William stepped into his path.

"It's none of your business. Stay out of my way and stay away from my girl," Jon said.

"You can't have both, Hastings. I won't allow it; she's too good for that. If you choose to let your head be turned by every pretty girl, or let your life be used up by drink like your pa did, I won't let you have Amelia. I promise you."

William wasn't interested in the younger man's response. He turned and started to walk away.

Jon called from behind him. "How do you know anything about my pa? Did Amelia tell you?"

"It's not hard to figure out, Hastings."

Especially not considering the things William knew.

"Oh, my goodness! What a surprise!"

Amelia turned from her position next to John at the counter of Hagaman's. Rebecca Sapp stood next to them, her hand on Jon's arm.

"I didn't see you standing there, Jon Hastings." She gave him a coy smile.

He gave her a polite nod. "Hello, Miss Sapp. Nice day, isn't it?"

"Why, it sure is! What brings you and your friend Miss Farnsworth to the store this afternoon?"

Jon looked uncomfortable. "Miss Farnsworth and I had some business to attend to."

Rebecca shifted closer to him, giggling. Amelia recognized something in her voice. It was almost manic, like old Mrs. Tibley back in Illinois, who stood on the street corner and told everyone's future as they passed by. She'd been sent to a sanitarium the second time she was almost run over by the stagecoach.

But Rebecca wasn't an old woman. She was young and beautiful, and far more intelligent than Mrs. Tibley had been. Surely it was Amelia's imagination.

"I came in for dress supplies," Rebecca said. "They're a bit more expensive at the dressmaker's. I don't care to be showy, but I do love having beautiful clothes. Jon, don't you just love this one?"

She did a graceful turn, holding the skirt of the pink gingham, complete with lacy trim and a low décolletage.

"Sure, Miss Sapp. That's a fine dress." Jon seemed nervous as Mrs. Hagaman came from the back room.

"Well, Mr. Hastings! Did you bring Miss Farnsworth in to show her the item you discussed with my husband yesterday?" Mrs. Hagaman gave him a knowing smile. Jon pulled at his collar.

"Actually, I think we'll wait for another time –"

"Nonsense." Mrs. Hagaman brought the catalogue from under the counter and started flipping. "Nothing to be ashamed of. It's all over town by now that you asked Miss Farnsworth to marry you. Everyone is simply going on about it."

Within seconds, Rebecca's face became bright red. Amelia likened the image to a steaming volcano erupting hot lava over its edge.

Mrs. Hagaman evidently sensed no danger. "I assume the rumors are true? There are those who think you are making a mistake, Mr. Hastings." She looked pointedly at Amelia. "No offense, my dear, but you know how progressive and outspoken you can be with your ideas."

"Oh, no offense taken," Amelia said with a hint of sarcasm and raised an eyebrow, wondering how Mrs. Hagaman could consider anyone else outspoken.

"But *I* think you are a handsome couple," Mrs. Hagaman assured them.

"Jon?" Rebecca turned to him, unable to conceal her wild anger. She gave Amelia a loathing glare before she put her hand to her forehead and sank to the floor, forcing Jon to reach out and catch her.

"Oh dear," Mrs. Hagaman clicked her tongue. "That girl is so flighty. Has been since her family passed in the fire."

Jon excused himself to help Rebecca out of the store. She seemed overly pressed against his chest to be unconscious.

"I've seen a picture at City Hall of a farm that burned quite a few years ago." Amelia turned back to Mrs. Hagaman. "That was Rebecca's family?"

"It was. What an awful day. First thing on a Monday morning all the men were called to the Sapp homestead. My Harold was there. After, he didn't talk about it much, it disturbed him so. Those burned bodies of the little children and their parents. Harold said it was eerie the way she just stood there in the field, staring at the smoldering remains of her home. Not a single tear in her eye. Poor thing was likely in shock, and hasn't mentioned it since. We all feel responsible for her. We all put up with Rebecca's nature because we know she has suffered."

Amelia felt guilty for her mistrust and judgmental attitude toward Rebecca. It seemed silly that she had wondered if the girl was evil. Miss Sapp was just troubled by her past.

"I had no idea. How awful."

Amelia was ashamed of herself.

Amelia was hoping for a quiet night at home. Maybe Jon wouldn't stop by. Maybe William would.

However, neither was not to be. Instead, there was a solemn knock at the door about seven in the evening. Not Jon or William, but Mr. Sommers of the school board. He requested that Amelia and

Amy follow him to City Hall.

When they arrived, Amelia saw a crowd had gathered, and she sensed the somber occasion was somehow because of her. Whispers ceased and all eyes turned her way upon her entrance. Fear seemed to claw from inside her stomach.

William leaned against the back wall, his arms crossed. He looked angry. Was he angry with her? Were they all?

She was directed to sit on the platform opposite the table of school board members. She obeyed with her face on fire. Her mind raced with the possibilities. As she searched her conscience, she realized why they were there.

"We have called this impromptu school board meeting because of a complaint that was sent to the board by anonymous letter. Miss Farnsworth has been accused of public intoxication, which allegedly occurred early in the school year."

Amelia closed her eyes in shame. How could anyone have found out? Amy had assured her she was safe. Had William turned her in? She dared to lift her eyes long enough to catch his.

He met her gaze without flinching and shook his head. She was relieved, but confused. No one else knew.

"Mrs. Amy Able, please stand."

Amy did as she was told, though her stance showed her disagreement with the proceedings.

"Mrs. Able, have you found Miss Farnsworth in a drunken state at any time since she has resided here?"

"Miss Farnsworth had an unfortunate reaction to medication she was given for her stomach ailment. Whoever is responsible for this has no idea what they are talking about."

Voices murmured. Jon stood beside Amy. "Why would you not come to Mrs. Able and Miss Farnsworth and ask them your questions privately? This is madness! I can't believe you have gone to these lengths and put this poor girl on display like a criminal! I insist you stop this at once!"

"We will officially note your protest, Mr. Hastings, but this meeting will adjourn when we are satisfied we have the truth. Please sit down."

Jon and Amy reluctantly sat, watching Amelia with concern. Amelia sucked in air and held her burning stomach. She stared at the piano in the corner with the cover over it and imagined herself crawling beneath it.

"Is Mrs. Dennis in attendance?"

"I'm here." The woman stood near the back, swaying and grabbing the chair in front of her for support.

"Mrs. Dennis, is it true that Miss Farnsworth visited your home?"

"Yessir," she slurred. Several people tittered.

"Did Miss Farnsworth leave your home with anything in her possession?"

"Why, sure. I gave her a bottle of my coca wine for her stomach. But I warned her – more than a few sips and she'd be drunk as a skunk."

The laughter and whispers escalated. Amelia's eyes found William's once more, the only pair in the room, other than Amy's, that held no judgment. He didn't smile, but he seemed to infuse her with strength. He'd faced worse and come through, and she could do the same.

"Miss Farnsworth, how do you answer these allegations?"

She tried to breathe. She felt faint, and gripped the arms of her chair until her knuckles were white.

She must tell the truth. There was no other option. She locked eyes with William and communicated her resolve. He stood up straight, shaking his head slightly and clenching his hands at his side.

After a tense pause, she opened her mouth to confess. But William's voice was louder than hers.

"You ought to be ashamed of yourselves. I'm guessing all of you are sitting in here because you have nothing better to do than gossip and make yourselves feel superior. Miss Farnsworth, don't answer to this sorry excuse for a town. It's no wonder we go through teachers so fast."

The room filled with the voices.

When Mr. Sommers finally regained partial order, he addressed

191

William. "Mr. Morehouse, you will be removed if you cause further disruption. Miss Farnsworth, you will answer the question."

William stalked down the aisle, pointing his finger at Mr. Sommers. "Mrs. Able already explained what happened. Amelia had a reaction to medication. You are treading on dangerous ground here, Sommers. You're accusing an innocent schoolteacher with a flawless reputation on the testimony of the town drunk. Are you really sure you want to continue?"

Mr. Dennis stood up and shook a fist toward William. "My wife is not a drunk, Morehouse! I'll knock your block off!"

Mrs. Dennis hiccupped.

The noise level became frenetic again. Amelia saw William's secret expression of satisfaction. He'd accomplished exactly what he'd intended.

He made his way through the audience, now standing in circles, discussing either side of the issue. He stopped at the board members' table and glared at every one of their sheepish faces.

"Look at what you've done to her. She's as pale as a ghost. If she becomes ill over this it will be on your heads. I'm taking her out of here immediately."

He came charging toward her and grabbed her arm, leading her toward the door in a manner that assured her he wasn't overly concerned over her delicate health. In fact, he seemed annoyed with her. She followed him out, and Amy and Jon came with them. Jon made sure the door fell closed as loudly as he could manage.

"Can you believe the nerve? Blaming Amelia for drunkenness? I hate to think ill of people, but they seem determined to run off every female teacher we employ."

Amelia felt miserable. "Jon –"

He took hold of her arm as if she might topple over without his assistance. She might have. "Don't give it another thought, Em. This town is full of people who are just looking for trouble. I'm sorry they put you through that nonsense."

"But Jon, I *was* drunk."

"Amelia." William narrowed his eyes. "Don't."

"She thought it was medicine," Amy insisted. Amelia could see her confession had caused Jon to go silent. Amy touched his arm. "I was there, Jon. Amelia did not intend to intoxicate herself. She was just too trusting and didn't have all the facts."

"But I should have known!" Amelia cried. "I deserve this."

William grabbed her again and forced her to look at him. "They weren't there for truth, they were there for a show, which you were about to provide them. There are times when you just shut up and let others take care of you."

She shook herself free of his grip. "There is never a time to lie! It doesn't matter what their intentions were, mine was to tell the truth."

Jon pushed William back before he could launch into another tirade. "Leave her alone, Morehouse. Come on, Em. I'm going to walk you home."

He grabbed her hand and pulled her away. Amy followed, giving William a lingering glance. He watched them go with fire still blazing in his expression.

As Amelia moved away, she noticed a figure sitting primly on the bench outside William's shop, hands folded in her lap. Rebecca Sapp stood, giving Amelia a wild, mocking grin. She waltzed into the darkness with her hands folded behind her back.

For the first time in months, Amelia was ready to catch the next train home.

THIRTY-SEVEN

"Oh, Miss Farnsworth," Connor said, peeking over the top of his newspaper as Amelia entered the kitchen. It had been three days since the meeting at City Hall. "Someone dropped you a postal this morning. I left it on the hall table."

Amelia thanked him and excused herself to get it, hoping it might be from William.

When she picked up the envelope, her illusions about a secret message in which William confirmed his undying love for her were dashed. It was not his handwriting on the front of the envelope. She opened it and unfolded the flowered stationary.

Dear Miss Farnsworth,

I would like to extend an invitation. Please join me for tea in my home this afternoon at five o'clock.

As well as to make amends for attempting to secure your job, I would like to discuss how I can help you as you seek to restore your good reputation to the citizens of this town.

Most sincerely,
Rebecca Sapp

She reread the note. She wanted to believe Rebecca Sapp was genuine. Perhaps a burden Amelia had been bearing was unnecessary, and she could set it down. But *was* the letter sincere? She reread it. There was no doubt Rebecca was eccentric, but the note was gracious. Mrs. Hagaman was right that the trauma she experienced as a child would set anyone off balance. That didn't make her evil. If she wanted to apologize and restore the relationship, Amelia had no right to hinder her.

So why did she still hesitate? She reached for a piece of stationary and dipped the fountain pen in the ink well on top of the desk.

Dear Miss Sapp,

Thank you for your kind invitation. I plan to join you in your home at five o'clock.

Sincerely,
Amelia Farnsworth

After a full day of teaching, she had almost forgotten the appointment. Polly had launched a heated discussion on why God could expect the Israelites to wipe out the inhabitants of the Promised Land. It had taken a half-hour to steer the class back to the history lesson.

She could only blame herself. She was the one who encouraged them to speak their minds. At least that was what Jon said at lunch with a chuckle.

Exhausted, Amelia thought she might go straight home and take a nap until she recalled the invitation she had accepted. She knew she couldn't break her promise.

She gave William a lingering glance as she passed by the open door of his shop. He was still working on the bed frame, but he was sanding now. His sleeves were rolled up to his shoulders; his strong arms flexing as they worked. She imagined the crease she couldn't quite see on his forehead. She loved that crease. She had imagined a time or two how it might feel to kiss that crease.

She blushed over her thoughts, reminding herself Jon had

195

proposed. But she argued to herself that she had not yet answered him and felt proportionally better.

She crossed the street near William's shop and walked the stone path to Rebecca's front door. The Gothic Revival cottage, painted blue, was pleasant at first glance, with whimsical gingerbread trim, but an aspect of it seemed cold. Out of place.

She knocked softly, hoping Rebecca had forgotten and gone out. It wasn't to be. She opened the door in a flurry of pink ruffled taffeta.

"Amelia! I'm so dreadfully pleased you have come!" Her voice oozed insincerity, but Amelia admonished herself to think the best.

"Thank you for having me, Miss Sapp."

"Oh, please, no need for formality. We're to be good friends, you and I. Call me Rebecca. Becca, even, I don't mind. Come right in and let me take your sweet little shawl."

Amelia was led into the front parlor. She had an immediate flutter of anxiety at the bright colors and haphazard patterns of the décor. Everything was stylish and contemporary, but with the furniture, wallpaper, textiles and pictures all shoved together, it was quite overwhelming to the senses.

Rebecca noticed her perusal. "I know, it's just lovely, isn't it? I don't have much to do with my time since I wasn't able to secure the position at the school. Not that I'm blaming you, dear, you've been just wonderful, but I seem to have taken up decorating as consolation. I lived here with my aunt until she died last year and I'm afraid she left the place awfully morose."

She pointed Amelia to a striped chair in the middle of the room. "Please make yourself comfortable, Amelia. Or what was that charming little nickname Jon gave you? Em? I'll be back quick as a wink with the tea."

She floated down the short hall to the kitchen, humming *Sunshine and Shadows*.

Amelia sighed and tried to focus on one item in the room to avoid being overcome by the garishness. Her eyes fell to the pictures along the mantle. Rebecca's family had been a somber bunch. Her parents seemed put out that they were being made to sit still for a picture, and her younger siblings looked like sad little waifs.

Amelia thought the practice of scowling in pictures was ridiculous. She knew by experience it was awkward to maintain an expression for the duration of the time it took to take the picture, but shouldn't they be remembered with smiles on their faces? All of their descendants would assume they were a rather unhappy lot.

She supposed it was true enough for some.

As she looked away from the fireplace, she noticed she could see the reflection of the kitchen from the elaborate mirror in the hallway. She saw Rebecca's back as she bustled around the space.

She was about to look away when something Rebecca held flashed against the sunlight. Rebecca took a pinch from whatever it was and turned back to the counter where Amelia couldn't see her.

It must be the tea tin.

She willed her stomach to settle. It was silly to be nervous over tea with a neighbor, however unfriendly the girl might have been in the past.

Rebecca returned in the same cheerful manner. She set the silver tray on the table and poured tea into two china teacups. They were edged with gold and painted with a picture of a man and woman strolling through a garden. She handed one to Amelia and smiled.

"I confess I bought them because I thought the man looked like Jon. He's so handsome, isn't he? Well, of course you would think so, being engaged to him."

Tea. Tea would help the pain. Amelia took a tentative sip. It was some sort of spiced tea. She took another sip.

"So, my dear Em, I have been thinking about that horrible accusation against you yesterday. I was just horrified that anyone would accuse you of such ghastly behavior."

Amelia squirmed, taking a few more sips to avoid responding. She didn't want to be forced to come clean with Rebecca Sapp, of all people.

"It's so fortunate you had Jon to stand up for you. He's such a dear. How nice that the two of you are to be married."

Amelia smoothed her twill skirt. "I haven't given Jon a formal answer yet."

She laughed. "Well, of course you won't turn him down. He's

the most eligible bachelor in Little Sicily! I must admit, I'm crazy with jealousy. And quite confused, since the cabinetmaker seems to have his sights set on you as well. It's almost scary how they fall for you. If I didn't know you to be so sweet and good, I'd wonder if you were a witch." Rebecca's smile faded.

A moment later Rebecca cheerfully urged Amelia to have a piece of cake, but she declined. She looked toward the door, desperate for an excuse to leave.

"Honestly, I can't imagine you'd even consider turning Jon down. We both know how capable he is when it comes to kissing and that sort of thing."

Amelia was confused, but she didn't ask for clarification. Rebecca covered her mouth and giggled as if she had just spoiled a birthday surprise.

"Oops! Sometimes I say things before I think. Jon and I have been friends for a long time, and one Sunday a few weeks ago he brought me home from church, and it just happened."

Amelia needed to leave. Her stomach was protesting against the tea she had thought tasted good. Uneasiness settled over her like a cloud.

"Thank you so much for the tea, Miss Sapp. I do need to get going."

Rebecca smiled, apparently not surprised. She handed Amelia her shawl and opened the door to let her out. Amelia passed by the other woman quickly, but not so fast she missed the whisper that she was almost sure she hadn't imagined.

"I know what you are."

As Amelia fled, she glanced back to the table in the parlor where she had set her garish teacup.

Thirty-Eight

It seemed fitting with the kind of day Amelia was having, William would, of course, be in his doorway frowning at her as she passed by. He must have known something was wrong, because he beckoned her.

She sighed, wishing only to go home and lay down. If she went to him, he would tell her to come in and sit down, and this time there were plenty of people to witness a breach of propriety. But when she pretended she hadn't seen him, he glared harder and called her name. She gave in and walked across the street toward him, trying not to meet his gaze and risk him reading her mind.

"What were you doing at Rebecca Sapp's house?" His voice held misgiving.

"I'm not entirely sure." She looked back at the house that now seemed eerie in the lengthening shadows of the evening. Was Rebecca watching from the front window? Her eyes refused to focus, so she rubbed them as she turned back toward William. He pulled her hands away and studied her.

"What's wrong with you?"

"I'm not certain... I need to lie down."

He pulled her inside the door and closed it behind her before anyone could see. She started to protest, but he reached for her waist and directed her to a chair away from the window. It felt so good to sit that she didn't argue.

He stood next to her, his arms crossed. "You had me worried last night. You almost gave that mob reason to get rid of you, and not a good reason at that."

Amelia shrugged and stared at the floor, trying to make her eyes focus. "They deserve to know the truth. If they want to take away my position over it, that's their right."

He scoffed. "Don't be such a martyr. Gossiping fools that can judge a person without hearing the whole story are not worthy of your so-called truth."

"Then why do I feel so guilty?" She felt a sudden rush of irritation. "I'm so tired of always feeling guilty."

He didn't answer, but he allowed his hand to fall, to brush against her hand. Hesitantly, she let it fall open and his fingers covered hers.

"I should have known better." She continued, shivering at a sudden chill. "My sin has found me out."

He gave her a dark stare. After a moment, he let go of her hand and moved to grab his coat from the hook by the door. Amelia thought he might be leaving and started to stand, but she sat back in the chair as he brought the coat and draped it around her shoulders.

She was overwhelmed by the scent of him all around her, sheltering her, warming her. He leaned over her, his hands on either arm of the chair. Amelia's heart started beating a rhythm of warning.

"Maybe it's time to go back to Illinois." She cleared her throat, trying to resume the conversation rather than look up at him in silence, which seemed a perilous idea.

He stood up, his expression one of disgust. "You mean it's time to give up." His tone was flat. Disappointed. "You're right. You should just quit what God called you to, so no one will find out you aren't perfect."

More guilt. Amelia felt as if she was swimming in it. Drowning in the feeling of not measuring up. Combined with the way her stomach raged and her head ached, she felt downright unreasonable at his inciting words.

"I never tried to make anyone think I was anything but what I am."

"Not even Jon?" he said scornfully. "You didn't lead him to

believe you are the kind of woman that would cheerfully give up everything just to be his submissive little wife?"

The truth of his words stung. She stood up, his coat and her shawl falling from her shoulders. She tried to move toward the door, but he took a sudden step close and captured her arms in an iron grip. There was no way she was going to stand there staring into his eyes, so she tried to come up with words. Preferably words to make him angry. Words that would set her free from the small room that now seemed impossibly warm.

"You're just bitter," she managed, feeling dizzy when she momentarily broke free of his hold on her. He steadied her and resumed possession of her arms. She looked down. Around the room. Anywhere but into his eyes.

"You are determined to live in regret and be spiteful to anyone who won't join you. Do whatever you want, Mr. Morehouse, but I will live my life the way I see fit. I will marry the person I believe I should marry and I won't spend a minute of my life regretting it. I will learn to love the way I want to love. With passion. Just try to stop me you selfish, callous −"

She dared a quick glance up at his eyes. Her words meant nothing to him. He discounted everything she said with one cold scowl. She took a tiny step back, hoping the door was located somewhere behind her.

But he took a larger step toward her.

"So, you think you know what passion is, Schoolmarm?"

She stepped back again, panicking when she realized she could not tear her eyes away from his.

"You think Jon's little kisses can even begin to describe passion, Amelia?"

Her name sounded smooth as butter wrapped in his low voice.

"You have no idea what the word means, even if you are a walking dictionary. Even if you can spell it and list every definition, you have no idea what passion does to someone who has come to understand it firsthand."

She could feel his breath on her face. The room spun around her. She matched his second step toward her with another in reverse, and

201

gasped softly as her back met the wall. She should beg that he let her go. But she only stared into his gaze, mesmerized.

His sneer had changed. His eyelids had fallen, as if he was tired. Instead of hardness, she read hunger in his expression. She gulped, frantic for words to keep the conversation going. She had never been more afraid; her stomach had never been so tumultuous, yet she kept talking.

"You call yourself a Christian. You sit in the back of that church, but all the while you are the same as the rest of them. Judging everyone. I hope that one day you grasp the meaning of kindness. Understanding. I hope you –"

"Amelia." His voice was rough and dark as the shadows covering them.

"Yes?"

"Stop talking. Now."

She felt a hum of the unfamiliar. He could sense it, but she had been oblivious, like a child talking in church. Or perhaps she had only pretended not to notice it. In turn, she wondered and dreaded and imagined what might happen next.

In a charge she would not have been prepared for had she received a full year's warning, he descended on her. His arms wrapped around her waist and lifted her up and toward him with a strength that stunned her. His mouth met hers in caresses she might have described as violent if she were a spectator to this unforeseen moment of time, but she had no trace of fear. No desire to flee.

Though she now understood the true nature of desire.

She tried to think. It occurred to her she should catalogue these sensations for later reference. In her library of feelings, was it? But she had no words for what was happening. This was no scripted novel's kiss. This was foreign and surreal, yet it satisfied something deep within her that had always hungered, had always craved fulfillment.

She wrapped her arms around his neck and returned his kisses, holding him tightly, wishing she could have more of him. It was as if a door within her had flung open, revealing a passageway into the soul of another. Nothing she had ever imagined or experienced – not even half a bottle of coca wine – could be more intoxicating than this.

His lips left hers and nuzzled her neck, just below her ear. She pushed her fingers through his hair and across his neck, trying to pull him closer. They were in a new place, all their own. There was a glittering sky above them and the whitecaps of an open sea below, and they were happily descending into the sweetest, murkiest depths to drown in the pleasure of what they were sharing.

Keep your heart with all diligence.

Words whispered in her father's voice interrupted the ecstasy.

Amelia cried out, pushing him back. "Let me go!"

She couldn't look back into his eyes. She suspected they would still register longing and she would not be able to resist again. She would recant her protest. Surrender.

Instead, she picked up her skirts and moved toward the door as fast as she could, ignoring the grinding of the corset against the raging pain in her abdomen, as well as the distant sound of his voice calling her name. Her breath came in short gasps, her throat was on fire. She only managed to find the doorway and escape into the street before she succumbed to the blackness that had spread across her consciousness and reached with hungry arms to swallow her up.

THIRTY-NINE

William watched her flee as he attempted to regain control of himself. "Amelia, wait."

Shame hit him full force when he realized what he'd just done. He'd made it no secret to her that he lived a different sort of life before coming to the cross for forgiveness. But this was without excuse. As he thought about what he had subjected her to, he felt sick. He had to go after her. Make sure she was okay. Apologize. Something.

Then he saw her fall. Not a fall that might occur if one tripped over a loose board, but the fall of someone who was injured or ill. White hot fear struck him like lightning. He took two large strides out the door and kneeled beside her, gathering her into his arms.

"Amelia?" He shook her, patted her cheek, but there was no response. How had he missed how pale her complexion was? How clammy and cool her skin was?

A crowd began to gather, but he ignored them, heaving Amelia up and pushing through the onlookers as he ran for the clinic.

"Doc!" William yelled as he neared the doctor's down on the edge of Main by the school. The door opened and he ran through it, panting with exhaustion as he lifted Amelia onto the examination table in the back room.

Doc followed him in, reaching for his stethoscope. "What happened?"

"I don't know." William struggled to breathe. "She was upset, and then she fainted."

Dr. Robert Stacy was a quiet man in his fifties, unmarried and dedicated to the task of caring for the health of the town. Everyone had called him "Doc" for as long as William had been in Little Sicily. He wore a serious expression as he held the stethoscope to her chest and felt for her pulse.

"Did she eat or drink anything?" He examined her eyes.

"Not that I saw, but I was only with her for a few minutes. She has a stomach ailment she mentioned was bothering her."

"Yes, I've treated her for her ulcer."

"Is that what's wrong with her?"

"It's difficult to say. Did she seem confused?" The doctor examined Amelia's fingernails.

William cleared his throat, realizing that he would have to share information that might get Amelia in more trouble. Would Doc keep a confidence?

"She was cold, now that I think about it. And dizzy. Had trouble focusing her eyes."

"Anything else?"

William looked back toward the door with unease. "There was a taste... sort of metallic."

Doc hesitated as if he didn't understand. "She said that?"

"Not exactly."

Doc nodded slowly, and there was an awkward pause. "I suppose it could be her ulcer or influenza, but if I gave my best guess at this point, I'd say she was suffering from poisoning. Arsenic poisoning, to be specific."

"Arsenic?" Anger and confusion flooded William's mind. "Are you sure?"

"Not at all. But it won't hurt to treat her for it. If she wakes up and her stomach can take it, we'll give her an infusion of garlic and onion tea. Maybe some eggs. I'll give her charcoal as a last resort."

"How would she have come by arsenic? Are you saying someone poisoned her?" He felt panic. This couldn't happen. Not again. Not before he even got to tell her how he felt.

William remembered watching her come from the Sapp house.

Seeing Rebecca's smug smile through the window. Could Rebecca have poisoned her?

"It could have been accidental," Doc answered. "Sometimes it gets into water sources, though I would think others would be affected, unless she's just more sensitive to it. There are even women that rub arsenic on their skin or take it with vinegar to improve their complexion. I can't think of a reason why anyone would hurt her. Can you?"

William remembered the message on the blackboard. Someone had threatened her a couple months before. Was it such a leap to wonder if someone had followed through on the warning?

William turned to leave. "I'm going to talk to Sheriff Tyler."

Forty

Amelia tried to wake up. She felt like she had been sleeping for days. Her eyes refused to focus at first, but gradually she recognized the plaster ceiling above her head. She tried to sit up, but nausea overcame her. She heard a moan and realized it was hers.

"She's awake." Amelia heard Amy's voice somewhere to her left.

Jon's face appeared in her vision, his hand holding hers tightly. "Em, you're awake! How are you feeling?"

Doc came across the room and held his stethoscope against her chest. She had a horrible taste in her mouth and the worst nausea she had ever experienced. Her head throbbed and she felt dizzy.

"I've felt better," she managed. "I'm thirsty."

"Of course, but start with small sips." He reached for a cup of water on the bedside table and handed it to Amy, who helped her raise her head to take a sip.

"What happened, Amelia?" Amy asked.

She looked around at the faces surrounding her. Everyone seemed so grave. As if all knew the possibilities but were unwilling to acknowledge them.

Jon cleared his throat. "The sheriff was here a few minutes ago. Doc thinks you might have been poisoned."

Amelia rested her head back on the pillow, gulping back the water that didn't seem to want to stay down.

"Can you think of anyone who would want to hurt you? Where were you before you were talking to Morehouse?" Jon's words held greater insistence than Amy's quiet inquiry.

Amelia stared at the ceiling, remembering the events in vivid detail. The strange meeting with Rebecca, the eerie feeling of foreboding that stayed with her.

The unthinkable things she did with William.

She felt her heart start to race and a scorching heat burned her cheeks. "I can't... I don't know."

She turned her face away and closed her eyes, pretending to sleep. She couldn't say anything against Rebecca, not without proof. She couldn't make an accusation of that magnitude on the basis of vague feelings.

Not if she wasn't going to say anything about what she had done.

She didn't move as she felt Jon kiss her hand and heard everyone leave the room. She breathed a sigh of relief at the sudden solitude.

Her mind raced with questions. Was she still considered a maiden? Had anyone seen them inside the shop? Was the line between a virtuous woman and a loose woman really so thin?

"Why didn't you tell them?"

She startled at William's voice. He was standing by the door, leaning on it. Two thoughts occurred to her. The first was the sort of panic that might make one dive out a window. The other was a fluttery sensation in her chest and a rather undeniable hope that what had happened before might happen again.

It shocked her enough to propel her to a sitting position. She searched for escape routes.

"You're not going anywhere." He pointed to her pillow as he scraped a stool across the floor and sat next to her bed.

"I'm tired, William. I'd rather you go."

His eyebrow turned upward in challenge to her words. He knew she was lying. He folded his arms across his chest and waited for her to answer his question. It occurred to her she wasn't sure what he meant. Didn't tell them about what happened at Rebecca Sapp's? Or didn't tell them what had happened with him?

"Tell them what?"

A flash of perception lit his eyes. "Tell them where you were before you were with me."

She nodded and felt a small sense of relief that he wasn't trying to address the other matter. And yet, now they were staring at opposite walls, trying to think of something else other than where the conversation had led them.

"You can't be here." Her voice was small. Humble. She would confess that she needed him to go to save her from herself.

His stance softened. "I'm the one who brought you here."

She tried to swallow whatever blocked her throat. "Thank you. But I don't –"

She stopped talking in order to will away the tears of shame gathering in her eyes. He was going to think her a naïve child once again. He might laugh at her. If he did, she was sure she would burst into tears.

He didn't laugh. He clasped his hands together in his lap and stared at them. Then he cleared his throat.

"I came to apologize. To beg your forgiveness, really. What I did to you was wrong."

She felt the tension in her chest lessen. "You didn't act alone."

He shook his head, his expression dark. "Amelia, we both know you had no idea what was happening before I... attacked you. And to think you were sick the entire time. You did the right thing by running away."

The words slipped out before she could stop them. "I didn't at first. And I didn't want to."

I could have stayed there forever.

He didn't look at her, but she felt his surprise that she would admit it.

"We certainly bring out the worst in each other," she continued with a soft sigh. "We should stay apart."

Hurt. She sensed his hurt, radiating like an electric light. But didn't he agree? Couldn't he see it was the only answer?

"Listen, I'm not going to sit here and agree you and I are all wrong just because we had a moment of weakness. It was inappropriate, I'll give you that. But I'm not convinced it was evil."

He found her gaze and held it. "What happened with you and me isn't an everyday occurrence, Amelia. Believe me, I've been

209

around, and plenty of married couples will never know something that intimate. We can't pretend that away. You may not see it yet, but I'm telling you, we'd regret it if we didn't at least consider why it happened."

Her hands trembled. She felt her stomach react and wondered if he would feel the same way if she vomited in his lap.

"That being said," he said, sitting up straight. "I promise I will not touch you that way again, for as long as circumstances remain as they are."

She relaxed. "You'll stay away?"

"I can't promise you that," he said firmly. "There may be someone in this town that wants you dead. I can't stand by and let that happen. Not again."

She could tell he hadn't meant to say the last part out loud.

He cleared his throat. "At least we have a suspect."

"Rebecca," she said.

"Why didn't you tell them?"

She fidgeted with the edge of the blanket, taking her time with an answer. "If I named her, and the Sheriff questioned her and found no evidence to link her to the crime, wouldn't that just make her more determined?"

"Doc thinks it was arsenic."

She nodded. "I was hoping in the back of my mind it was just my sensitive stomach, but that seems unlikely now."

"I'm guessing you don't take it with vinegar for your complexion?"

She smiled and shook her head. "But now that I know, I'll have to give it a try."

He chuckled.

They both went quiet. The questions remained, shouting through the silence, demanding answers. Doc came in a few minutes later and gave her a dose of laudanum.

In the first few moments of her dreams, she felt a hand reach for hers. It gave her a comforting send-off toward her sleep. If it really happened, she was most grateful.

FORTY-ONE

William knew there was something wrong before he made it all the way into the back room where Amelia slept. Doc had come to the door in his robe and slippers, looking bleary-eyed enough that William knew he woke him up. But Doc could only blame himself for not letting William stay the night at her side.

"Something's wrong," William said as he touched her hand. It was like ice.

William searched her face, finding her pale. Before Doc could find his instruments, William had already taken her pulse.

"Doc!"

He was waved out of the way.

"You're here early," Doc said as he assessed her.

"Wanted to see how she was before I started working."

"As I hear it, Miss Farnsworth is engaged to the schoolteacher, Hastings."

"Depends on whom you're asking."

"If I was asking you?"

"Doesn't matter what I say. But I haven't heard her say it."

Doc nodded. "And you and Miss Farnsworth are…?"

William hesitated. How in the world would he even classify their odd relationship? Friends? Fire and ice, and some neighborly good will for appearances? Should he explain that some days he couldn't imagine going another second without taking her in his arms and experiencing every last part of her soul there was to explore?

That might sound disturbing, so he just shrugged. "Friends."

Doc filled the basin with water from the pitcher and washed his hands, splashing his face as well. He dried off with the towel and turned back to William.

"She's bleeding."

"I don't see any blood." William's eyes passed over the parts of her he could see.

"No. I wish it were visible, because that would mean there was an easier way to stop it. I think her ulcer must have been irritated by the poison or the vomiting, and it started to bleed. It's sometimes called chlorosis, but these days, doctors studying hematology call it anemia due to blood loss."

There was a long pause. "Don't tell me she's going to die."

Amelia had opened her eyes and was watching the two men. She gave William a curious look. He sounded as if he might be irritated with her for almost dying.

Though she was not about to die. She had taken Doc's words in stride. She knew that ulcers bled sometimes, and it wasn't the first time she had been anemic after a bad episode. The times she had nearly died as a child had been much more severe.

"I'm not going to die."

Her voice betrayed her. It was small and weak – the voice of someone knocking on death's door. Doc turned to her, thoughtful.

"I can give you medication to help your stomach heal. Hopefully with time and rest the bleeding will subside."

Amelia nodded, satisfied. But William didn't seem to be convinced. "What if it doesn't?"

Doc turned back to him. "I have high hopes, Mr. Morehouse. But if you're asking the next step, there isn't much I can do safely."

William leaned over and pressed a finger to his temple. After a moment he reached for her hand and squeezed it. She wanted to assure him she was fine, but couldn't deny she enjoyed the attention.

"What's wrong?" She squeezed back.

He eyed her with a dark expression. "I don't want to lose you."

Doc and Amelia both stared at him. He cleared his throat. "I don't want us to lose you. The town."

Doc raised an eyebrow, and a smile caught the corner of his mouth. "Of course."

Jon came through the door. "I'm sorry to come barging in, but I had to know how my Em was doing."

Doc gave William a pointed look as he answered. "She's anemic. Her ulcer must be bleeding."

"Bismuth and diet?"

"She's having trouble keeping anything down. We'll have to keep her sipping water for now."

Jon nodded as he glared at William, who at least had the good sense to let go of Amelia's hand and cross his arms over his chest.

"What are you doing here, Morehouse?" Jon demanded.

"Same as you. Visiting Miss Farnsworth," William said evenly.

The suspicion in Jon's expression wasn't missed by anyone. The two men stared at each other and Amelia imagined an icy breeze blowing through.

"Well, now you know. Shouldn't you get back to work?"

"Shouldn't you?"

Doc chuckled and pointed at the door. "There's nothing either of you can do right now. I'm quite capable. You're welcome to stop back later."

They both left with reluctance. Doc gave her a conspiratorial smile.

"And may the best man win."

That night, Amelia began to feel worse. By the following morning, she was very ill. She remembered little of the following days as she grew sicker. Doc kept her on laudanum, so she slept most of the day. People came to visit, and she had vague memories of conversations, but she didn't truly feel herself again until she opened her eyes one morning, finding herself in the Ables' downstairs guest bedroom.

Jon sat at the desk marking papers. He looked up and smiled

213

when she moved.

"Good morning."

"Good morning." Her voice was raspy with disuse.

He crossed and poured her a glass of water. She sipped it.

"You've had a long week," Jon said gently.

"A week?"

"Since you first collapsed. You've been sleepy. Doc said it was from the sedation. He gave you heavy doses to settle your stomach. We thought we might lose you Sunday night."

His voice was troubled. She wondered if he was rethinking the wisdom of tying himself to an invalid for the rest of his life.

"We wired your family. They said they would come, but when you started getting better yesterday, we wired again and caught them before they boarded the train."

Amelia sighed. "I'm glad they didn't have to go to all the trouble and expense."

"Are you hungry? Doc says you'll have to start eating before you can start feeling stronger."

"I think I could try."

He pushed back a strand of hair from her face. "I'll let Amy know."

He moved toward the door, but turned with a hesitant expression. "Em, do you think you were poisoned?"

Amelia looked down at her hands. "I don't know what happened."

He nodded, accepting the half-truth. She could see it wasn't really what was on his mind.

"What is it, Jon?"

"Nothing. I've just been thinking. It's probably trivial, but I can't seem to stop wondering."

"What?"

"Did something happen? Between you and Morehouse?"

She had to take a deep breath to overcome the wave of nausea from the sudden anxiety. She swallowed, closing her eyes until the feeling passed. When she opened them again, she knew her response had given him his answer.

He nodded once and left the room, clenching his jaw.

"I'm sorry," she whispered after him.

She didn't know it would happen. She didn't know she would respond the way she did. But when she put herself in Jon's place, she felt immense guilt. There was no excuse for her behavior.

She needed to stay away from William. She simply did not make good decisions when she was close to him. If she could put some distance between them, maybe she would have more clarity. Maybe she would be at peace with her future.

Her future with Jon.

FORTY-TWO

"Hello, sir," William spoke into the mouthpiece of the telephone at Hagaman's. The voice on the other end on the line seemed to crackle. It was odd, hearing a man hundreds of miles away. What next, flying?

"Mr. Morehouse, I received your wire. I wanted to make sure all was well before we called off our travel plans." He heard Reverend Farnsworth's voice.

"She's doing much better. Doc says he thinks the bleeding stopped, and she's keeping liquids down."

"Wonderful news. Now tell me what you're hiding from me. What brought on this attack?"

"What do you mean?" William stalled. At first, he thought the reverend knew how he had assaulted his daughter. Then he remembered that Rebecca was probably the one responsible for Amelia's brush with death.

He wasn't comfortable announcing either on the public line.

"The sheriff was making a few inquiries, sir," he continued when the older man didn't speak. He didn't think Reverend Farnsworth would be convinced. There was a long silence on the line, until William wondered if they had been disconnected.

"Is my little girl safe?"

William eyed Mrs. Hagaman, who was making no attempt to hide her curiosity as she listened to his end of the conversation.

"For the moment, sir. And I assure you, I'm not going to let

216

anything happen to her."

"Good man. I will be praying for the both of you."

As William replaced the receiver, he wondered if Reverend Farnsworth was at ease after their conversation.

He wouldn't have been if it was *his* daughter.

William knocked on the door. He had stopped by Doc's that afternoon to see Amelia and had discovered she had gone home.

As he waited for Amy to answer, he looked out over the quiet street, ruminating over the past week. He'd sat in the back of that room with everyone else, hearing her labored breaths and seeing her ghostly skin. It had been torture, not even being able to whisper a goodbye or hold her hand as he waited for her spirit to fly away.

No man should have to face that twice in his life.

He hadn't wanted God giving Amelia a choice, because she'd most likely choose being with Jesus. William knew how she felt about Jesus. Considering the miserable selection of men she had down below, she'd not have to labor long over the decision. William argued with the Lord that it wouldn't be fair – him losing *both* Clara and Amelia.

As he was praying about it, he was reminded that Amelia wasn't his to lose. It got him thinking. Did he remain indecisive over what he wanted where Amelia was concerned? He still didn't relish the idea of ruining her innocence with his decided lack of it. More than that, he might put her in danger by getting closer.

But if he went after her, he would have to be completely committed to the idea. There would be no turning back unless Amelia became the wife of another man.

"You show me how to win her over, Lord, and I'll do it."

His prayer was interrupted by Amy, who opened the door and saw him talking to the sky.

"Hello, William." Her voice was strained.

"I'd like to see Amelia." He pushed the door open and stepped inside.

"I'll ask her, but –"

By Amy's tentative stance, William assumed Amelia had told her what happened.

"Look, Amy, I know what I did wasn't proper, but it's not as bad as she probably made it sound."

"What are you talking about?"

He hesitated. "Nothing."

She narrowed her eyes, but didn't press the issue. Instead, she went into the bedroom and closed the door. She returned a minute later, shaking her head. "She's not up to visiting today."

"I'll be hanged if she thinks she's going to turn me out, the stubborn little..." William started toward the bedroom, but Amy stopped him with a hand on his arm.

"She doesn't want to see you. She asked you to leave."

William fumed. Amy gave him a look of challenge, as if she was interested to see how he would respond. He shrugged out of his jacket and threw it on the hat tree.

"She can keep me out of her room, but she can't keep me out of my own sister's house." He spoke loudly enough for the obstinate girl hiding in the bedroom to hear him.

"Kathleen was just saying she'd like a Checkers partner." Amy smiled and stepped out of his way.

"Well, tell her to get the board, because I have *all day*."

Around suppertime Jon knocked on the door, and William made sure he was the one who answered it.

"What are you doing here?" Jon glared at him.

"Last I knew it was a free country," William said with a shrug.

"When are you going to accept that she doesn't belong to you? She's marrying me. You lost."

William scoffed. "The only one who keeps saying that is you. Don't you think it's her decision?"

Jon came through the door. "What did you do to her? What happened that she's afraid to talk about?"

"If she doesn't want to tell you, you sure aren't going to hear it from me."

Jon pushed him. He balled his fists as if he was planning more than that, but Amy came into the room.

"Jonathan Hastings, what do you think you're doing?"

"I have every right to defend what's mine."

"She's a person, Hastings. She's not your property." William kept his voice low. If Amelia heard anyone yelling, it wasn't going to be him.

"She will be my wife. That's as good as saying that she's mine. You have no right to be here."

"I do, actually. Amy is my sister."

That made Jon pause. Confusion mingled with anger.

"You're William." Recognition flooded Jon's eyes, but they did not soften. "I remember you now. You broke my mother's heart when you left. All the more reason to stay away from Amelia."

"You know what I think, Jon? I think you're worried. The fact she's yet to give you an answer tells you all you need to know."

Jon grabbed William's shirt and pulled him forward. "Stay away from her."

Amy wedged herself between them and pushed Jon back, gesturing for him to leave. He went, slamming the door so loud the windows rattled. Amy sighed and smoothed the wrinkles from William's shirt.

"Aren't things tense enough without you having fun at his expense?" she chided in a quiet voice, so Amelia wouldn't hear.

"That's not what I was doing." He tucked his shirt back in.

She gave him a curious look.

"I was staking my claim," he said.

She gasped softly. "When did you decide?"

"Tonight. I thought it best for him to know he's got competition."

She smiled a victorious, told-you-so sort of smile.

He made a face. "Go ahead, gloat."

She shook her head. "I'd rather you tell me what you did to that poor girl that was *not as bad as she probably made it sound.*"

He eyed her with a hard stare. "Kathleen, what's taking so long with that board?"

"You know it only makes it seem worse when you won't say anything." She clicked her tongue, wagging her finger as if he were a naughty schoolboy.

Ah, but that was exactly what he was.

FORTY-THREE

"Are you really going to ride that?" Kathleen said as Amelia pushed the bicycle along the path that led out to the wooded path. "What if you fall?"

"I'm sure I will," Amelia said. "That's part of learning. Falling down, getting back up."

"I'd be too scared."

"I think you are more courageous than you think." Amelia was reminded of William's words.

You are stronger than you think.

Standing here, alive after almost dying, she wondered if he might be right. Since her first bad bought of sickness, she had assumed she was weak and delicate. But had she been using her illnesses as an excuse not to try, because she was afraid to fail?

When they reached the secluded path, Amelia bunched up her skirt and climbed on. She admired the shiny white contraption with firm rubber tires and smooth handlebars. She pushed off with her foot and tried to move the pedal forward, turning the handles wildly as the bicycle inched along the ground. Without a bit of grace, she fell.

"Ouch."

Kathleen giggled as Amelia rubbed her backside. She stood up and tried again. The second time she did a little better, managing to stay on for a few turns of the pedals before she crashed.

"Want to try?"

At first Kathleen seemed like she would decline, but with wide eyes she suddenly moved forward and climbed on. Amelia helped her onto the seat. After Amelia pushed her up and down the path several times, Kathleen climbed off and turned shining eyes toward Amelia. "Do you think Mama would let me ride a horse?"

"I think it might make her a little nervous, so you would need to be patient and let her get used to the idea. But I'm sure she'd be open to it if she saw it was something you loved," Amelia said.

She nodded. "I do love horses. I want to sit on top of one with no saddle, just holding his mane and letting him run free."

Amelia raised her eyebrows in surprise. "That sounds a little dangerous, young lady."

"Dangerous like a bicycle?"

Amelia laughed as she climbed back on. She pushed forward on the pedals, imagining escaping all the troubles that loomed behind her. They were no match for her speed. She'd ride and ride until she pedaled all the way back to Illinois, to people who loved her and folks who appreciated the concept of understanding and acceptance.

Her attempt at escape ended in another bump and crash. She sat on the ground and resigned herself to her fate. She'd finish the month of school, which meant she'd probably have to face the crazy and perhaps murderous Rebecca Sapp. She'd have to walk down the street and smile at people who thought she was a drunk. She would continue to wonder what happened that made it so hard for them to trust. She'd have to make up her mind whether to marry Jon.

She'd have to decide if she was ever going to look William straight in the eye again.

And that might have been her greatest fear of all.

On Sunday morning, she dressed in her new blue dress and straw bonnet. When she stepped outside, she felt the hint of warmth in the air and smelled the earthy scent of new life beginning to emerge again. She walked slowly, relishing violet-hued crocuses and buds on lilac bushes starting to push forth green hints of life. She pondered that she was alive, in that one moment of time, never having been there before and never to be again. God had gifted her with this very second to enjoy his creation. Life went on, and she had been allowed to go on with it.

When she came to the familiar white building, she passed through the doorway and on to her usual seat, drinking in the sight of faces that had become dear to her. She heard the creak her bench always made as she sat down. She looked out the window into the meadow beyond the churchyard and cemetery.

She intended to refocus on creation and the miracle of being alive, but her worship was interrupted by the sense of someone behind her, watching her.

She thought of the two times recently William had moved from his back row seat to sit with her. He'd received the standard disapproving stares, but it had felt natural to Amelia.

The nearness of his arm had radiated heat though they didn't touch. She had covertly breathed in his indefinable, almost piquant scent. Watched his thick, work-roughed hand rest on his worn Bible. She'd imagined one or two of those long fingers reaching across the space on the pew between them and entwining with her own...

Don't think about William.

Amelia had given herself no room to fail in her endeavor to forget the man existed. Whenever she was tempted to give her mind a reprieve from the prohibition, she reminded herself of the shameful kisses she had shared with him. She beheld the images of the memory just long enough to prove it wasn't a good idea to think of him. Thoughts led to... actions.

William suddenly sat down next to her. She gasped and scooted over as far as she could. Her hip bumped the arm of the pew, which promptly reminded her of the incident in the shop, when her back had met the wall and he had given her that look of victory before he...

Exactly like the wicked smile he gave her now as he scooted closer.

"Glad to see you alive and kicking, Schoolmarm."

"William, please," she whispered. "Go back to your seat."

"Not until you say you'll talk to me. I love Kathleen, but I'm getting awful tired of losing to her in Checkers while you hide in the next room."

"What is there to talk about? I don't want to see you. I do not wish to continue our acquaintance." She looked straight ahead. There was no use getting a glimpse of those green eyes. Nor that dear wrinkle in his forehead, which she imagined was quite pronounced at this moment.

"Acquaintance?" He scoffed.

"That's correct."

He looked angry. "Well, that's where we got a problem. Because I do wish to continue our *acquaintance*. And I got a feeling *Someone* is on my side."

The pastor began to pray. The next hour and a half proved a battleground between opposing forces: her awareness of William and her conscience instructing her to forget him and pay attention to the sermon.

There was an easy winner. By the time the benediction began, Amelia realized she hadn't heard a word Pastor said. She had, however, imagined most vividly every soul in the room removed save her and the man next to her. From there a continuation of what had begun in his shop threatened to evolve.

When the last amen had been spoken, she hurried out. To her chagrin, he followed her.

"Leave me alone, William." She marched down the path that led home.

"I can't." He easily kept in step beside her. She heard a tone in his voice that she had never noticed before. What was different about him?

She peeked at him, and he gave her a smile that almost completely loosened the wrinkle in his forehead. It was a tender smile. One that reminded her of the smiles her father gave her mother. Connor gave Amy. She thought she'd even seen such a look on Mr. Hagaman's face when his wife was chattering on and didn't know he was watching her.

But why would William look at her that way? He was rough. Dark and cynical. She didn't know how to respond to him without the layer of protection their banter and arguing provided.

"We need to talk," he said, watching her.

"I have nothing to say to you."

"Are you going to marry Jon?"

She bit her lip and tried to increase her pace. He matched it without trying, since he hadn't been recently poisoned. When her breath became labored, he took her arm and made her stop.

"Amelia, there's no sense in making yourself sick again trying to get away from me. I'm not going to let this go."

She wondered if he would feel the same if she told him why she was trying to get away. What if she was honest and said she was having a hard time thinking of anything except being in his arms?

"Alright, if you won't talk, listen. I don't want you to marry him."

She hesitated. "I can't imagine how that's any of your concern."

"I care about you, and I wouldn't be much of a friend if I didn't tell you, I think Jon is wrong for you. I don't want you making a mistake you can never undo."

His words sobered her, but she felt frustration well up. "Are *you* the right person? Have you forgotten what happened? Is your conscience so deadened you can't feel the burden of that sin?"

She was looking him in the eye now. And he smiled. He reached across the distance between them and swiped a thumb across her cheek, across the evidence of the tears she was unwilling to acknowledge.

"Remind me what particular law was broken."

She narrowed her eyes. Did he really think she would begin reciting verses about "fornication" and "lust of the flesh"?

"Have you read the Bible?"

"It seems to me the spirit behind God's Word is as important as the words themselves."

"Meaning?" She turned for home again. She was relieved to see her destination was only five doors down. He followed.

"Meaning that sometimes God's law, and our inability to follow it perfectly, sort of leads us on the path to where he wants us. Like how Christ saves us right out of our sin. He couldn't do that if we didn't know we are sinners – if we weren't painfully aware of it. Amelia, look at me. I can't say this if you aren't looking me in the eye."

He caught her shoulders and swung her around. "God created men and women differently on purpose. He made the feelings that made us do what we did. I won't lie to you; God has forgiven quite a lot more than that on my account. I think he wants us to learn from it. Figure out why it happened."

She shook her head and crossed her arms across her chest, over her Bible. "I know why. Because of your past."

"Partly. But as you said – I didn't do it alone," William reminded her.

She blushed. "No, that's not what I mean. I know why you think you have those feelings, but they don't really have anything to do with me."

His forehead wrinkle deepened. "Go on."

"When you look at me, you see *her*. Clara." She hesitated, giving him a moment to process her words. "I remind you of her, maybe more in spirit than appearance. But I'm not her, William. I could never be. We are both pretending I am, and you expect I will do the things she would have done."

They stood the same distance apart, but it seemed that iron bars had locked into place between them.

Amelia continued in a tone hardly more than a whisper. "I can appreciate she was exceptional. She must have been to leave such an empty place inside you. But I'm not as courageous. If we tried to be together, we would realize it in the end, and we'd both be disappointed. And, as you said, it would be something we couldn't undo."

Amelia dared to reach to him, placing her hand over his heart. She felt the steady rhythm and ached for his arms. "I can't fill the hole she left. I wouldn't even think to try."

It seemed the whole earth paused for a moment of contemplation. The air held back the breath of the breeze and the trees stood still as a witness to the moment when they untangled themselves and went their separate ways.

William exhaled and dragged his gaze back to hers. "Tell me what you want, Amelia. Out of life. What's your dream?"

She was jarred by the unexpected turn. "I... suppose I want a home and a family. I want to belong."

"That's it?"

She sensed where he was leading. "You think I have big dreams that will require big faith. But I'm not so convinced. What's wrong with being someone's wife and making it my highest goal to please him? Isn't that what a woman is created for?"

He watched her from under the shadow of his furrowed brow. "Nothing wrong with that. As long as it's what *you* are meant for."

She turned and started walking again, though more slowly this time. "When I think about being married to Jon, it seems reasonable. I would know what he expected. What scares me about you is that you won't settle for anything less than... everything."

He grabbed her again and turned her around, forcing her to look at him. His eyes were full of that same terrifying and exhilarating expression she'd seen that day in his shop. She told herself to run, and promptly ignored herself.

"You're right about that. I'm not a half-hearted kind of man."

His gaze dropped to her mouth for an agonizing moment before he looked back into her eyes. "So, Amelia, are you willing to spend your life doing the normal and expected? Or would you like to see what God does when you give it all you've got?"

Her heart cried out the answer. He was right. She wanted more. She wanted God to use her and somehow make her life matter. Through teaching, through writing, with the blessing of a home and family – whatever it was that could give him glory. She wanted to step out on nothing and find him waiting to catch her. But it wasn't safe.

"What if I failed?" She could only manage a whisper, as if she was afraid someone would hear her even considering it. What if she dreamed and worked and spent years of her life for something that in the end meant nothing? That would be worse than never trying at all.

And what if she ended up in an institution, wasting away with consumption? Would his acceptance extend that far, or would he simply demand she pull herself out of bed and get on with it?

His smile was kind. "You will fail." His voice matched hers, soft and insistent. "And I will be right there to pick you up and demand you try again. I will make sure you do your best, and you'll learn to do the same for me. Sometimes we'll yell so loud the neighbors might call the sheriff, but we'll sharpen each other something fierce. When you hate me, you'll have to believe that Jesus is enough. You'll need the faith to accept that you are where you belong, even when nothing is working out as you planned."

She felt dizzy. The moment was capable of spinning her world upside down. It was a turning point, if she allowed it.

"Is God enough, Amelia?" He didn't let her go. He didn't let her wiggle away and allow the moment to escape. He held her and forced her to answer the question.

"Of course he is." It was an easy answer. But his deeper question remained unanswered, and he waited. "But I'm not sure I'm enough for you, William."

"You are far more than I deserve. And for that reason, you'd have to be able to depend on God."

She thought about it. She imagined her life with William, stretching out before her in a continuous line of passion and expectation. It was exciting just to dream of the adventure.

But it was also exhausting.

She considered a life with Jon. It would be disappointing in feeling. She would feel restricted and held back. She wouldn't get to the heights – or depths – that she could reach with William. But she would know what was expected of her and she'd do it with all her heart.

"I'm sorry, William. But I'm not Clara."

She tore herself out of his arms and left him standing in the road. He watched her, a black expression fixed on his face, his hands fallen to his sides, still open from holding her. She looked one last time. Her heart wrenched inside her. He wore his dark countenance as a mask, but she saw hurt beneath it.

He seemed so... alone.

Forty-Four

"I want you to know how much I have loved being your teacher this year." Amelia looked out over her classroom of girls as she realized with dismay that she would only have this one year with them. Their faces had become so familiar, so dear. She felt an ache at the thought of saying goodbye forever.

Laura spoke up. "We loved it too, Miss Farnsworth. We never had a teacher like you before."

Others nodded their agreement with shy smiles. Amelia blinked away tears and looked at the clock. "Time to go home. I'll see you tomorrow. Don't forget your essay about the most important thing God has taught you this year."

Laura came and hugged her, followed by Wanda and several of the smaller girls. She smiled until she saw Polly sitting at her desk with her hands folded on top. She noticed a particular glint in Polly's eyes. She was staying for something, and Amelia was fairly sure it wasn't to give her a hug.

To say she was alarmed when Rebecca Sapp entered the room would have been understating things. She backed up, gulping in air to lungs that didn't want to work. Was she here to finish her off right there in the classroom with children everywhere and Jon in the next room?

Amelia tried to breathe. She had no proof Rebecca had meant to harm her. She doubted Jon would allow her to be murdered in her own school.

She could not speak, and she didn't try. She backed toward the corner. Rebecca was followed by the school board members, all wearing somber faces.

"Of course, I feel just awful having to be the bearer of this sober news."

Amelia heard Rebecca's words to the men as Polly grinned and gave Amelia the slightest nod.

"But I care too much about these girls to allow a negative influence over their lives to continue."

Amelia swallowed hard, staring at Polly. Rebecca must have seen what happened in William's shop, probably because she followed Amelia to make sure the poison did its job. She gripped the edge of her desk.

Jon came across the hall with a curious expression. Her throat burned with mortification.

"It's my duty to inform you that this poor child has divulged to me a terrible secret. I am sorry to say she happened upon Miss Farnsworth one day several weeks ago, alone with Mr. Morehouse in his carpentry store. They were engaged in a most brazen embrace. I mean to speak delicately, but it seems it was the kind fit for a saloon."

Amelia forced herself to look up. If she stared at the floor, she would appear guilty. Though she was guilty, and there was no escape from the truth this time. She saw uncertainty cloud Jon's expression, especially when his gaze fell to her shaking hands.

"This is a serious accusation, and it most certainly better have merit this time, Miss Sapp," Mr. Hubble said in a warning tone. He turned to Amelia. "Do you have any response, Miss Farnsworth?"

William wasn't there to keep her from speaking the truth this time. She had no choice. She considered reminding them she had been poisoned and saying she remembered nothing of that day, but she couldn't do it. She felt peace invade her spirit when she made the decision to speak the truth.

"I'm sorry to say it is true."

Jon side-stepped the other men and approached her, still unsure. "Amelia, from what you told me, it was a moment you did not anticipate. And you left immediately."

She nodded. "But I never should have entered his shop alone."

The men exchanged glances with each other while Polly and Rebecca sneered at Amelia. When Mr. Sommers turned, they hid their smiles like accomplished actresses.

"Child, what did you see?"

Amelia watched Polly sadly, wishing she could will her to speak the truth. To tell them she had been bribed by whatever means, most likely a dish of ice cream, to say that she had seen them.

Amelia wasn't sure why Rebecca wanted the accusation to come through a child. Maybe she knew her own reputation was questionable. Maybe she thought it would seem more insidious.

"I must protest. A child should not be made witness in such an accusation." Jon stepped in, his voice strained.

Mr. Hubble nodded, though Mr. Sommers seemed perturbed. "He's right, Sommers. Polly Dennis, you are not to speak about this to anyone else. You may leave."

She shrugged and gathered her books, waltzing out of the room.

"Miss Sapp, we need nothing further from you, since you weren't a witness. Thank you for apprising us."

Rebecca seemed upset about being made to leave. She walked close to Jon as she left. "I simply don't know what she was thinking, Jon. I'm sorry you had to find out this way."

Amelia saw a look pass between them, and a resignation in Jon's eyes she didn't expect. He had the right to be furious. Rebecca left, though Amelia doubted she went further than hearing range.

"Amelia has already told me – her fiancé – what happened, gentlemen. I believe Miss Sapp is making it seem more than it is to implicate Miss Farnsworth out of spite. I assure you; she is above reproach. She has made mistakes, as have we all, but they have been twisted and magnified today."

"That may be, Hastings, but a child witnessed it this time. And Miss Farnsworth is a teacher. Miss Farnsworth, I must insist you tell us what happened and allow us to draw our own conclusions."

She cleared her throat. "I left Miss Sapp's home feeling ill."

"She was ill from arsenic poisoning. Just after tea at Miss

Sapp's," Jon interrupted, but Mr. Hubble motioned for her to continue.

"Mr. Morehouse saw something was wrong and insisted I come in and sit down. We argued. In the midst of it, he... kissed me." Amelia felt her face burn with shame at being made to report such an intimate moment. "I felt uncomfortable, so I pushed him away and ran out, and I fainted. Mr. Morehouse has since apologized and promised to conduct himself honorably."

"Forgive me, but are you saying that you did not encourage this kiss?"

Was she softening the truth? She wanted to be honest. She needed to be. "I suppose you might say it takes two... I would be lying if I tried to make you think he assaulted me –"

Jon stopped her. "I think that's enough. I'm sure no one in this room is really qualified to throw stones. If you want to pursue it further, I suggest you talk to Morehouse. He's the one who should have known better."

The men were reluctant, but they moved to leave, still wearing serious expressions. Mr. Hubble turned to Amelia as he was leaving. "You would do well to avoid this situation in the future. Especially if you have an enemy who wishes to capitalize on your mistakes. Be above reproach. Don't allow yourself to be alone with a man."

She fought back tears at the reprimand. "Of course."

Jon was harder to face. She quickly stepped outside into the sunlight, mindful of Mr. Hubble's warning.

He followed and closed the door. He was quiet as he walked her home.

On the Ables' front porch, he finally spoke. "I know you haven't accepted my proposal. I'm willing to give you the benefit of the doubt that nothing happened beyond what you've confessed. But you need to understand one thing: If you agree to marry me and anything like this happens again, it will be the end of our association."

He stared at her for a long moment. When he left, she sank to the porch swing and covered her face with her hands.

FORTY-FIVE

Amelia came home to find a bundle on her bed with a letter addressed to her in William's familiar scrawl. It only served to deepen her sadness when she realized how she missed him.

She touched the masculine script, marveling that the same hand that wrote the beautiful letter from the trunk had written this letter to her. How could Amelia possibly compare to the beautiful Clara? Why did he bother with her? She opened it with a lump in her throat.

Dear Amelia,

I have read your story from start to finish, twice. I wish I could speak to you in person so you would know how sincere I am when I say you have a gift for words. You have a grasp of characters similar to Jane Austen, and a serious, inspirational tone that reminds me of Dickens. In fact, I can see hints of all the stories you love as if you took them and made them part of you. The result works well.

It is easy to see you are Gwendolyn. You might disagree, but she has your determination and your honesty. (And your beauty.) I was moved by the scene in which she offers her life for her beloved. I can relate to loving a woman such as that.

The theme of your story is one I have learned the hard way. I don't know how you came up with the idea of showing the reckless, uncertain nature of love. You don't know this, but you spoke Clara's last words. When she was dying, she said "Love ain't safe, Will." I think she would have loved your book. Maybe she does from her home in the clouds.

I think you should try to publish. I know it will scare you, but this is one of those times when I hope you will rise above the commonplace and attempt something drastic. It's a big dream, but you have a big God who gave you the ability in the first place.

I miss you, Amelia.
William

The knock on the door brought an unexpected balm to Amelia's wounded spirit. Ella stood in the doorway with her customary half smile. Amelia laughed with disbelief and pulled her inside.

"What are you doing here? Did you come all by yourself?"

"Father sent me to see if you were okay. He wanted the truth; he knew you'd say you were fine no matter what your state, and he thought Mr. Morehouse wasn't giving him the whole story over the telephone wire."

"That sounds like Father. I'm really fine. I know I look pale, but I am feeling much stronger now."

"Cheeks rosy, eyes bright. I'll report as much to Father." She gave Amelia a thoughtful stare. "Something else, too. What is it?"

Amelia blushed, and Ella nodded. "I thought so."

"How is mother?" The question escaped Amelia's lips before she was sure she was ready to hear the answer.

Ella sighed, her smile fading. "She's not any worse."

It was all either of them could manage to say on the subject.

When they were upstairs in her room, Amelia told Ella what had happened since Christmas, except for the part about suspecting Rebecca poisoned her. She thought her father might insist she leave if he knew. She confessed her guilt over what happened with William and then showed Ella the letter she had received just that day.

"I agree with him. Send the story in. And then marry that man."

Amelia wished it were that simple. Ella would scoff at her reasons for choosing Jon, so she kept them to herself.

They took the bicycle out and Ella declared it the best fun she'd had in her eighteen years, although it wasn't saying much considering the doldrums her life had been.

Ella discovered from Amy the town's founding celebration was that weekend, complete with an ice cream social and dance, and insisted Amelia would be going. She also rejected the new blue dress. "You need a princess dress."

And so, the afternoon of the social, Ella opened her trunk and revealed a dress of elegant ivory with lace overlay and a form-fitting bodice.

"Where in the world did you get this?" Amelia fingered the trim in awe. It was not the standard dress of a preacher's daughter.

"You'll never believe it! It was in the donations at church. Perhaps it was for a wedding."

"I've never seen such a lovely dress."

"You'll have the full skirt to twirl when you dance." Ella pulled out a pair of delicate white boots to match.

"Your feet are bigger than mine."

"No one ever died of wearing shoes that were a bit big."

"I don't know why you are going to all this trouble." Amelia sighed as Ella pinned up her hair in ringlets and let the rest of the curls fall down her back. "I'm practically an old married woman."

Ella pulled Amelia's hair, making her squeal. "Emmy Jo, if you were seriously considering Jon's proposal you would have said yes when he asked. You are never unsure of major decisions."

"None of them were ever this important."

"Not even when Father asked you to move to Ohio and teach school? As I recall you gave your answer rather quickly."

"I could see the wisdom, even if I was terrified."

"But you can't see the wisdom in marrying Jon?" Ella paused

with the comb and raised an eyebrow at Amelia in the mirror's reflection.

"I didn't say that."

"I wouldn't say Jon is an unwise choice. He's just not William. Isn't that right?"

"Ella," Amelia sighed. Her sister was undeterred.

"I may be wrong, though I'm not. And since I'm not, we're going to make you look like you stepped out of a fairy tale."

That was exactly what she did. When she was done, Amelia stared, quite horrified.

"It will all be for nothing if you make that face the entire time." Ella mimicked her expression.

"I don't want everyone looking at me. You don't understand these people, Ella. They already think of me as a drunken... lady of the night." Amelia wouldn't have used such language with anyone but her sister. "My goal is to stay in the shadows and not be noticed."

"Which is why I made you noticeable," she said, rolling her eyes. "Trust me."

"You are fortunate I adore you, Ella."

As Ella made a few adjustments, she frowned. "Why do you think the people of this town have been so against you since the moment you came?" she asked. "And how does every secret fault somehow come to light? It's almost as if someone is orchestrating your demise."

It was just like Ella to speak the truth in a simple sentence. The truth Amelia had been trying to wrap her mind around for months.

"I have wondered the same thing."

The beautiful evening and the pleasant atmosphere of the gathering spoke of possibilities Amelia was too afraid to consider.

A large dance floor had been constructed in the grass next to the church, and young people dressed in their finest clothes danced to lively music or milled about in cheerful conversation.

She tried to ignore the glances from the men and the compliments from the women. No one attempted to hide their surprise that the odd little schoolteacher possessed any sort of beauty. Amelia fumed when her sister disengaged their arms and danced away with the handsome young Edwin Harrington.

Jon was at the punch table nearby, laughing with several other men, so she found a set of steps behind the refreshment table where she intended to sit and stay hidden.

Almost immediately, someone sat down on the step just behind her. She braced herself for conversation and a hasty retreat until she smelled the scent of pine. Her heart began to race.

"I suppose you've been told how good you look."

Amelia refused to answer him, though a thrill coursed through her. The dance finished and couples applauded.

The Viennese Waltz began. Amelia didn't like dancing as much as the average young woman, but if there was a dance she'd be willing to participate in, it was the Viennese Waltz. She swallowed hard, praying he wouldn't ask.

"I don't see anyone sitting this one out." He leaned close to her ear and said the words in a soft, teasing sort of tone. As if he could read her thoughts and knew his proximity made her long for him. She felt his finger trace the length of her back.

"I wonder if your suitor would mind if I asked you to dance."

She bit her lip and stole a glance at the punch table. Would Jon object? It seemed harmless enough – a dance in full view of the other young people of the town. But Amelia noticed the close quarters on the dance floor.

"It's so crowded."

"Tight spaces make you nervous. I remember."

"I'm sorry," she said, relieved but also disappointed.

He stood up and reached for her hand. "Come with me."

Amelia narrowed her eyes. "I'm not sure that's a good idea."

He only watched her, still waiting and reaching for her hand.

She let him pull her up, though Ella's delicate white boots dragged with her uncertainty. She allowed him to lead her behind the church along the path where the forest met the town.

There were benches along the edge of a peaceful pond where several other couples roamed in quiet conversation. The sweet smell of cherry blossoms infused the air with pleasant ambiance; graceful weeping willows bowed politely as they passed. The social atmosphere that had choked her gave way to the wonderful solitude of nature at eventide.

The sound of the waltz followed them. William turned to her, his free hand skimming her waist in a manner that felt possessive. Once again, she was proving herself weak. But she was tired of caring what other people thought. She wanted this perfect moment with the man that stirred her soul, even if they would not have a future together.

Keep your heart with all diligence.

She let the bold, rhythmic music lead her away in a happy march. They turned in circles until they were both dizzy and laughing. It was a heady feeling, being in his arms in the dim light, under the privacy of gentle swaying trees that seemed to enjoy the music as much as they did.

"You're beautiful." He murmured the words so softly she wondered if he really said them. His arm wound tighter around her as the music changed moods. The tender fiddle strings mingled with the piano.

"*O Lovely Rose.*" Amelia recognized the tune. He nodded, his eyes never leaving her features, the enraptured frown fixed on his face. They swayed slowly as she hummed, affected by the gentle melody.

"I feel like I could break into song," she said.

"With anyone else that might make me nervous."

She felt warmth spread across her face and neck despite the cool evening. The low tone of his voice seemed to chase away her reticence. She began to sing the slow, haunting melody.

O lovely rose,
No flower that grows,
Is half as fair as thou, as thou,

He was still frowning, but his eyes shone with appreciation. "I warn you, I might have to sing along."

She gave him a curious grin.

"You don't think I can sing?"

She raised her eyebrows in unspoken invitation as she continued to sing. He offered a harmony, deep and resonating. Their voices mingled in opposite tones in another sort of dance, one that seemed more intimate than their physical nearness.

O cruel rose,
Thou dost disclose,
A loveliness divine. But had I seen,
Thy thorns, I ween, I'd all thy love decline.

She was overcome. "Oh! That was nicer than a kiss."

She realized with embarrassment she had spoken the words aloud. He stopped moving, the crease on his forehead deepening. She was embarrassed she had broken the spell of the perfect moment.

"I don't know." He raised his hands to either side of her face, barely touching them with his fingers. "There's nothing wrong with a good kiss."

And he kissed her. Not rough and demanding as before; this time he was tender, chaste. She could hear the story of that kiss as if the words wound around them, whispering lovely ideas into her soul.

Promise. Endurance. Kinship. Understanding.

Belonging.

The words formed sentences as she responded, moving her lips with his in a silent song. She hoped he would understand what she couldn't say aloud.

I love your frown, and the crease in your forehead when you are thoughtful or hiding something or teasing me. I love the way you lecture me when you are mad at yourself. I love your beautiful past with all its shadows. I can feel the ache of your love for Clara and the tender way you have held her memory. I'm amazed at how the darkness inside you met the light and burst forth in the sunrise of your faith, just like the colors of the sky at the moment of the dawn.

Amelia would have been content to remain in his arms forever.

She had begun to wonder what one might do to deepen a kiss when the reckoning became necessary.

"Amelia?" Jon's angry voice shattered the beautiful dream.

Forty-Six

William felt Amelia push away from him, covering her mouth as if she might hide what they had done. Again. He made sure she saw the small smile of satisfaction he wore, as if he had just made an excellent point in the midst of a heated debate.

He knew Jon was going to hit him. But he figured he owed the younger man the dignity. So, he took a right hook to the chin, and grunted to let Jon know it hurt.

"You no-account, scheming snake! Why can't you just leave her alone?"

"She wasn't complaining." William rubbed his face and tried not to show his amusement. "Shouldn't you ask yourself why this keeps happening?"

"It keeps happening because she is too kind to refuse you, and you take advantage!"

William could not help his chuckle. Jon clenched his fist as if he was gearing up for another punch, so William prepared for a fight. Amelia stepped between them and put her hand on Jon's fist.

"Jon, don't blame him. It's my fault."

William was irritated by her words. "Your fault? How in the world is anyone at fault, leastwise you?"

Her eyes pleaded with him. "We can't go on this way."

"I think we are all agreed on that point." Jon grabbed her wrist. She winced and pulled back.

"Let her go." William took a step toward them, willing to start throwing punches if Jon injured her.

Jon gave her a hard look. "Your contract with the school is complete, as is mine. If you are still agreeable to marriage, we're leaving. In two days."

William watched her body stiffen in protest.

"Two days? Jon, surely you know that is unreasonable. I don't appreciate being given an ultimatum."

Jon narrowed his eyes in disgust. "I don't appreciate walking out to find my fiancé mugging with the town carpenter for all to see. For the second time! I'm leaving in two days. If you don't show up within the week, I'll consider our arrangement over."

She hesitated, still trying to free her wrist from his grip. "Where are we going?"

"Home."

William saw hope in her eyes. "Illinois?"

Jon scoffed. "*My* home. Indianapolis." He let her go and walked away, kicking a stone into the pond.

Amelia watched him go as she rubbed her wrist.

"Are you okay?" William spoke.

"I'm fine." She sounded annoyed.

"You don't have to do this."

"I haven't been given much choice."

He reached for her arm. She jerked away from his grasp. "Why must everyone grab me?"

"Sorry." He held up his hands. "You don't have to do something you aren't sure about. You can let him go."

"I'm the one who's sorry." Her voice was edged with cynicism. "I'm sorry for being afraid. I'm sorry that I'll never be enough for you."

She turned away from him. As she walked away, William saw her form shaking as if she was crying, but didn't want him to know. He started to follow her, but stopped. Had he reached the line? Maybe he would only push her further away if he persisted now.

There comes a time when you have to let people go. We couldn't control what our father did to our family. I can't control what my husband is doing to mine. All we can do is let them go and pray that

242

they find their way home.

His older sister, Elizabeth, had said the words when he found her, bloodied and shaking. Her home had been torn apart by the raging of a drunken fool, who ripped through hearts as completely as pillows and curtains. He wished she hadn't had such a hard life. But her words were full of wisdom for it.

If he loved Amelia – and he was enough of an expert on the subject to know he did – maybe it was time to prove it, and let her go.

As sure as William was about stepping back, he found he didn't want to think about anything besides kissing Amelia Farnsworth. He was sitting on his bench hours later, reliving the moment. He hadn't planned on kissing her. He had some sort of speech in mind to convince her to choose him over Jon. But she'd given him the opportunity and he gladly took it.

It surprised him when Ella turned the corner and headed his way.

"It's a little late for a young lady to be out for a constitutional," he said as she sat down next to him.

"Not when the young lady needs to discuss something important with her soon-to-be brother-in-law."

William eyed her with doubt. "It didn't appear to be going in my favor tonight."

She shrugged, unconcerned. "You had her weak in the knees. If Mr. Hastings hadn't come along when he did, she would have marched straight to the church and married you on the spot. Trust me."

William chuckled. He liked Ella. She was brutally honest, but her quips were fast and smart.

"Do you have any idea why she's so determined to marry Jon?" William asked her.

Ella gave a small sigh, turning thoughtful. "Amelia has a low view of herself. She thinks she's average and she doesn't see why she should have the best of anything."

"You're saying I'm the best?" William gave her a wry smile. "Because if you are, she hasn't told you my story."

"I'm saying you're the best for her and you and I both know it's true. She's blossomed since she met you. She's started to believe she can do the things she dreams about."

William nodded. "She can. And she will, if I have anything to say about it."

Ella watched him. "That's why God gave you and me to Amelia. To push her past her fears. I know God wants her to do those things. She has it within her."

William met her look. "I agree."

Ella smoothed her skirt and surveyed the quiet street. "I expect you to win, no matter the cost. I'm leaving tomorrow, so I must depend on you to make her see reason."

"Miss Farnsworth, I don't deny that's what I want, and I'll do what I can, but neither of us can force her. She's stubborn. She always thinks she's right. And she usually is, unless she's scared."

Ella nodded and stood up. "That's why you have to play your cards correctly. You don't realize that Amelia is terrified of disappointing you. In fact, I think it's the only true reason she resists you. You can use that to your advantage, of course."

He eyed her as a smile played at the corner of his mouth. "I'll think on that."

FORTY-SEVEN

"Amelia, don't act on anything until you are sure," Ella said as she waited to board her train bound for Illinois.

Amelia chafed. It wasn't what she wanted her sister to say. She had half a mind to buy her own ticket and join her sister on the train.

"There's nothing to think about. William makes me do things I regret."

"William makes you do things Jon regrets," Ella said with impatience. "You can't tell me you regret it, Amelia Josephine. I saw you. You were dancing like a blushing princess at a ball. He cradled your face in his hands and kissed you as if you were a work of art. He loves you, and you love him."

"But Jon –"

"I'm tired of hearing about Jon." Ella heaved a dramatic sigh. "You say you don't know what to do, so do what I say. Marry William."

Amelia frowned at the train as if it was at fault for all her consternation. Ella pulled on her gloves.

"You know very well that if you marry Mr. Hastings, you will never be able to write that time travel novel we've been talking about since we were children. I want the time travel novel. I'm afraid I must insist on William, if only for that reason. You promised, Amelia."

Amelia couldn't help a smile at her sister's words.

"I expect to be called right back to Ohio to attend your wedding.

The one in which you will become Mrs. William Morehouse."

Amelia's heart skipped a beat at the words.

The boarding call was announced. Ella picked up her bag. Amelia started to argue as they moved toward the train, but she was shushed by Ella's severe expression and her finger wagging in Amelia's face. Her graceful sister climbed aboard and only turned once before she found her seat.

"Mr. Morehouse." Ella pointed her finger in the direction of town, as if she expected Amelia to immediately go and find him.

Amelia stepped back as others moved to board. A moment later Ella's pretty yellow bonnet poked out of a window near the back of the car.

"So help me, Emmy Jo, I'll marry him myself. Don't think I won't do it just to spite you."

It was a tragedy of irony. All Amelia had wanted, when she first arrived, was to leave Little Sicily and never return. Now that the time had come to depart, she wanted nothing but to stay.

She sat back on the bed and tried to memorize the room that had been her sanctuary for the last nine months. Every knot in the wood, every scratch on the floor.

When she was a child, feverish and hallucinating, she remembered how she noticed every detail of her room as if they had been magnified. When she tried to describe it to her mother, she knew she sounded insane. Yet the images she saw which no one else seemed to notice were as real to her as her mother's gentle touch.

Had the sobbing man also been a hallucination? A product of her imagination as she tried to give form to the letter writer who had left his imprint on the room? She knew now it had been William, but the information only made the mystery more compelling. She had never asked him how his letter came to be in a trunk of old baby things in his sister's attic. She supposed he had stayed here after Clara died, but there were pieces missing of the story. Her intuition told her that the pieces had been removed on purpose.

She went to the trunk a final time, reaching underneath and

retrieving the letter. She read it again. Part of her, a great and important part, wanted to unlock the mysteries. But her rational side reminded her that when she got on the train tomorrow, she was choosing Jon. Her life would not be full of mystery and stories anymore. William's account would not matter.

She had not forgotten William's arguments. Was he right? Was she made for more? Was she making the greatest mistake of her life?

She rubbed her face with her hands. She wasn't even sure what he meant.

If she stayed, and allowed whatever might happen with William to progress, what would be different? Wouldn't there still be a certain routine, even if they ended up as husband and wife? Life could not be exciting every moment.

She felt confused. Alone.

She wandered to the backyard and sat on the swing, lost in thought. She was surprised when she turned her head and saw Polly Dennis standing next to her. Watching her.

Amelia's first response was dread. What mischief was she involved in?

But Polly's expression lacked its usual obstinacy. "My mama got so drunk last night she almost died."

"I'm sorry, Polly." And she was.

"I know I act tough, but I do it so no one knows I'm afraid," Polly said.

Amelia nodded, ashamed at not believing the best of her. "I think I understand."

"You won't understand. Not when I tell you what I did."

Amelia waited for her to explain.

"It's my fault – why everyone thinks bad of you. I've been talking to Miss Sapp, giving her ideas about how to get rid of you." She lifted watery eyes. "I told her about Mama's wine. And I lied about seeing you and Mr. Morehouse doing things you shouldn't. And... I wrote the note on the blackboard."

Polly looked down. "I deserve the mama I got and I deserve the bad stuff that happens to me."

Polly tried to run away, but Amelia caught her and pulled her into her arms. She hugged the girl hard before she led her to the steps

247

and sat down.

"Polly, we all deserve punishment. We're all sinners. I'm not any better than you and I don't blame you. I forgive you, and I hope you'll forgive me, too."

Polly stared at her in surprise. "How can you forgive me?"

"That's the wrong question. The one that doesn't make a bit of sense to me is why Jesus would ever forgive *me*." Amelia felt the meaning with a rush of emotion that stung her eyes and made her throat feel tight.

"But you're good. You always do the right thing. God has to be pretty proud of you."

Amelia shook her head. "No, I'm not. The only good you see in me is there because Jesus forgave me and the Holy Spirit came to live in me. He's helping me to learn, but I still do wrong sometimes. Your mama didn't force me to drink too much wine, and Miss Sapp wasn't completely lying about Mr. Morehouse and me. And the truth is – I wouldn't have the courage do anything right if Jesus hadn't died on that cross in my place and rose again with power to help me."

Polly seemed confused. "So... God ain't interested in me getting all clean and shiny before I ask him to forgive me and let me go to heaven?"

"Not at all. You can't. We can't do anything without his power. All he wants from you is exactly what you're doing. He wants you to come to him, humble, and ask for his forgiveness and help. He'll do everything else, Polly. You just have to be willing to follow his lead."

Polly glared at the ground for a time. Then she suddenly fell forward on her knees in the grass and closed her eyes. When she opened them again, she smiled shyly. "I guess that's that."

Amelia hugged her shoulders with a teary smile. "There's no guessing involved."

Polly turned to go, but looked back with a curious expression. "You're different than most, Teacher. I expected you to be mad and yell at me. I guess being forgiven and that Holy Spirit coming to help does make a difference."

"You'll see."

Amelia nodded.

"One more thing, Teacher. Be real careful around Miss Sapp. I'm not sure what she's all fired up about, but I think it's her aim to hurt you."

Amelia nodded. "Thank you for letting me know. And I think you should also stay away from her for your own safety."

"You tell your Mr. Morehouse so he can protect you. That's what a man's for."

She left before Amelia could tell her Mr. Morehouse would not be her protector, after all.

For Amelia had decided. She would send a telegram to Jon and tell him to expect her on the next train to Indianapolis.

A steady hammering that oddly matched the cadence of her heart caught Amelia's attention as she walked with Amy and the girls to the train station. She peeked across the wide street into William's shop, unable to deny herself one last look.

She could see him just inside the door. He was banging away at an unfortunate board, until he hit too hard and split the wood. He threw the hammer on the table and came to look out the door, as if he knew she was watching the whole time. He stared at her through narrowed eyes.

She stuck her chin in the air, determined to show him her confidence in her choice. Even if she possessed none.

He waved her off, as if she wasn't worth the time, and disappeared back into the store. Amelia felt a little hand slip into hers. When she looked down at Kathleen, she saw tears in the girl's eyes.

Amelia could hardly bear the sadness. Would she ever find a friend as dear as Amy? And even if she saw Kathleen again, she would never be the same as she was right at this moment. She would grow older without Amelia watching. She would change and forget her.

"I'm going to miss you so much!" She kissed Kathleen's cheek and hugged her once more. Kathleen's brow furrowed and she turned away as if she was angry.

"She's going to miss you. I think she doesn't know how to express that," Amy said with apology.

"I understand." Amelia fought the lump in her throat.

"Good thing someone does, because I sure don't get it."

William was standing behind her. She whirled around. He was standing with his arms across his chest. There was hurt in his expression.

Amy said a last goodbye and guided the girls away to a bench where they would wave when the train moved out.

William glared at Amelia. "Even *acquaintances* say goodbye."

She couldn't look at him. She stared down at her folded hands.

"Maybe you aren't who I thought you were," he said.

People surrounded them as the final boarding call was made. Amelia couldn't look him in the eye. "William, please. This is hardly the place."

"I thought you were something special. Now I see you're just one of those feeble-minded girls with nothing on her mind but getting a husband who will tell her what to think for the rest of her life." He spoke with disgust, and her cheeks heated with anger.

"And someone like you would save me from that?"

He leaned closer, reminding her of the way he had held her face and kissed her. This time she sensed no tenderness. "You're going to get there. Trust me. He won't love you the way you need to be loved. There will be no *passion*. And you know you don't love him. Can't even work up a tingle when he touches you, I reckon."

She gasped in disbelief, looking around to see if anyone had heard him. "You are an awful man!"

"So I hear. But someone's got to say it. Maybe only *awful* men make you tingle."

Amelia wanted to slap him, but she didn't want to cause a scene. People were already staring. Instead, she turned toward the train, where most had already boarded. It was now or never. She had hoped William would come. She had hoped he would give her a reason to stay. She wanted to hear that he needed her.

That she belonged with him.

It was time to face reality. He was more upset over losing the game than he was over losing her.

"I need to go." She picked up her valise and turned away.

"I don't know why I wasted a second of my life caring about you," he said.

The harsh words gave Amelia the courage she needed to walk away, though a tear escaped and fell down her cheek. The conductor offered her a hand with a sympathetic look. Once aboard, she went to the first seat. She wanted to pull the shade and hide from him, but she had promised the girls she would wave.

She looked out the window, searching for them, but she could only see William. For a moment he just stood there, staring up at her, his frown deep and unrelenting. As the train began to move, he walked alongside.

"Don't go."

There was no platform, so he walked along the ground, well below her window. She had to lean out to be able to see or hear him over the train engine, groaning as it came to life.

"Why shouldn't I?" she said in a desperate tone. "Give me a reason to stay."

"I have my reasons."

"Give me one!" She had to yell over the noise.

In one fluid motion, William grabbed the hand rail and pulled himself up on the side of the train that was inching along, metal squealing against the tracks. Eternity seemed to pass in the moment he stared at her, his face taking on a rare expression of vulnerability. Amelia leaned close to hear his coarsely spoken words.

"Because I love you."

He let go and disappeared from her view.

FORTY-EIGHT

Indianapolis immediately made Amelia long for the simple quiet of Little Sicily. Jon found her in the crowd of immense Union Station, standing on the furthest wall of the atrium, watching sunlight stream through the large circular window that dominated the front balcony.

It had been five days since she had seen him, though she had sent him a telegram to let him know when she would arrive. He smiled and kissed her cheek, but something seemed missing in the gesture. His took her bag and guided her out of the building to the waiting horse and carriage. She watched him, looking for signs that he was either overjoyed at their reunion or still angry at her.

At least he didn't seem to think his life was wasted in caring for her.

They spoke of the weather and the interesting aspects of the city as they drove through the busy streets in his mother's carriage. She noticed the lack of meaningful conversation as if it spoke in louder tones than what was actually said. They were avoiding questions that must be answered. She wondered if he sensed she was only more conflicted about her decision.

They arrived at his mother's home, a modest but well-kept little house between two larger buildings. There was a bit of lawn and a flowerbed. A tiny porch with a rocking chair lent a homey appearance in spite of the location.

When she first laid eyes on Elizabeth, she could only think of William. The family resemblance was strong. Her mind went back to the train station.

I don't know why I wasted a second of my life caring about you... I love you...

Amelia's eyes stung. *Well, which is it? Which one am I supposed to believe?*

She knew she could not burst into tears the first evening with her potential mother-in-law, so she attempted to swallow her grief as they had dinner together.

Immediately after supper, Jon left, saying he had business to attend to. Amelia sat in the parlor with his mother and tried to carry on a polite conversation, but she could think of nothing to say.

"What do you think Jon had to do?" She looked out the window, noticing the shadows that marked the setting of the sun. Elizabeth sighed.

"That boy could never stay in one place for long."

Amelia was troubled by her tone. In a crushing feeling of regret, she remembered William hanging off the train and professing his love. Her hand went to her chest.

Why did I go? He loves me, and I left him!

But did he? Why did they only fight if he truly loved her the way a man should love a woman?

"What's wrong, dear?" Elizabeth touched her arm. "Jon mentioned you have a stomach ailment. Is it giving you pain? I could make some peppermint tea for you."

Amelia knew why her stomach hurt and she deserved it. She sat back and closed her eyes until the feeling passed. "I'm sorry, I'm fine. Yes, tea would be lovely."

At breakfast the following day, Jon asked if they had made any wedding plans while he was out.

Amelia shrugged and pretended to be interested in her food.

"If you don't want a big wedding, maybe we should just visit the preacher and have him say the words."

"Jon," Elizabeth chided.

"Plenty of folks do that."

Both of them looked to Amelia for her response. She bit her lip and stared hard at her eggs.

"I really haven't thought about it." She tried to hide the tremor in her voice. Actually, she had thought a great deal about her wedding, starting at about the age of seven. And in recent days, the groom in her grand and glorious plans had acquired a face. But it wasn't Jon's.

She had never felt so conflicted, and yet not conflicted at all. The only true battle, if she was quite honest, was in accepting what her heart had decided the moment she first read the letter from the trunk.

But had she gone too far? Would she have to live by the choices she had already made?

FORTY-NINE

William wouldn't admit it to his sister, but when he saw Amy approaching from across the street, he had to drag himself out of his morose thoughts and the chair he was supposed to be staining. When she came in, he pretended he was so lost in his work he hadn't heard her. Her only response was a skeptical raised eyebrow.

"How are you?" She set down a basket covered with a tea towel. The smell of freshly baked bread tempted his senses from their apathetic state, and his stomach told him it would appreciate sustenance at some point.

"I'm fine," he said with a shrug. Amy rolled her eyes.

"I think we both know better." She sat down at the chair by the desk and folded her arms, as if she was intent to stay there until he confessed the truth.

"Why wouldn't I be?"

"Oh, I don't know, maybe because a young lady with pretty blue eyes left you with your heart on your sleeve at the train station today?"

"Green."

"I beg your pardon?"

"Her eyes are more green than blue. At least most of the time."

"Well, you would know better than I." She tried not to show her amusement, but he didn't miss it.

"I'm glad you think it's so funny," William said in a sullen voice. Amy smiled and came across the room to lean against the

255

counter next to his chair.

"I don't think it's funny, William. I'm glad you are able to feel that way about someone again."

"And what has it gotten me?" He leaned back and stared at the ceiling. "I promised myself I wouldn't do this again."

"Love someone? I don't know that it's completely a choice," she said with sympathy. "Amelia is unique. You wouldn't be the man I know you to be if you didn't fall for her."

"Doesn't matter now."

Amy shrugged. "She seemed torn to me. I think she could be convinced, if you found a way to say it *gently*."

He grimaced. "She's not as fragile as she tries to make everyone think. I've seen her spunk. It's part of the reason I... love her. But if she felt the same way, she would have stayed." He kicked at an empty can of wood stain at his feet. "She's safer with him anyway."

"Love isn't always safe," Amy reminded him with a pointed tone.

They were quiet for a long time. Finally, Amy stood and put her hand on his shoulder. "You know what surprised me the most when she first came here? What still gives me pause?"

He looked at her, waiting for her answer.

"Kathleen loves her so much. Every day she cries and asks if she's coming back."

William took a deep breath and clenched his jaw. "What are you saying, sis? You want me to go bring her back?"

Amy smiled. "I think, in this case, you should follow your heart."

Amelia, Jon and Elizabeth took a sightseeing tour around the city. She noticed several familiar places from the times she had visited her grandparents.

"My father preached revival services at the Third Presbyterian Church on the corner of Ohio and Illinois." She pointed across the street at the building, now abandoned. "It was my grandparents' church."

256

They crossed and went inside the old Gothic building. The sound of their footsteps echoed through empty halls as Amelia marveled how life went on, never stopping, never remaining still. At one time, this place had been filled with people and the mighty sound of her father's voice preaching the Gospel to needy souls. Now all had moved on. She closed her eyes, wishing she could travel in time to be there again as an idealistic seventeen-year-old.

"What a beautiful old place," Elizabeth said. As she turned, Amelia was struck by a sudden memory. She pushed open one of the two sets of heavy oak doors.

"What is it, Em?" Jon followed her and put his hands on her shoulders.

"I remember something." She tried to recall the way it had happened before she spoke. "My stomach had been giving me trouble, and I left the service. I came out here."

Elizabeth joined them and they all stared down the broken stone steps.

"She was sitting right there, on the bottom step, looking at the sky. Her hands were open on either side, like she was waiting for something to fall into them. I'd never seen such a lovely woman."

"Who was she?"

"I don't know. She never gave her name. But when she saw me standing here, she started to leave. I stopped her and invited her inside to hear the sermon. She said she was too ashamed to go in, but she could hear. She heard him say there was hope for the vilest of sinners."

Amelia stopped, lost in thought.

"What did you tell her, dear?" Elizabeth's voice sounded far away. Amelia closed her eyes and remembered everything.

"Do you believe that, little girl? That God loves the vile? Because there's a whole mess of people who believe God hates us. That's what I've heard my whole life. I'm too ugly and used up inside to matter to God."

Amelia felt sick at the hatred the woman had endured. "No!

That's wrong. God is love. God is Jesus, hanging on a cross and taking the burden of sin just so we wouldn't have to carry it. There isn't a single thing you've ever done or ever could do that could possibly take away God's love. The Bible says *nothing* can separate us from that love."

Amelia came closer and sat next to her. Touched her arm. The contact seemed to startle the woman.

The woman looked up with fathomless eyes, filled with tears that didn't spill over. "You're just a young, innocent girl. You probably don't realize what I am."

Amelia gulped, suddenly aware of the black lace and red silk peeking through the folds of the woman's long coat. "It doesn't matter. To God, we are all the same."

She stared out over the street. "It wasn't my fault at first. But I stayed. I was afraid."

The woman looked back at Amelia. "Do you think God can forgive me for not making it out?"

Amelia reached for her hand and gripped it tightly. "Jesus died and rose again so he could forgive you of that and everything else. He loves you. He's the only one that can wash you – whiter than snow."

The other woman's eyes were big, as if they could not contain the idea that her soul could be spotless. "What would I do? If I was interested?"

"The work is already done. Just ask. Believe he can save you and accept his gift. Give the rest of your days to him and follow him."

The woman took a deep breath and blew the air out, staring at the ground again, as if she was trying to add it all up. Count the cost.

"I'm scared," she admitted with a chuckle. "Do you think if I asked him to save me, he'd watch over me? Help me get out?"

Amelia considered her question. "God doesn't promise our lives here will be easy. But he promised to be with us and make a way for us to do right. The Bible says he will 'provide a way of escape.'"

Her face broke into a smile, and Amelia was speechless at her beauty.

"That's real good, little sister. I'll think it over."

Before Amelia could find her voice to ask if they could be of any practical assistance, the woman got up and walked off into the night.

Amelia opened her eyes and saw Jon and his mother watching her. "She was wearing a man's hat. I remember thinking it was odd because she was so beautiful."

"You never saw her again?"

"No. But I thought about her. I prayed for her every day for months."

Elizabeth reached over and squeezed her hand. "Then I'm sure she was looked after."

FIFTY

That evening after dinner dishes had been washed and Jon left for whatever business he had in the city each night, Elizabeth asked Amelia to join her on the porch.

"I'm glad we have a few moments to ourselves." There was hesitation in Elizabeth's voice and Amelia felt anxiety at whatever the other woman was about to say. "I want to ask you something."

Amelia shifted with unease.

"There's something I need to understand, since you say you are going to marry my son, after all."

Amelia nervously wrung her fingers in her lap.

"You are hesitant to marry Jon," Elizabeth said.

Amelia swallowed hard.

"Do you doubt his character?" From the quiet, regretful tone of the other woman's voice, Amelia could tell she believed that was the problem. Elizabeth lowered her eyes and stared thoughtfully at the closed book on her lap.

"If I had met Jon without other… occurrences, I'm sure it would be different," Amelia said softly.

"What happened?"

Amelia could hardly bear the disillusionment in the woman's expression.

"It wasn't anything Jon did, really." Amelia looked at her, hoping she would accept the half-truth. She hated to be completely honest about Jon to his mother. She sensed Elizabeth already felt helpless.

"There is someone else. Back in Little Sicily," Amelia explained.

Elizabeth met her eyes. "And you are uncertain of whom you should choose?"

Amelia sighed. "I thought I had chosen. But when I was on the train to come here…"

She tried to find the right words.

"This man, well, for the longest time we were enemies, always fighting. We still always argue but when the train was pulling out, he… he said he loved me."

Elizabeth nodded. "And does this other gentleman have a name?"

"Yes, well, he's William. I believe you know him."

She sat up, her hand fluttering to her chest. "Know him? I practically raised him myself."

Amelia nodded. "He told me you were like a mother."

"We haven't spoken in many years. He left when he was hardly more than a boy. I'm afraid I wasn't even aware he was living in Little Sicily. I've wondered." Elizabeth's voice was even, but her expression darkened. "William spent time in jail. He's been involved in some shameful things."

"He allowed God to change his heart. After Clara died."

She nodded, but Amelia wasn't sure her words had been accepted.

"I heard a little about Clara through Amy. She never said so, but I've wondered if he was running from someone or something he'd done," Elizabeth said.

Amelia had never considered the possibility. Could that be why he was so secretive about his past and the people he was connected to? Why he had worried over involving her in his life?

"William has always been stubborn." Elizabeth shook her head and sighed.

"If I had to describe William in just one word, 'stubborn' would be a good choice," Amelia said. "Though he would probably say the same of me."

Elizabeth smiled, but it quickly faded. "Why didn't you go back? Why did you come to Jon anyway, knowing how William feels?"

Amelia hesitated, feeling like she was in City Hall again, having her character questioned.

"With Jon things are simple. I wasn't sure I wanted to feel so completely overwhelmed for the rest of my life."

Elizabeth eyed her with an indecipherable expression. "Love is never easy. It makes us the most vulnerable to hurt."

Amelia nodded. She'd been trying to run from God just like Jonah on the ship to Tarshish. It was an exercise in futility.

"Amelia, we are responsible to let people know where they stand," Elizabeth said, her voice quiet as she looked down at her hands. "You came here and gave Jon and me the impression you are going to be part of our family. If you love someone enough to be doubtful of the right path, you simply cannot agree to marry someone else just because you are afraid. In the end you will only cause everyone pain."

Amelia had not expected the lecture. She could tell Elizabeth was frustrated. Her cheeks felt hot with shame. "I'm sorry."

"Do you love Jon?"

Elizabeth had come to the heart of the matter, and the question made all the pieces fit together.

"No," she answered, and the saying of the word was what she needed to be sure of it.

Elizabeth's eyes slid from Amelia's face to the porch stairs. Amelia saw Jon leaning on the porch railing, his hands buried deep in his pockets, wearing a somber expression assuring Amelia the direction of her life had changed.

FIFTY-ONE

Jon volunteered to take Amelia to the train station the next morning, as wounded as he was, but Elizabeth went with her instead. Amelia was not sure it would make the trip any less uncomfortable.

In Union Station, she worried while they waited in line to purchase her tickets. What would William do when she came back? Would he forgive her for leaving? What if he wouldn't even speak to her?

Perhaps a ticket to Illinois would be more prudent.

As she contemplated, someone jolted her from behind. She turned and saw what she supposed was her first genuine outlaw. At least he looked the part. He had stringy hair and shifty eyes, and his hand never strayed far from his gun holster. She noticed he had a significant limp, and he walked with another man who wore a sheriff's badge. She watched them with a curious frown. The sheriff appeared no more civil than the outlaw.

She shivered, glad they had ignored her.

They were nearly to the front of the line when something prompted Amelia to look to her right. In that moment she could not have been more surprised if she had turned and saw someone riding an elephant across the pavilion. She gasped and dropped her bag.

"What is it?" Elizabeth turned. Amelia couldn't answer. She couldn't move. She stared across the room, overcome.

William was leaning against a post, his hands in his pockets.

His features were guarded, but she thought she glimpsed

vulnerability. Was he there to see her? Was this just an unfortunate coincidence? Should she go to him or wait for him to come to her?

And then his expression became a smirk.

She smiled, feeling breathless. She took two steps out of the line as he started to come toward her. Then she moved faster, seeing that he did the same.

When they were no more than a few feet apart, two men stepped between them, facing William. Amelia realized they were the same two men who had bumped into her moments before. Her utter joy quickly became alarm as she abruptly stopped.

William's face went dark. His hand reached for the gun he no longer carried. The man with the limp placed a confident hand on his own pistol.

"Look what we found, Sheriff. Hiding right here in plain sight. I guess our man in Little Sicily was right."

Amelia had never seen William so serious.

"What are you doing here, Clint?" William spoke, his casual tone mismatched to the concern she saw in his expression. He stood taller. "No, I don't care what you're doing here. Turn your sorry self around and get out of this station before I give you more of what I gave you last time."

Elizabeth picked up Amelia's bag and grasped her arm to pull her back.

The man William had referred to as "Clint" sneered. "Bet you didn't know I was still alive, Morehouse. Did you think you finished me off? Didn't I tell you I always get what's mine?"

For the first time since she'd known him, Amelia saw fear in William's eyes. No one else would recognize it, for his expression was hard, but Amelia glimpsed it. Why was he afraid? Certainly not for himself. He was the bravest man she'd ever met. She covered her stomach with her arms, and the movement caught his attention.

He stared at her, narrowing his eyes as if he was trying to send her a message. She heard the gist.

Get out of sight.

Elizabeth and Amelia backed away until they rounded a corner nearby. Amelia peeked around and continued to watch, her heart pounding.

"William Morehouse, you're under arrest for the murder of Clara McCloud."

"You want someone to blame for her murder, you got him right here. Clint's man is the one who shot her." William's voice was like steel.

"Not how I remember it." Clint shrugged.

"But he's a lawman!" Amelia whispered.

Elizabeth shook her head. "I don't think he's the trustworthy kind."

Amelia covered her mouth with her hands. She needed to get help. But where would she go? She didn't know anyone in the city. She didn't even know the location of the police station.

Elizabeth held her fast by the arm as if afraid she might bolt out between the men. Her hold tightened significantly when the sheriff quickly pulled a gun and pointed it at William's heart. Amelia struggled to break free. People gasped and began to murmur as they backed away from the three men.

"You can make this easy or we can give you your sentence and execution right here in front of all these nice folks."

"No," Amelia moaned softly.

Clint limped toward William, dragging his bad leg behind him. "Now if you told me where the girl is, maybe we could work something out."

"She's safe. Where you'll never find her," William said with an even voice.

"She belongs to me!" Clint growled. "Because of you, I lost Clara. Because of you, my leg don't work. I will have her or you will die. You and everyone you care about."

Amelia gasped again, and the sheriff turned his head at the noise. She crouched back and held her breath.

William didn't look away from Clint. "If you shoot me here, people will question. There are good lawmen that don't take bribes from low-life scum."

"That's quite a story." The sheriff waved his gun, speaking loudly for the sake of the onlookers. "It's your picture on the poster in my jail. Dead or alive, it says."

"Where is she?" Clint seethed. William didn't answer.

"Who is he talking about?" Amelia whispered to Elizabeth, but the older woman shook her head with a shrug. Did he mean Amy? Nothing added up.

"Let's go." Clint motioned to the sheriff, who reached for his handcuffs and forced William's wrists behind his back.

"You're going to regret this," William warned.

"Not as much as you will regret ever thinking to take what's mine." Clint pushed him as they moved in the direction of the door. "You won't be alive to protect her when I find her. And I will find her. I got men everywhere. I got men in your town."

Amelia could hear no more of their conversation; they had exited the ticket area. She ran to find a police officer. Elizabeth trailed behind, still carrying her valise. Amelia finally located a man in a blue uniform monitoring the entrance to Union Station. He peered at her with suspicion, maybe due to her disheveled appearance and breathlessness.

"A man was just abducted! I demand to speak to someone now!"

The policeman proved to be rather unhelpful, but after a ten-minute walk to the station on Alabama Street, another officer helped Amelia make a telephone call to Sheriff Tyler in Little Sicily. She had never placed a long-distance call before. She waited nervously on the line until she heard the dispatch operator.

"What number?"

"Little Sicily."

The operator connected her and she waited again to hear a response.

"What number?" a familiar voice said.

"Sheriff Tyler, please. I'm not sure of the number."

"Miss Farnsworth? Is that you?"

Amelia recognized Mrs. Hagaman's voice, but she had no time for pleasantries. "Sheriff Tyler, please."

She heard the connection and the phone buzzed twice before the

Sheriff answered.

"Sheriff Tyler, this is Amelia Farnsworth. I'm calling from the police station in Indianapolis because Mr. Morehouse has been captured by two men, one of them posing as a sheriff. I'm hoping that you or perhaps Amy Able might have an idea where they have gone."

"What do the officers there say?" Sheriff Tyler's voice sounded fuzzy and false, like a copy of his real voice.

"They don't see much hope for finding him, and they are convinced I am hysterical."

"I promise you I'll do some checking, Miss Farnsworth. Now hold on while I run over and get Amy for you. I just saw her go into the store."

A few moments later Amelia heard Amy's voice, crackling in the dissonance of the line. "Amelia? What's wrong?"

She immediately had the desire to burst into tears, but she remembered that everyone who owned a phone in Little Sicily would, no doubt, be listening in on the conversation.

"It's William," she said with a gulp of emotion.

Amy hesitated. "Is he…"

Amelia shook her head before she remembered Amy couldn't see her. "No. They took him. Someone named Clint. And a sheriff who seemed to be doing whatever Clint wanted."

Amy was quiet.

Amelia was desperate for answers. "Do you know where they took him? What is this about?"

"I'm not supposed to say." Amelia could hardly hear Amy's quiet words. "It's not safe."

"Not safe for whom?"

"Everyone he loves."

It was Amelia's turn to have nothing to say in response. Finally, Amy spoke again. "If you find him, tell him you called me."

"He said he had men who knew about Little Sicily. They could come there, Amy."

"I know what to do."

"How will I find him?"

267

"There's a town in Indiana called Sage. If they've taken him somewhere, they might go there. But don't go with the policemen, Amelia. William wouldn't want it. Let them do their job."

Amelia didn't answer. She said a quick goodbye and hung up the receiver. The two policemen stared at her with incredulity.

"They may have taken him to Sage. Do you know where that is?"

They exchanged glances. "Maybe."

"Well, are you going to go after them?"

"I looked up your William Morehouse." One of them leaned back in his chair and put his hands behind his head. "He's a criminal. He's done time for robbery and he's killed men."

He spoke slowly, as if he was waiting for his words to sink in. She nodded, hoping Elizabeth might speak up on her brother's behalf, but the older woman remained silent, her gaze on the floor and her mouth set in a line.

"He paid for those offenses. He's turned his life around! Now he has been unjustly taken against his will by men who already made it clear they plan to murder him. You can't allow that to happen!"

"If we have any other evidence to go after them, we'll look into it. But Sage has its own sheriff."

"The sheriff in Sage is probably the one that took him," Elizabeth finally spoke, but her voice was quiet and she did not meet their gaze.

"Look, Mrs. Hastings, we're sorry about your brother, but there's really nothing we can do right now. You'd best just go home and wait. We'll send a message if we hear anything else."

"You can't just let it happen!" Amelia banged her fist on the table, tears burning her eyes. "It's your duty to protect him!"

"Thank you, gentlemen." Elizabeth took hold of Amelia's shoulders and directed her away. "We understand your position. We appreciate your time and the use of your telephone."

When they reached the street, Amelia turned to her in anger. "We can't just leave him! They'll kill him!"

"Don't you think I know that?" Elizabeth's voice trembled, and Amelia could see the same grief in her eyes. "He's my brother. I wish there was a better option. But William made his choices in life, and one of them has caught up with him. I wouldn't know the first thing to do to help him, Amelia. Would you?"

"I have to find him," Amelia said. "I can't sit and wait to hear that he's dead, not if there's a shred of hope that I can do something to save him. I have to go to Sage."

"What would you do when you got there? You're a schoolteacher. You don't own a gun or know how to use one. All you would do is get yourself killed, and William wouldn't want that. Don't underestimate the power of waiting and praying."

Amelia considered her words, but in her heart, she knew she would not change her mind. There was only one choice. No matter what it would cost her, she had to go.

"I will go on the strength of your prayers." Amelia squeezed Elizabeth's hand before she turned and headed back into the night alone. Elizabeth called after her, but Amelia kept walking, determination in every step. Her mind was made up, and thank goodness, a plan seemed to be forming there, as well. William wasn't going to die alone and helpless. Like Gwendolyn, like Clara, if she had to die to save the man she loved, she would.

It would be an honor.

FIFTY-TWO

There was no train to Sage, Indiana. It could only be reached by stagecoach, so Amelia purchased her fare and walked onto the busy street outside Union Station.

She saw by the large clock tower she had two hours before the stagecoach would arrive. She was sure that would be enough time to get the items she needed. She marched into the crowd with all the purpose her timid heart could muster and made her way down two blocks until she came upon a two-story, red brick building. The sign read *Black Eagle Tavern*. From the raucous noise and women milling around the porch, she guessed the nature of the business.

She turned around and saw the spires of the church she had visited with Jon and his mother. The woman she had spoken to that night when Amelia was seventeen had walked this direction. She was sure of it. She scanned the group of women in front of the tavern.

The plan her mind was conceiving seemed outrageous. She could never pull it off by herself. And she was not completely sure God would bless her efforts, knowing what she was about to do.

But her feet wouldn't listen to reason. They wanted to find William. And so they led her up the rough board steps to the women as she begged God's understanding.

"I'm looking for someone. A blonde woman, maybe four inches taller than me?" She surveyed the blank looks. These were faces that had seen the worst. She couldn't begin to fathom the darkness they lived in from day to day. And not all by their own choice – some of them might be little more than slaves. Her heart ached.

"She wore a Stetson," Amelia said. Near the wall in the back, a woman sat on the railing with a flimsy shawl pulled around her revealing red shirtwaist. She looked up at Amelia's words.

"What's going on out here?" Amelia heard a lazy drawl. All the women snapped to attention, returning to their avid search for potential clients passing on the street. A man with a thick waistline walked through them and rested lustful eyes on Amelia.

"This ain't no place for decent women. You run along and find your family."

She took a deep breath and forced herself to say the words. The lie. "I got no family. I'm looking for work."

He snorted, and some of the girls snickered with him. "Get on."

"It's true." She shrugged with her best sullen expression. "Who do I talk to about getting a job?"

He came closer, walking around her so he could survey her from all angles. Her face burned.

"You know what goes on in there?" He nodded toward the noisy saloon, raising his eyebrows. She nodded.

The standoff lasted a few seconds. Finally, he gestured to a nearby girl. "Take her up and get her a dress. I'll be up to see what she's made of."

Amelia almost ran away. She was completely terrified. The woman on the rail jumped off. "I'll take her."

Amelia fought back a wild attack of fear as she stepped away from the man and followed the young woman inside. She wished she could close her eyes the moment she stepped into the dark, smoke-filled room. She was surrounded by drinking and gambling men. Dancing girls on the stage teased the men with skimpy outfits and lewd movements. It was more depravity than she had witnessed in her entire life, combined into one deplorable moment in time.

She reminded herself of the plan. Her only plan to save William. And that was enough to make her feet move.

She followed the woman up a winding staircase covered with worn velvet carpeting, feeling a growing dread with each step. She didn't want to imagine what took place behind the closed doors.

And yet she could not deny a certain level of curiosity as well. Not to know the shameful ways people mistreated their bodies, but to know William's world. To know where he was before his life was transformed by grace. She wanted to feel his rush of emotion as he climbed the stairs to his Clara.

The woman opened a door and motioned her inside.

When the door closed, she turned to Amelia. "You get out of here quick, Miss. Trust me. It's better to starve than sell your soul to the devil who owns this place."

"Who?" Amelia tried to still her own trembling limbs.

The woman seemed afraid to say his name. She came close and whispered in her ear. Amelia smelled her gaudy perfume and saw the hint of bosom peeking from her corset-like shirtwaist.

"Clint. He don't like decent folk coming around. He's been known to shoot before he asks questions."

"Is he here?" Amelia's heart jumped from either fear or excitement or both. Had she found William? Was he alive?

"No, but he could come back anytime. You get out now."

There was a loud knock on the door and the woman went to a trunk. She sorted through and pulled out a sleeveless chemise with exceptional flounce, and a lacey black corset with red ribbon... everywhere. Amelia waited for the rest of the outfit, but she was given nothing else. Another woman stuck her head inside the door.

"He wants to know what's taking so long, Mercy."

"She's got a few questions. Tell him to hold his horses."

When the door closed, the woman called Mercy gestured to Amelia to begin to change. Amelia swallowed her protest and allowed her to help undo the buttons of her travel outfit and her own plain white corset, camisole and pantalets.

"You wanted to know about Clara."

Amelia stopped changing and stared at her in surprise. "Did you say Clara?"

"That was the woman you were talking about. Clara McCloud."

Amelia covered her face with her hands as she put the pieces together. The woman she had met that night at church had been

272

Clara? William's Clara?

"She died," Mercy said with a mournful voice as she pulled the laces impossibly tight on the corset. "There was never anyone like her, Miss. She stood up to Billy and even escaped for a time. But in the end, he killed her for standing up to him."

"I'm sorry, Mercy." Amelia touched her hand. Mercy pulled her hand back in surprise.

"No one decent has touched me in a long time," she said, her eyes going soft. It made Amelia wonder about her story. Was Mercy one of the girls who never had a choice?

"Then it's high time someone did," Amelia said and gave Mercy a small hug for good measure. "You helped me figure out a puzzle, and I'm thankful. Now I'm afraid I'm going to have to ask you to help me climb down the outside of this building before your gentleman friend comes looking for me."

She snorted. "He isn't a gentleman or a friend. And I don't know how you know Clara, but you sound a lot like her."

Amelia squeezed Mercy's hand and hurried to put her travel jacket and skirt over the clothes she had been given. She took a quick glance in the mirror. Her curves were more exaggerated than before, but she didn't think anyone would guess what she was wearing under her sensible clothes. It would have been amusing had the situation not been so dire.

Mercy opened the window and tied a length of rope to the leg of the bed. She held it while Amelia tied it around her waist and let herself down the side of the brick wall. She was only on the second story, and managed to arrive safely on the ground. After giving her rescuer a wave, she took off as fast as she could with the tight stays sucking the breath from her body.

She arrived back at the stagecoach landing with no time to spare. They were loading the last of the luggage and closing the door.

"Wait!" She held her skirt and hat and ran the last few steps, her chest heaving from the exertion. The man opened the door again and helped her in.

The stagecoach slammed and the whole carriage swayed as the driver climbed up into his seat. Amelia realized the wretched-smelling compartment filled with strangers might well be the final

273

part of her journey. When the door opened again, she would be in Sage. And she would have to complete the rest of her plan or die trying.

It wasn't the dying part she feared the most.

FIFTY-THREE

After two hours of the jarring motion of the stage, alternately praying and fretting the entire time, Amelia saw the little settlement in the distance. Before she was ready, the coach stopped with a sudden creaking and swaying. Amelia waited for someone else to move.

They all stared at her as if she was holding them up. She realized she was the only one who would be ending her journey here.

She allowed the driver to help her down and quickly looked for a place to hide. She ducked behind a shed and sat there until the sun went down.

She smelled someone's supper and her stomach growled. She realized she hadn't eaten anything since dinner the night before.

To distract herself, she reviewed her plan, and as she did, she recognized it wasn't much of a plan at all. It involved several assumptions she could not be sure would happen as she expected. She looked around in the dark to ensure she was alone before she quickly pulled off her skirt and jacket. She removed her hat and let her hair down. She tried to pin it up in a fashion like some of the women she had seen in the tavern, but without a mirror or a brush she was afraid her efforts would look ridiculous. She shook it out and let it be. She hoped she could pass for the part she was playing.

She wouldn't even look at her clothes. Could she walk through town dressed this way – in no more than frilly undergarments designed to lure men?

What would William think of her? What if he no longer loved her after seeing her in such a state of undress? She gulped at the thought of him staring at her with disgust.

She took a deep breath and told herself that saving his life was more important than winning his love. After making a sincere apology to the Lord, she stepped out into the night. She located the jail, the third building in a line of four. She suspected two were taverns.

Praying that Billy Clint felt more at home spending his evening drinking in one of the saloons, Amelia headed for the small building with bars on the windows. She peeked inside. Her heart jumped with affection when she saw William sitting on a thin cot and staring out of his cell with a furrowed brow.

"Yes, sir, when that judge gets here in the morning, we are going to have us a hanging. I wouldn't mind shooting you now, but it is nice to kill a man and call it legal." The sheriff leaned back in his chair and took a long puff from a cigar. "What's the matter, Morehouse? Nothing to say on your last night of living?"

"I'm not afraid to die." William didn't look up.

The sheriff snorted. "You some kind of religious boy?"

"Didn't used to be. Clara changed that."

"Too bad you killed her." The sheriff gave an insufferable laugh.

William didn't respond. Amelia figured it was as good a time as any to make her move. Whatever her move might turn out to be.

She took a deep breath, resisted the urge to try to pull the chemise higher on her chest, and went inside.

At first the sheriff was confused, but a light of appreciation replaced the question almost immediately. Amelia gulped, never having had a man ogle her in such a fashion before. She peeked at William, her back to him. He must have decided to avert his eyes when he saw her dress, so he didn't know it was her. Yet.

The thought of him being unwilling to look on her made her feel faint. But she forced herself to approach the sheriff, who pulled her into his lap without hesitation.

"Did Clint send you over to keep me company, little lady?"

She smiled as best she could manage, fighting the instinct to pull away, and nodded.

"Oh, a shy one! He snaked a possessive arm around her waist. "You new? I haven't seen you around here before."

She nodded again, pretending she was a character in a novel and not Amelia Josephine Farnsworth, pastor's daughter. She even managed to come up with what she hoped was a coy expression.

"Well, honey, I'll give you a schooling; don't you worry." He leaned in and placed a repulsive kiss on her mouth. He tasted of stale jerky and cigar. She felt a wave of nausea and tried to still her natural response, which would have been a hard slap to his reprehensible face.

"Leave her be," William said quietly. Amelia didn't dare look back at him. She was afraid he might rip the bars off and kill the man if he knew it was her.

"She's not complaining."

"I am."

The sheriff gave Amelia a conspiratorial look. "He's complaining now, sweetheart. But there was a time Morehouse here couldn't get enough of your kind. Even murdered the one he couldn't have."

She suppressed her objection to the lie. "Oh, my! How frightening," she whispered close to his ear.

He stood up, his hand still on her waist. "But I'm a fair man." He pulled her across the room and made her stand in front of the cell. She braced for William's reaction, hoping he wouldn't start yelling and give her away.

"What do you say, Morehouse? Are you too religious a man for a visit with a *fine* lady on your last night breathing?"

William glanced at her. Then looked again. His expression changed from resigned to... amused?

Amused and very, very angry.

He stood up and sauntered the few feet across the cell. Amelia noticed his face had bruises and cuts as if he had been beaten. He stood in front of her, his hands on the bars on either side of her. He gave her a silent earful of a lecture Amelia was confident contained more than one foul word.

"Oh, I know this one. She's a handful. But I could teach her a few things," William said.

The sheriff burst into a wheezy laugh. "You got five minutes. Might want to save the religion for tomorrow."

Still sniggering, the foul man found his hat and wandered out into the night, most likely next door to find a drink.

"So, what's next in your little plan?" William raised an eyebrow and allowed himself an unhurried look at her uncovered arms and neck.

"Shame on you!" She reached through the bars and pinched his arm as hard as she could.

"Shame on *me*?" He traded his leering for severity. "What do you think you are doing, Amelia? Do you realize the danger you're in?"

"I did it for you."

"Why in the world would you risk the rest of your long, safe life for me? Don't you understand? I came from this. I deserve to die, even if it's not for what they're going to kill me for."

"We all deserve to die. If I died trying to get you out, I'd deserve it just as much. I'm a sinner as well."

He breathed a soft laugh. "You say you're not like Clara, but if I squint my eyes just a bit, I could pretend this whole conversation was with her."

"I have something to tell you about that." Amelia gave him a small smile, prepared to tell him about what she had learned at the tavern. He nodded.

"Later. First I'm going to make use of my five minutes."

He grabbed her waist and forced her close, so that her body was pressed against the bars. He used his other hand to bring her face to his so he could kiss her.

If he wasn't holding her up, she would have melted to the floor. When he allowed her a breath, she remembered the other thing she hadn't told him.

"Oh! I almost forgot... I love you, too."

He chuckled and threaded his fingers through her hair. "Yeah, I kind of figured."

He watched her for a long moment before he spoke. "Amelia, did your plan involve anything more than dressing up and coming in here to make a man regret his imminent death?"

"It didn't at first," she admitted. "But I do have this."

She held up the ring and key she was holding, snagged from the sheriff's belt. He stared at it in surprise.

"Well, why didn't you say so?"

"You distracted me!"

"Hurry up, woman!"

She unlocked the door. He grabbed a pistol from inside the desk before they ran. He untied the sheriff's horse and swung her up to the saddle before he jumped up behind her and kicked the animal in the sides.

The creature protested loudly to the treatment, taking off at a gallop just as the sheriff and Clint came out of the saloon. Amelia might have made a face at them if they hadn't pulled out their guns and started shooting.

William fired back as the men mounted horses and rode after them. In the dark, and riding at top speed, William was able to get far enough ahead to maneuver into the woods and dismount in time to find a place to hide.

He held her hand, pulling her through the dark forest. She was terrified, but if she focused on their joined hands, pale in the moonlight, she found she could manage.

He found a cave and pulled her inside.

It was chilly inside the dark cavern, and he must have felt the goose bumps on her bare arms. He scooted her back against his chest and encircled her with his arms.

"Don't get me wrong, Schoolmarm," he said, pressing a kiss to her jaw below her ear. "I am furious that you risked your life on my account. And you better never pull anything like that again... but thank you."

She nodded against him. "Are they going to follow us?"

He nodded with a grim sigh. "As soon as there's enough light to see, we have to move. We aren't too far from Indianapolis. I'll take you to Elizabeth's and she can get you food and clothes and keep an eye on you."

"I don't need someone to keep an eye on me." She jabbed him in the side.

"You most certainly do, little girl."

She was quiet for a moment. "What's going to happen to you?"

"You gave me a chance. I have a weapon. But you need to understand something, Amelia. There's no easy way out. When this is over, either Clint or I will be lying on the ground, waiting for a pine box."

She swallowed hard. The gentle words were the confirmation she didn't want to hear. "I just got you back. I don't want to lose you again," she whispered.

He pulled her tighter and buried his face in her hair. "I know."

"We could run. Just go as far away as we can get."

William sighed. "It would be nice. But we can't. For so many reasons, but one especially."

She waited for him to explain, but he didn't say anything else.

They were quiet for a long time, both lost in contemplation.

"Will you tell me your story?" Amelia finally asked.

He hesitated. "You aren't going to like parts."

"I'll manage."

"You know about my wild days."

"Generally," she said.

"Some things don't need repeating. After I met Clara, she became my weakness. I didn't want to roam with the boys anymore, stealing and picking fights. I stayed close to her, even tried to hold a job so I could buy up her time. That's how I learned the carpentry business. But Clint had owned Clara since she was a child, and he didn't like that I was falling for her. He tried to keep us apart. She'd sneak out early in the morning sometimes and come to me."

He paused, and she ran her fingers along his arms. Amelia wondered, and not for the first time, if she should feel jealous over his intense love for Clara. But she didn't. Something about his devotion showed her his character and gave her faith that he could love her just as much.

"She started getting really sad. Questioning everything in her life. I told her I would get her out. I'd kill him if I had to. One night I helped her escape. We hid in Sage. At first, we did okay. I had a few carpentry jobs that kept us fed and we stayed in an abandoned house just outside the town. For a time, we had peace. But eventually, we ran out of money and the old habits were too strong. I went back to stealing, and she got a job at the saloon. It wasn't long before Clint found us.

"Another few months passed where I hardly saw her. He would beat her every time we were together, and I couldn't take seeing the bruises all over her and the spirit gone from her eyes. One night she came to me, late, and I noticed she had a spark of hope in her eyes. She said she'd been to church, of all places. Said she'd found out God could forgive her for not making it out."

Amelia sat up and turned around, searching for his features in the darkness.

"I can tell you this part of the story." She reached a hand to feel his bristly cheek. "I was there."

"What are you talking about?"

FIFTY-FOUR

Amelia wished she could make out the surprised expression she was sure he wore.

"I was there. I only remembered this recently. Jon, your sister and I were sightseeing, and we found a church where my father had preached a few years ago. It all came back to me, how I found her sitting on the stairs and listening through the door because she didn't think she was worthy to come in. I told her God could forgive anyone because of his Son, no matter what we'd done."

"Amelia," he whispered. She felt his quickened breath on her face. "You're sure it was Clara?"

"She was wearing a Stetson. And the girl I met at the Black Eagle told me about her."

He laughed in disbelief and drew her closer.

"Thank you, Amelia. Thank you for saving us."

"Jesus saved you. He just put me in the right place at the right time. Because of my stomach pains, of all things."

His hand pressed against her abdomen. "Most people wouldn't have spoken a word to her."

"It wasn't me. It was Jesus," she argued. "Finish the story."

"After that night, Clara was different. She wasn't afraid anymore, and she was done with that life. She asked me to help her get out, but said she'd understand if I didn't want to risk it. I was more than willing to die trying. I loaded my gun and went with her to get her things and sneak out. This time we were going to do it right. We'd find another town further out, and get married."

Amelia closed her eyes and pictured the story.

"Clint was waiting for us at the stagecoach, shooting in every direction, sending everyone running for cover. He had two gunmen with him. I jumped behind barrels set out in front of the store. Started shooting. I got his two men, and then went out into the street to settle the matter.

"As I was walking, a third gunmen jumped out of nowhere just behind me and took aim to shoot me in the back. Clara saw him and ran in front of him just as he fired. He shot her in the stomach. Twice."

Tears stung Amelia's eyes.

"Clint got me in the shoulder, but Clara had given me the time and motivation to take out both of them. It cost her life."

"Oh, William," Amelia said. He took a deep breath, and his voice caught.

"She told me as she was lying beside me bleeding, that she was dying for me because she knew she was ready to go be with God. She said she was buying me time, and she wanted me to use it wisely. Told me to get right with God, and live for love instead of hate. When she couldn't talk anymore, and blood was gurgling out of her mouth, she pulled a letter out of her coat and handed it to me."

Amelia thought about the letter she had found. His letter to Clara. She almost mentioned it, but somehow, she couldn't. It was too sacred.

"At the time I stuck it in my pocket and didn't think about it again. But when I found it later, I realized it was the letter I'd smuggled in to her when she was back at the Black Eagle. Asking her to marry me. I thought she was giving it back so I could keep it to remember her, but then I realized she'd written something at the end. I don't know when she wrote it. Maybe before she ever left her room."

"What did she say?" Amelia was breathless at the hush of his voice. Whatever Clara had written amazed him still. He didn't say anything for a moment.

When he spoke, it was like he'd forgotten Amelia was there.

"The note said *Take her to Emmy Jo*."

Amelia gasped and sat straight up, her skin prickling in response to the eerie message.

"What on earth...?"

She felt him shrug. "Clara had a sense about things. After hearing Ella call you that name at Christmas, I thought maybe she'd seen the future. But you must have told her your name that night."

Amelia considered the conversation from years before. She didn't remember either of them exchanging names. "Even if I had, I would have said my name was Amelia. The only one who ever calls me Emmy Jo is –"

She remembered then. "When we had finished our conversation and she was walking down the steps, the door opened and Ella came looking for me. She was calling me."

He chuckled. "Well, that explains a mystery I've been trying to figure out." He pulled her head back to his chest. "It's still amazing to think that she knew I'd find you and had the presence of mind to write me that note before we left."

"Maybe someone else knew."

William wrapped his arms around her and sighed with a wistful contentment. Something occurred to Amelia.

"But wait—who is *her*? Take whom to Emmy Jo?"

"That's the final piece of the puzzle, Schoolmarm. You see – Clara had a daughter."

She sat up again, banging her head against his chin and eliciting his grumbling. "Ow! Will you please be still?"

"A daughter? Where is she?"

He hesitated, and she knew she would learn no more tonight. "That's a story for another day. Not because I don't want to tell you. If I live past tomorrow, I will. I promise."

She leaned back against him. When Amelia slept, she dreamed Clint was coming after William, a gun pointed at his heart. When he pulled the trigger, she jumped between them and felt the bullets blast into her stomach.

FIFTY-FIVE

Amelia realized the pain in her stomach was real when she woke – unrelenting and sharp. She tried to be still to allow William a few more minutes of sleep. She huddled close to his warmth, trying not to think of the day ahead.

William stirred, his hands running the length of her back. He groaned with what she thought might be pleasure, but maybe he was just sore from her laying on him all night. Or was he remembering Clara? Did he think she was Clara?

"Amelia," he growled. He captured her chin and kissed her, managing to silence her doubts. She kissed him back until he pushed her away and stood up, bringing her up with him.

"We better get going." He led her out of the cave and gave the area a cautious scan. When he was satisfied it was safe, his eyes caught on her dress. Amelia felt her face flush, realizing it was dawn and she was quite scantily clad. He took off his jacket and draped it around her shoulders.

"I think it would be best for both of us if you wore this."

Amelia pulled it on, but not before she risked one look that might be construed as flirting. He narrowed his eyes.

"Careful toying with a man, Schoolmarm. He might not be able to help himself if you pass out too many glances like that."

She sobered right up.

After they had walked for a couple hours and the sun had fully risen, Indianapolis came into view. They practically fell into Elizabeth's front hall when she opened the door.

"Thank the Lord," she said, ushering them into the parlor. She turned and looked down at Amelia's dress under the coat. "May I ask what you are wearing, young lady?"

Amelia pulled William's coat more tightly over the risqué costume. "Something I hope not to be wearing much longer," she said, embarrassed. William smirked, and she flushed.

"I mean I hope to change…"

"Of course you do." Elizabeth gave William a look of reprimand.

William and Elizabeth considered each other, both hesitant.

"How are you, Elizabeth?" William's voice was tight.

"I'm fine. I won't ask the same of you." Amelia heard the quiet rebuke in her tone. Elizabeth crossed her arms. "Tell me what happened."

"I'll let Amelia fill you in," William answered. "I've got business with Clint."

Elizabeth lifted her chin. "What business?"

"You need to eat. He's not here yet," Amelia protested, taking off his jacket and handing it to him. He pulled it on and even averted his eyes just like a gentleman.

"It won't take him long to figure out where we are. And being in a busy city won't stop him. I'm going to walk out and meet him to lessen the chance of someone getting caught in the crossfire."

Amelia knew there was nothing more she could say. He was settled in his mind, and she trusted his judgment, as much as she didn't like it. She felt a certain measure of peace in that trust, but no joy. She could lose the only man she had ever loved. The only man she wanted for the rest of her life.

Please, God. Please keep him safe.

William made her sit on the couch and crouched in front of her. He took her hands in his and looked at them. "I'm not going to lie to you. There's about a fifty-fifty chance I won't come back. I think you understand that."

He waited for her response, and she finally nodded.

"I don't want to walk out of here with those kinds of odds without making sure you know I have hopes. For our future," he said softly.

The room was quiet for a long moment. But he wasn't finished.

"Amelia, I want you to understand something. I wouldn't have done any of it. I wouldn't have done all the things I've done if I had any idea *you* were in my future. I wish I could go back and change it all." William's tone was full of the tender regret he tried to convey.

She nodded again, unable to speak. The bittersweet words fell on her ears like a heart-rending strain of music. She reached for his face and pulled him toward her, kissing the line on his forehead.

"Jesus, please bring him back," she whispered.

William twisted his fingers through her hair. She held her breath, hoping he would stay, but he stood and walked to the door. He stopped in the doorway and looked back at Amelia.

"Look at it this way. If I don't come back, at least it will make a great ending to a novel – eh, Schoolmarm?"

Amelia thought she would burst into tears. She was afraid it would make him feel even worse about leaving, so she subdued her response with effort. He must have known by her red face, because for a moment he watched her as if he was torn. Elizabeth came and put a hand on her shoulder. Finally, he put his hat on and stepped out.

Amelia stayed put as long as she could. But her mind wouldn't stop reminding her that this might be their last goodbye. Before he closed the gate behind him, she ran after him, tearing down the steps and path. He turned as she launched herself into his arms.

"I love you!" She hugged him with fierceness. "I always will."

He didn't say anything, but his eyes were gleaming with unshed tears when he set her down and let go. He turned and walked away without looking back. Elizabeth came to join her, pulling a shawl over Amelia's shoulders. They watched until he was out of sight.

The day wore on. Amelia couldn't imagine what was taking so long, but her intuition warned her it couldn't be a good sign. Jon came home around dinnertime and the three of them ate in a pensive silence. Though Amelia was physically famished, her throat was so tight she could only swallow a few bites before she gave up. She sat in the parlor for the rest of the evening, watching the door as if she might summon William if she concentrated hard enough.

Jon left again after barely saying a word to either of them. Elizabeth waited with Amelia, peering over her glasses every few minutes as she read from a large medical encyclopedia.

At a quarter to one, there was a quiet knock. Amelia froze; her eyes glued to the door, dread and hope warring for control. She panicked, realizing the direction of her future stood just outside that door. Why would William knock? He'd know they were there waiting for him. Was it a policeman, coming to tell them he'd been found dead? Even worse, what if it was Clint and he was coming to torture them to learn where Clara's daughter was hiding?

She reminded herself that it was unlikely Clint would politely knock.

Elizabeth crossed and opened the door. Amelia squeezed her eyes shut. The ache swelled in her throat when she became convinced they weren't talking because no one wanted to tell her he was gone. Tears began to escape from her eyes and roll down her cheeks. She heard heavy footsteps on the floor and shook her head, willing the bearer of the news away. She didn't want to hear he was dead.

"Don't say it," she begged.

There was a creaking of leather boots as someone kneeled next to her. Was it the horrible policeman who called her hysterical? Was it Clint?

Amelia felt a kiss on her shaking hand. And then strong arms went around her.

He was alive.

FIFTY-SIX

Elizabeth went to bed, but left her door open so they could talk. Amelia was suddenly so hungry she could have eaten an entire chicken by herself, so she suggested they find a snack. He followed her into the kitchen.

"I waited out by the edge of town for hours. I saw them coming long before they got there. Clint slid off his horse and approached me. Said he was calling me out. I said it was high time."

"Did you trust that the sheriff wouldn't shoot you while you were watching Clint?" Amelia tried to envision the proceedings as she prepared sandwiches from the remainder of supper in the icebox.

"Nope."

Amelia nodded with eyes wide.

"We stood there glaring at each other for a time before Clint made his move. He and the sheriff both went for their guns at the same time."

"But how did you –"

He shrugged. "I figured it had mostly to do with a certain schoolmarm praying. They barely touched their weapons and they were flat on their backs."

There was no pride or satisfaction in his voice. Amelia heard humility. She heard regret.

"They're dead?"

He took his time answering. "May God have mercy on their souls."

289

"How sad."

"I pray it's the last time I ever have to take a life."

They ate their sandwiches and shared a glass of lemonade

"I expected to have trouble explaining it to the police, especially given my history, but they were accommodating." He grinned at her. "It seems a young lady came in a day or two ago, demanding that justice be sought for her lover who had been abducted and was to be murdered by Clint and a rogue sheriff."

"I never said you were my lover." She was indignant at the misinformation. He chuckled.

"Give us time, sweetheart. Give us time." He reached for her cheek. "But not tonight. Time for bed."

"Where will you sleep?"

"On the sofa. I'll probably wake up with a few sore spots but it's better than being dead, I figure." He stood and walked with her to the stairs.

Amelia smiled. "I don't know. Seems like being dead would be the best scenario, wouldn't it?"

He eyed her with amusement. "Sometimes I wonder about the way you think, Schoolmarm."

"Until recently, I assumed everyone thought the same way as me," she said.

"I've never met anyone who thinks like you," he said, kissing her nose.

She sighed. "I'm coming to understand that truth."

Amelia realized in that moment she had not a clue what they were supposed to do next. The possibilities overwhelmed her.

"We'll head home tomorrow." He seemed to read her thoughts. "And when we get there, I'll tell you the last part of the story."

Amelia thought she should probably be worried about being seen as William walked her home from the Little Sicily train depot the next evening. But she couldn't find a single part of her that cared what anyone thought as she leaned against him. When they came to stand in front of the Able home, Amelia noticed it was dark and empty.

"I wonder where they are." She traded contentment for concern. "Do you think Clint really had a man here?"

"You told Amy what happened on the telephone call, didn't you?"

"Yes. And she said to make sure you knew I had told her."

He relaxed. "They should be fine. She knew what to do. They'll come home when I send word that it's safe. I'll talk to Sheriff Tyler; see if anyone suspicious has come in on the train. I suspect not, because I think Clint was bluffing. I'll wire Amy if Tyler hasn't seen anything."

He pulled her close and kissed the top of her head. "I don't think we need to expect any more trouble."

"We can live happily ever after," she said with a smile.

"Something like that."

Amelia reached for him and kissed him, delighting in the conclusion of their love story. Only the sweetest parts remained.

"I'll be back," he said, and rather unwillingly let her go.

But when Amelia turned to walk up the steps, Rebecca Sapp was blocking the path.

FIFTY-SEVEN

Rebecca stood primly with her gloved hands folded in front of her. The grim slant of her smile was arrogant with the wild look of madness Amelia had observed before. The force of Amelia's intuition made her gasp. Rebecca was here to kill her. She could read it in the chill of her beautiful eyes.

Rebecca reached for her handbag, but stopped. Amelia wondered if William had noticed the movement. Her eyes fixed on the bag as Rebecca watched her.

"I suppose you thought you'd won." Rebecca's voice was so serene, so peaceful. "You should have known better than to take what was mine. You grabbed that teaching position for yourself, never mind all the studying I had to do to get that certificate. I was able to forgive that, since I knew no man would have you. It was easy enough to get rid of the last three teachers; I could find a way to persuade you to leave, too. All it takes is a few whispers in the right ears for gossip to spread like wildfire.

"But then you stole him. You seduced him because you are a witch." Her voice gained intensity and her eyes seemed black as midnight. "Our ancestors knew how to handle people like you. I follow their courageous example."

She took a step forward, and William held out a hand in warning. Amelia wanted to tell him what she feared Rebecca hid in her purse, but the words stuck in her throat, as if interrupting Rebecca's speech would set off the destruction Amelia sensed was forthcoming. "Witches don't die easily, do they?" Her voice carried an odd, musical tone. "I tried to get you to follow that child into the cave and perish. Arsenic didn't get the job done, either, though I gave you more than it took to finish off Auntie. But even witches aren't a match for guns. Your carpenter won't be, either."

She pulled something out of her purse as she spoke. The last of the sunlight filtered through the trees and reflected off the shiny steel glint of her Derringer pistol.

There were no options left. Amelia knew it was pointless to argue with her. She'd had no qualms about luring Kathleen into the cave; she'd killed her own aunt, so this would be nothing to her. Tears stung Amelia's eyes when she realized William would also die that day. She knew he wouldn't just stand by and let Rebecca kill her.

Amelia peeked at him as Rebecca sighed, her voice far away as she continued. "My parents died when I was twelve. In a fire."

William stared hard at Amelia, as if he was trying to say something without words. She looked down at his hand. He held two fingers to his leg.

She looked back at Rebecca. What did he mean?

"Only, they didn't really die in a fire," Rebecca continued. "They weren't fit to be parents, anyway. I was nothing but their little slave. One day, I'd had enough. I was tired of Daddy's orders and Mama's refusal to stand up to him. And then there was my little brothers' constant bickering and foolishness. I just wanted them all to be quiet."

She smiled at the gun as if she was recalling a fond memory. "I shot them all. Not with this, no, I took Daddy's rifle from the wall. After, it was so blessedly quiet. And how easy to make the town think it was an accident! It only took a spark from the fire to kindle the newspaper on the floor. Before I knew it, the house was in flames, and I was free."

A chill shook Amelia when she considered the darkness of the young girl that would do something so horrifying to her own family. She forced it from her mind as she tried to focus on William's message.

Two? Two what? Two steps? Two blows? She took a deep breath as Rebecca laughed in glee and turned in a circle, swiftly bringing her aim back to Amelia's head.

William took the opportunity and charged. Rebecca's black laced gloves seemed surreal against the flash of the weapon. Her finger was on the trigger when he lunged at her, waging a war of time that Amelia's life depended upon.

She stared at the black lace, realizing these might be her final thoughts, but the gloves triggered the memory of William's letter to Clara.

I felt the lace of your red dress in my fingers, stiff and feathery all at once as it clung to satin.

William had been here before. This was his turning point. When he faced the barrel of a gun, God had changed everything.

He knocked Rebecca's smaller frame to the ground and she screamed in a frenzy of anger. She fought to keep hold of the Derringer as she struggled against his grip. He grabbed for the gun, but too late. She squeezed the trigger, and Amelia cried out as she saw him grab the side of his face.

Rebecca had shot him in the head.

Amelia barely had time to recognize it had only grazed his temple when she saw Rebecca pull the trigger again. This time her fleeting hope that William would live crumbled in a pile of ashes. Rebecca's bullet had met its mark. He clutched his chest and fell.

Rebecca turned with evil eyes, pointing the gun back at Amelia. "Your turn, witch."

William struggled on the ground, holding his chest, face contorted with pain. His jaw was tight and his teeth clenched. "Only... two... shots!"

Amelia looked back at Rebecca, who screeched and threw the gun, grabbing a thick tree limb that must have fallen during a storm. She lunged. Amelia dodged her first swing, but tripped in the process and caught the next blow across the back. She battled to stay conscious and stood back up, grabbing the limb when Rebecca swung again. They fought for possession until Amelia managed to twist it away as a branch raked down the side of her face. In the moment when Amelia was distracted by the sting, Rebecca ran at her again. Amelia pushed her, and she fell back.

She ignored the pain and stood, poising the limb over Rebecca's head. It only took one glance at the red spreading in tragic contrast to William's white shirt. Dread seeped into her spirit just as the blood leached into his clothing. She brought her weapon down as hard as she could on Rebecca's head, either imagining or sensing a flailing evil presence slink away into the trees as Rebecca was rendered unconscious.

As quickly as she could manage and heaving with sobs, she tied Rebecca to a tree with her bonnet strings. She ran back to William, who was laboring for every breath. He didn't speak. His look seemed apologetic, yet she knew he wasn't sorry at all.

"Why did you do that?" She barely managed the words.

He took several breaths that all seemed cut short, and forced a slurred whisper. "I know what it is to have someone die for you. It's okay."

She shook her head, surveying the wounds. "No, it's not." As gently as she could, she lifted the blood-soaked shirt from the hole in his chest and watched helplessly as the blood flowed. She had the overwhelming sense that there was too much blood. There was no possible way a man could survive such a wound.

It's hopeless.

Amelia felt the dark spirit lurking. Foul fingers seemed to put their loathsome thoughts in her mind, pressing down on her hope until it smashed into pieces. What would hold him back? William had nothing to fear, staring up into that great beyond and knowing he faced a Savior this time. There would be no judgment. More than that, his Clara was there.

"But what about me?" Her words caught in a soft moan. She had no interest in walking the earth and living out her days without him. She clutched his hand, and he seemed to rouse from the painful chore of taking another breath long enough for one weak squeeze.

In the midst of the bleakness, a sudden spark of light danced in her mind. It was a verse. How many times had she read the words and been unaffected? Now they were her lifeline; she clung to them.

"Nothing is impossible with God. Nothing is impossible with God!" She stood up. William tried to stop her.

"Don't go," he said faintly. "Stay with me. Until the end."

Only a second of indecision passed before Amelia shook her head. "No! It's not over." She ran to the back of the house and grabbed her bicycle from the side of the shed. She rode it back to where he lay, refusing to let the temptation to despair override her mission. "God says it's not over, William! You hold on. Promise me!"

She waited only a moment for a response, not even sure she saw the nearly imperceptible nod. She pushed off against the pedal, carried down the road and back toward town, almost positive she could hear the angels' wings giving her flight.

FIFTY-EIGHT

William lay on the ground, his senses acute as he waited, helpless. Waiting to die?

He considered the thought as he felt his limbs go numb, his mind become slow and his eyes tire. He felt peaceful.

It was different from the first time he was near death. He'd been defiant then, and without hope. Now so much hope flooded through him he thought he'd overflow with it. He stared up at the sky, shrouded by the trees but growing brighter by the minute. Were those angels beckoning? Or was it Clara?

He strained to see, feeling excitement at the thought of seeing her again. He could let go. He could fly away toward that light. No more darkness. No more pain. No more living alone. All he had to do was fly.

But in his feet that had long since lost all feeling, he felt sudden pressure. Someone was holding him down.

"No." He tried to struggle, but the force that held him was infinitely stronger. "Let me go."

The arms of iron would not release him. The light began to fade and the searing pain replaced the peace.

He let the pain overwhelm him. He remembered why he couldn't fly away, and she was reason enough and more to live.

"Amelia, hurry," he groaned before he passed out.

The next thing he knew, William opened his eyes in Doc's examination room at the clinic. He tried to focus and take account of his body. As long as he didn't move, it didn't hurt too badly. The foggy state of his brain told him that was due to a large dose of morphine.

"He's awake," Amy said in a hushed voice. He heard footsteps on the floorboards, and Elizabeth came into his view, checking his pulse and listening to his breathing.

"How do you feel?"

He gulped and tried to speak. His mouth was dry. Elizabeth helped him take a sip of water from the cup on the stand.

"Amelia" was the only word he managed.

His sisters exchanged hopeful smiles. "She's been here the whole time, William. Praying her heart out," Amy said. "You wouldn't believe anyone could actually spend an entire night on her knees in prayer, but she did. She must have done something right, because here you are – alive. You shouldn't be."

She smoothed the hair on his forehead back, and Elizabeth reached for his hand. "I believe you are going to be okay. I can't explain it, because I've never seen anyone recover from those kinds of wounds, but Dr. Stacy and I both think you are going to live."

His sisters waited for William to respond.

"Amelia." He wasn't going to waste breath asking for anything else.

They both chuckled.

"She had an important errand," Amy said in a reassuring tone. "I'm sure she'll be back in a few minutes."

FIFTY-NINE

Gwendolyn touched the pale face of her beloved. She felt as if her heart was being torn from her chest. Her throat ached with terrible pressure.

"This is why I didn't want to love you."

She gave his dear features one last glance, dreaming of the ability to will his spirit to return to his body.

"I never told you to give your life for me," she said.

She turned to leave, as if the act of turning might erase the years she'd spent learning to love him. Reaching for the door handle, she found she could not open it. How could she walk out of the room and return to a life void of the one person who had broken through every wall she'd carefully built around her heart? How could she take another step without his arms holding her up?

Did life matter anymore? Did it make sense to continue to breathe if he returned to dust?

She turned back to him, kneeling beside the bed and pleading with her heart not to listen to each rasping breath. She took hold of his arm with one hand and his head with the other.

And she prayed.

Not a timid prayer. Not the prayer of a saint who had learned to trust, who had developed a quiet acceptance of heartache. It was an urgent, desperate pleading with the only One who could change the inevitable future.

She reasoned. She begged.

She lamented.

"Your name is more powerful than any force on earth. In that name I was saved and in that name I am confident, just as your son rose from the dead, just as Lazarus walked out of his tomb, just as a little girl died and lived to feel her mother's embrace again... I know you can save him – this man I love.

"That I have come to love him at all is a great miracle in itself."

In that moment, when she opened her eyes, nothing was changed. When she placed her hand on his chest, his heartbeat was still erratic.

His skin remained cold and pale. He struggled for every breath. So she prayed on through the night until she finally fell asleep, emptied and exhausted.

When sunlight hit Gwendolyn's face, she opened her eyes, forgetting for a moment where she was. She drank in the beauty of the sunrise. Something felt different.

A new beginning?

Her eyes fell to her beloved. He was smiling, reaching a trembling hand her cheek.

"I heard you praying. And so did God. You saved me."

Amelia placed the final page on the stack and tied it with string. She placed it in a box, and took the bundle under her arm to the postal office. She stopped outside, hit with a wave of doubt.

Be humble. Have nothing to prove. Give me your offering.

She opened the door, went to the desk and handed the box to the clerk, feeling both relief and terror as he took it from her.

"Robert's Brothers in Boston?" He looked at her over his wirerimmed glasses with a polite smile. "Are you a writer, then?"

She tried not to gasp aloud when he tossed her treasure into a pile of mail behind him.

"Yes." She nodded, inhaling deeply. "I suppose I am."

SIXTY

My dearest daughter,

I received the letter you sent, telling me of your recent adventures and of sending your novel to a publisher. I'm having Father write this for me so that I can tell you how proud I am. You have embraced the talent I always knew you possessed.

I know that you understand my days are short. Soon, I will cast off this suffering shell and fly to Jesus.

Don't let that fact rob you of this most exciting time in your life. Don't let the road God has allowed for me to walk make you afraid of the road he has given you. They are not the same, and he gives us grace for the path he means for us.

When it is all said and done, the number of our days will always seem short. When we look back from eternity it will only seem like a breath. Live with abandon, Amelia Josephine. Be all that God meant you to be, and run full force at the opportunities that will open. He will use you in wonderful and lasting ways. You need only trust him and do the hard work.

I'm so weary. I cannot dictate any longer. Should these be my last words to you until we meet again in heavenly places, know that you are loved with all the love a mother's heart can hold.

And run.

301

> *Affectionately,*
> *Mother*

"William Morehouse, are you trying to break open your stitches?" Amelia chastised as she saw him trying to maneuver the back porch stairs, holding the railing so tightly his knuckles were white.

She came and stood before him, her hands on her hips, giving her best schoolmarm frown. "Honestly, it's only been two weeks since you all but died. Why must you be so stubborn? Elizabeth says if you don't rest, you'll prolong your confinement."

William narrowed his eyes. "Hush up and walk with me."

She heaved an exaggerated sigh and went to help him conquer the final step. She held his arm. He stopped to rest, and chuckled when he saw the tree swing merrily swaying in the breeze.

"What?" She made a face and pretended she didn't know what he found amusing. He answered with a smirk. But then his gaze became solemn, and he reached for her hands.

"I have something to tell you."

Amelia felt a wave of anticipation. Would she finally hear the end of the story?

She noticed he was trembling. She wondered if it was from the exertion or what he was about to say. She felt lightheaded at the possibility of hearing something that made William Morehouse tremble. But she gathered her courage and waited for him to speak.

The girls ran up and down the hill, shrieking with laughter. Amy surreptitiously watched Amelia and William from the garden where she was planting. Amelia noticed that William sent a solemn nod in Amy's direction.

"I told you that Clara had a daughter."

Amelia nodded. She certainly hadn't forgotten.

"A kind woman near the brothel kept the baby for Clara. Clara visited her when she could, but Clint knew. We might have made it out of town in time to avoid the gunfight if we hadn't stopped to get the baby. Of course, Clara couldn't leave her."

William was looking at their hands as he spoke, but his gaze wandered to the children.

"I owe you an explanation, and I haven't been able to think of a way to tell you other than just to say it." He hesitated. "The thing is, I only have one niece."

He watched the girls, waiting. Amelia looked at him in confusion. "What are you talking about?"

His head turned and he gazed straight into her eyes. "Jennifer is my only niece."

"And Kathleen?"

He smiled, affection shining in his eyes. "Come on, Sherlock. Where are those brilliant deductive powers?"

It dawned on her. She stared at Kathleen in shock. "All this time…" she whispered. "Kathleen is Clara's daughter?"

"Not only that." His face grew serious, and his grip on her hands tightened. "She's mine."

If Amelia could have uttered a sound in that moment, it would have been a most unattractive squeak. She could only stare in amazement at the five-year-old.

She had always noticed the differences between the girls, but now the missing information caused the picture to slide into place. Jennifer's dark brown hair contrasted with Kathleen's blonde locks. Jennifer's calm and cheerful manner that matched her parents, and Kathleen's deep thoughts and solemn expressions. Even the crease in her little forehead matched William's perfectly. How had she never seen it?

Amelia took an unconscious step backward. William sought her eyes, and she saw his fear.

"How do you know for sure?" Her voice faltered.

William nodded, as if he had expected her question. "Kathleen was born when we were living in Sage on our own."

"What happened after Clara died?"

"I was laying on the ground, planning on dying myself, when I heard her. Kathleen. She was barely a year old, and she was terrified, just sitting there in her basket where Clara had left her behind the store barrels. The sound of her scared little voice was enough to convince me I had to live. If for nothing else, I had to take care of that baby. It was the least I could do for Clara, and for my own flesh and blood. So, I got better, and I took Kathleen east."

He clenched his jaw. "I knew Clint would be looking for her. He felt since he had lost his best girl, he was owed her daughter, as sick as it is to consider it. He probably figured that was the best way to get his revenge on me. That's when I came to live with Amy and Connor. I was trying to figure out what to do next, but when I saw how Amy was with Kathleen, I knew she'd be safest here. I asked them to raise her as their own."

William watched the little girl with emotion. "I almost gave in to the grief after that. But Jesus held on tight and didn't let go. He saved me. And not too long after I climbed out of the pit, so to speak, you showed up."

Another silence fell as the comforting warm breeze of early summer teased errant strands of hair across her face.

"I'm sorry." His voice was soft. "I know my past is a burden. I understand if it's too much."

"I don't know what to say." She heard her voice, small and afraid in the face of everything he had told her. Moments passed as she looked away from him.

"What is it, Amelia? Talk to me. If you don't feel the same way about me, say so. Have it out."

She met his eyes, letting him see the truth. "It's not a matter of affection."

"Then what?" he asked. "Whatever it is, we'll work it out."

She looked away again. "I never thought it would be like this when I finally found myself here, at the end of the story. I thought I would feel complete, like everything was settled. There are so many questions. I don't know if I can live with the uncertainty."

He watched her thoughtfully. "This isn't a fairy tale, Amelia. This is real. We are real. As much as you want every moment to feel like a scene from a novel, this is us. We'll have storms and heartaches ahead, there's no doubt. You just have to decide if you're up for going through them together." He lifted her chin with his fingers. "It's not an ending, it's a beginning. With more potential for life than you can imagine in that creative mind of yours."

Before William's speech, she had wondered if she would need more time to consider what it all meant. But she remembered Ella, scoffing at her belaboring of decisions. Her sister was right. She had a first instinct, and it was rarely wrong. She grasped his hand and looked him in the eye.

"I'll understand if it hurts too much to get down on one knee."

EPILOGUE

Everyone went on about what a beautiful wedding it turned out to be. Even when the bride sat down at the piano, bridal dress and all, and sang to her new husband.

Some argued that just wasn't done, after all.

Controversial or not, a good part of the town still crowded into the little white church on the edge of town. Though some complained they should have moved it to one of the larger churches. For everyone's comfort, of course.

When the morning ceremony was over, and Amelia's father proudly announced they were "man and wife," William marched his bride down the aisle and out the door, where he promptly put his arms around her waist and lifted her up, kissing her quite thoroughly, as he had on one other occasion.

That earned them a few sniffs as well, but neither noticed.

He let her slide back down to the ground as they turned to greet their guests. He whispered in her ear something about a man being impatient for the privacy of their hotel room later that night.

She reminded him with a tolerant smile that he should have picked a closer destination than a sandy shore in Michigan.

He reminded her that she was the one who wanted to feel sand between her toes.

After the wedding breakfast, just before William and Amelia endured a shower of rice as they boarded their train, Ella dutifully recited all the ways they might doom their marriage.

"Don't stumble, whatever you do, Emmy Jo. I know you. You stumble. Don't do it today, or you will cause a bad omen to fall over your life."

"And this from the preacher's daughter."

Even so, Amelia tossed the bouquet straight to her, as promised.

They waved goodbye as the train pulled out of the station. Amelia leaned out the window until she couldn't see her father, sister or the members of her new family any longer. The last to be found still waving was Kathleen, who ran beside the train. Amelia sighed as she watched her fade away. She wanted to know the future. Would Kathleen be her daughter? How would they go about making a decision like that?

She felt a tug on the back of her new travel outfit and fell into William's lap.

"Careful! You're going to rip my dress."

"If necessary."

He kissed her. She forgot to worry about all the strangers who were trying to pretend they didn't notice such a bold display of affection.

William gathered her trembling hands in his. "Scared?"

"No," she lied, shrugging. She tried to think of something brilliant to say. Something to make him glad he married her. She smoothed her skirt and adjusted her hat that had been set askew.

"Stop that." He caught her hands.

"Stop what?"

"Stop wondering if you look okay."

"I'm not."

"You are." His voice was quiet, meant only for her. "You don't have to be perfect. You don't have to make sure every moment is like a storybook. This is life, Amelia. We're sharing life. That means for every ordinary day and a few extraordinary ones, for the rest of our lives, you, in whatever form you happen to be, will be everything I want or need."

She couldn't help her smile.

"I belong with you, Amelia. And you belong with me. You don't have to be anything else. I want you just the way you are."

She reached for his face. "You love me for love's sake."

"I do, Schoolmarm."

She relaxed against him and they fell silent, contemplating the rest of their journey. She wondered when they would discuss Kathleen, but he was right. They'd find their way, one step at a time. Her thoughts returned to memories of the day. She didn't want to lose them. She would need to write them down. As she searched through her bag for her notebook, she chided him.

"You know, you really shouldn't have told Mrs. Hagaman to 'get her silly speech done so we could be on our way.'"

"Why? You think I hurt her feelings?"

"Not in the least. But you know how she talks. Everyone is going to know what you meant before we're five miles out of town."

He smirked. "You think the whole town doesn't know what we're planning to do next?"

She blushed and pushed him away, scanning their nearest neighbors to see if anyone had heard him. "Are you going to spend the rest of our lives embarrassing me?"

"I didn't know you were so interested in the rules of polite society."

"You aren't interested in them at all, so I have to be."

They argued all the way across Ohio and into Michigan. After they finally stepped off the train that evening, Amelia imagined the whole car erupted into applause.

But it didn't matter what anyone else thought. She was hand in hand, for better or worse, right where she belonged.

William leaned close to her ear. "Oh, and don't worry, Schoolmarm. I remembered to bring your coca wine."

Acknowledgments

I must give credit where it's due. My sister Kathy, not unlike Amelia's sister Ella, has been both my biggest fan and my harshest critic. A few years ago, she suggested I write more of what I know personally. Her words sparked the idea for *Where We Belong*. It's written in my favorite time period, with a mixture of my favorite genres (although I couldn't find a way to fit science fiction into the story!) It takes place in the Midwest, where I have lived all my life, and though Amelia became her own person, she started out quite a bit like me.

As Amelia, I've learned through this process to get out of God's way and allow him to lead. So, thanks for the advice, Kat. I'm sorry for shamelessly exploiting our relationship in this story – please don't sue me.

I also want to thank my relentless and passionate editor Tanya Dennis. (tanyadennisbooks.com) You always know when something's not right and you are the best at offering solutions and seeing it through to the end. I'm amazed by your tireless ability to get the job done, and I'm so incredibly thankful for your unique mastery of words and how they should go together. I apologize again for all my comma issues. Thanks for loving these characters so much you had to take time outs to deal with the emotional trauma they were giving you.

Thank you as well to my mom and dad. I inherited my passion for words and stories from both of you, and I'm thankful that you've always been available to offer criticism and encouragement where needed. Dad, now that you're living it up heaven-style, I promise to measure up to the standards you taught me, both grammatically and spiritually. Thank you for always believing I could do it.

Thank you to Marissa, my level-headed and ever-available sounding board. You know your stuff and I can always count on your complete honesty no matter what outrageous story I have come up with.

Thank you to my husband, who has been known to disappear with all four children for an entire day just to let me have some quiet to write. Thank you, my love, for believing in me in your practical and down-to-earth way and listening patiently to all my rants about the state of book publishing. I love you.

Thank you to my readers. You don't know it, but I've thought about you and prayed for you for years before I was ready to introduce myself. My life's passion is to write stories that you will benefit from. I bypassed traditional publishing because I thought this would be a more fulfilling reading experience for you. I pray you found something you can take with you on your journey. It will always be my ultimate goal to see that you are entertained, encouraged, inspired, and just a little bit more in love with Jesus.

Because, after all, he is the reason I can sit down and write one word, let along the next ninety-thousand or so. He is the inspiration for every story that finds root in this brain and heart. His amazing love, that went all the way to the cross and came all the way back from the grave, is the theme of my life story. So, tell it the way it needs to be told, Savior! I am yours.

About the Author

Miranda Shisler started writing stories when she learned to read. From that point on, she could usually be found either reading or writing.

She pursued music education and vocal performance at Cornerstone University, but after marrying the love of her life and starting a family, she clearly felt God's call to a writing ministry.

These days she can be found homeschooling four energetic kids, serving in the music ministry of her church, hosting Bible studies and small groups, reading all the quality fiction she can get her hands on, and spending her evenings quite literally writing her heart out.

Note to Readers

YOU are important to me. I could not sit down to the daunting task of writing entire novels if I was not thinking of YOU, the reader, the entire time, and gauging your reactions. That's why I need your help.

I did not begin my writing journey recently. In fact, writing has always been a big part of my life. It is how I think. But twelve years ago, God surprised me with the call to pursue fiction writing professionally.

At first, and until recently, my heart was set on traditional publishing. I had no interest in self-publishing. I only wanted to write stories and skip the hard part of publishing and marketing.

I began to interact with the publishing world. I endured the early disinterest and rejections, taking each one personally and using it as an excuse to feel sorry for myself and procrastinate instead of persevere.

Looking back, I know why I was rejected early on. I wasn't ready. Writing is hard, and it takes a lot of practice before someone is ready to confidently create worlds and invite readers into them. However, there is a lot of negativity in the world of publishing, and it was sapping me of creative energy.

In the end, though I worked for almost a year with an agent on this book, and did benefit from that relationship, I decided to Indie publish.

Why? If I wanted to go traditional, I would need to chop my story down to the skeleton that fits cookie-cutter Christian fiction romances. Agents and publishers want stories the masses will buy. I have different goals. I want to appeal to the thinkers, the feelers who want a story to surprise them, to take them on a journey, to make them consider ideas and questions. I know this type of reader well, because I am one of them. And I know how hard it is to find stories that are unique in the present market – and it's just getting harder.
With these things in mind, I ask you to do two things. I thank you in advance. Your help will increase my ability to keep sending great stories your way.

First of all, if you enjoyed this book, *please* leave a review on Amazon and Goodreads! There is nothing more precious to a serious Indie author (or any author) as a review – a recognition that someone did indeed read the book and found it worth the time and expense. It's easy to do and doesn't require you to display any personal information.

Second of all, let me know what you thought. Visit my website, mirandashisler.blogspot.com, or send me a private message on my facebook site.

Thank you for taking this journey with me! I value you, I pray for you, and I write for you.

You can find me online at Facebook, Pinterest or Goodreads:

facebook.com/authormirandashisler
pinterest.com/mirandashisler/ (See the *Where We Belong* board!)
goodreads.com/mirandashisler

Everything Kathleen Able has ever known was a lie.

After discovering the truth about her parents, she leaves home on a quest that brings her to the saloon where her mother died. Thinking she won't stay long enough to be compromised, she agrees to sing and dance so she can uncover more details about the parent she never knew.

Now she's in over her head and fears for her life. There's only one glimmer of hope left. The deputy, Joshua Whitley, has been kind to her. Desperate, she asks him to marry her.

Joshua is a devoted man of God with a scarred past he intends to overcome. The idea of marrying a saloon girl flies in the face of everything he hoped for. Would God really ask him to risk his reputation for her? Is there more to Kathleen than he assumes at first? Find out in book two of the *Midwest Maidens* series.

May 2016